THE CLOSET GOTH

THE CLOSET GOTH

RAIN NOX

For Ann, who introduced me to Austin,
and for Tony, who gave me a reason to stay.

ISBN-13: 979-8-9925092-0-5

Printed in the United States of America

1

The Cure's "Just Like Heaven" blasts from my car stereo and the sun shines so bright I'm squinting with my sunglasses on. No excuses for me now, flying down the highway towards a cloudless future. A sign says only four miles left to go and my heart flutters in anticipation.

Maybe this is all crazy, because who needs the extra stress of setting up a new apartment, making friends, starting a new job. But it will all be worth it because I get to reinvent myself, moving far away from my hometown with its cold and gray winters to someplace warm, someplace sunny.

Texas.

I can practically feel the shadows disintegrate around me.

Waze interrupts the song to announce my exit is approaching. I follow the directions to Creekside Manor, a fancy name for what is really a budget apartment complex, a series of three-story brick buildings, next to a water feature that looks more akin to a drainage ditch. I stop the car in front of the leasing office to sign the final paperwork and pick up my keys.

"You made it, Kat," I whisper to my reflection in the rear-view mirror before I get out of the car. "It's only going to get better from here."

The face that gazes back with less certainty sports expertly applied eyeliner, long lashes plumped with mascara, smokey eyes framed by dark brown asymmetrically parted bangs, and deep garnet lipstick. I'm going to miss this look, perfected since I first tried it at fifteen and felt like a goddess of the night. My morning makeup routine will be different, starting Monday.

I slide the key in the lock and open the door to my new abode.

"Aaaaa!!! What the hell is that?" I screech and put my hands up when something launches right at my face. It's brown and about two and a half inches long. What in the realm of Hades? There are giant flying cockroaches here. How do people exist in this environment? My first instinct is to get in the car, and drive back where I came from. But I can't, because this is supposed to be my new beginning.

Welcome to Texas, where they claim everything is bigger, apparently even vermin.

This isn't going to work. No way I can sleep knowing that monster bug might crawl over me in the night. I march back to the leasing office and the property manager promises to send someone out when she sees how distraught I am.

On the way back to the apartment I grab a few boxes from my trunk, then scan the room cautiously as I rest them on the floor. Might as well start unpacking, because I'm not chancing leaving for even one second, in case I miss the exterminator.

First, I open the oblong package that contains my carefully rolled and rubber-banded posters. I still like to decorate like I did in high school—band posters and strings of blacklight. With a bit of sticky tack, my She Past Away poster finds its new home in the bedroom and the transformation begins from a blank-walled, cookie-cutter one bedroom, to budget gothic lair.

Next, I open the only suitcase of clothing I brought with me in my car. No way I could risk it getting lost by the movers because it's packed with my most treasured possessions—irreplaceable concert t-shirts. When I slip one on, I'm immediately transported back to the venue, the music washing over me, the energy of the crowd hugging me like a blanket. These simple pieces of cloth represent some of my most special memories.

I hang the t-shirts up in the middle of the rod, then think better of it and push them all to the left. From now on the wardrobe will be split in two, half for the old me and half for the new me.

The whole goth thing is problematic for me. Back in high school, I fell in love with old-school eighties and nineties goth pretty hard. It felt like company to my darkness, but I soon discovered that goth and depressed are not synonymous. It can be a fashion choice, which makes sense to me, because I always thought and still do think that goth is at the top of the fashion charts.

The velvet and lace and zippers and collars and boots and chokers. It's all fantastic, glamorous, but elegant. I'm partial to mixing black with scarlet or deep purple, long skirts, tops with lace up bodices, ruffled sleeves. Fake Victorian jewelry, beaded black and pewter earrings, cameos or lockets, giant rings.

It was disappointing to learn that the other goth kids weren't kindred spirits. They thought darkness was fun; they weren't haunted by it and trying to escape it like me. Still, the music was comforting, and the clothes alluring, so I stuck with it throughout high school and college, and it became part of my identity, my true self.

When I decided to move to Texas, I made a choice. I don't want my story to be the depressed girl anymore, and the goth look probably reinforces that to the people around me. So, I'm becoming a closet goth. Being goth will be something I keep just for me.

My apartment will still be covered in band posters and after work I'll still slip into my favorite black jeans and my old, ratty Lacuna Coil t-shirt, sink into my purple velour couch, and let the voice of Siouxsie Sioux transport me somewhere far away. But during the day I'll be Katie, the non-depressed, highly functional twenty-six-year-old.

I'm almost finished putting away what I had been able to pack in my car when there's a knock on my door.

"Pest control," a man's voice yells.

I let him in gratefully and tell him what happened. He tries his best to sympathize instead of laughing at my disgust, and assures me he will do what he can, then begins to treat the apartment. I wring my hands as I wonder how soon it will work. When he's done, I ask and am horrified at the answer.

"You might still see some for a few days, but this should take care of it," he says, as if that will make me feel better. It does not.

The second I close the door behind him, tears threaten to flow again. I'll be sleeping on the floor tonight since my bed hasn't arrived but there is no way I can sleep thinking about the giant roaches skittering around me and possibly over me. Bleaggh!

"Not yet, Kat," I tell myself as I choke back the tears because there will surely be more obstacles to face in the coming weeks, and I'm determined to stay strong.

I used to cry a lot more, but now crying is emphatically reserved for the worst of days. Supposedly it's therapeutic, but that must be for people who mourn for something briefly, then get over it. After I'm done crying, the darkness lingers on.

Now that the exterminator has come and gone, I'm free to leave the apartment. One odd joy I've always had in my life is going to the grocery store. All the choices—a hundred or more types of cereal alone; it's mind boggling, and I'm excited to see what regional items they have here in Texas that they didn't have up north.

A quick search on my phone tells me the nearest store is called H-E-B and it's only a couple of blocks away. That cheers me because it's right on the way home from work, and only a five-minute drive from the apartment. Time to fill up my fridge.

Even from the parking lot, I can tell it's nicer than my old grocery store up north. Outside the entrance there are cast iron grill pits and orange chimineas, a small selection of garden pottery, and tables with flowering plants and vegetable starts.

Inside, the produce section greets me to the right, and there's an entire display of guacamole. Yep, this must be Texas. I happen to love guacamole and throw the spiciest one in my cart. The bakery section boasts freshly made tortilla chips and those get tossed in as well. Chips and guac sound like a perfect Texas dinner to me, even though I generally eat healthy out of necessity—can't afford to feel physically run down in addition to my mental sluggishness.

There are so many aisles to peruse, and although my cart is mostly empty due to a tight budget, my mind is making notes of things to try in the future. I spend over an hour meandering inside, which is fine because there is plenty of time to kill. My internet isn't hooked up yet, and there awaits only a long evening alone in my apartment with nothing to entertain me. But eventually I've covered the entire store and have no choice but to make my way back to Creekside Manor.

I'm carrying my grocery bags up the sidewalk that leads to my unit, when someone tramples down the metal staircase from the second floor, making a pounding sound with each step. Black combat boots come into view first, then faded dark blue jeans with a hole at the knee, a worn-out Iron Maiden shirt, long, wavy brown hair, and finally, a distracted face looking down at the ground.

This guy almost runs into me as he turns at the base of the stairs but stops short just before we collide. "Sorry about that," he mumbles and sweeps the hair away from his face.

Whoa. For a moment I'm caught staring, noting the tiny flecks of gold in his steel blue eyes but I forcibly tear myself away from his handsome face and say, "No worries," then sidestep around him and continue towards my apartment.

I have zero interest in dating, having just moved here, not to mention my long history of failed relationships generally doomed by my mental status. But upstairs guy is certainly my type, aesthetically speaking.

Goth and metal are not the same at all, as any goth or metalhead would tell you, but there is a certain amount of shared attitude, subversiveness, plus the whole depression is the flipside of anger concept.

I unlock the door, turn on the light and immediately something flies at my face again. I shriek, "Fucking little monsters!"

I'm about to have a nervous breakdown. Footsteps approach behind me, and I swing around. It's metalhead guy.

"Hey, you alright?" he says, his eyes wide with concern.

My face flames and I'm sure I'm blushing like a tomato. "Yeah, yeah, I'm fine. This roach tried to attack me, that's all. It's like a Hitchcock film or something."

He laughs. "They don't bite, you know."

I narrow my eyes at him. "Even so, they're disgusting."

"They are. I guess you're not from around here?"

"No, I'm from New Jersey."

"I can't believe there aren't any in New Jersey."

"There are, but they aren't giant and don't fly at you."

He purses his lips in sympathy. "Let the management office know and they'll come exterminate."

No point in explaining that I already did that.

"I'm Damon."

"Kat—I mean, Katie." I nearly forgot that as part of my reinvention I'm going with the least alternative version of my given name, Katherine. Kat served well as a goth name, but that is behind me now. Katie sounds like a well-adjusted person with no baggage and that's who I want to be in Texas.

He tilts his head, puzzled that I'm unsure of my own name. "I'm upstairs if you need anything, bug killing or whatever."

I know he's making light of it, but it's not funny because I'm dreading just being in my apartment. "Actually, could I use your wi-fi for a few minutes? I need to do some things on my laptop and mine's not set up yet."

"Sure. I'm just going to pick up dinner but come up in an hour. Unit 242."

"Cool."

I watch Damon walk away, his long tresses bouncing against his back, and I shake my head. What am I thinking? I don't want any entanglements with my new neighbors and definitely do not want to get romantically involved with anyone. I want to build a career, make friends, and start a new life here, as Katie. Damon seems like a hot piece of trouble. And now I'm going to be alone in his apartment. Great freaking start, *Katie*.

2

Buck it up, girl. You're in Texas now and you don't need a man to kill your bugs for you. Hopefully, the bastard that flew at me this morning and just now is the same one and I put my terror aside to switch to Rambo mode. The high-pitched strings of a horror movie scene run through my head as I creep around searching for my nemesis.

It appears in the corner, scurrying up the wall and I run towards it, unleashing a battle cry, and smash it with my shoe before it can fly at me. My slain enemy falls to the floor, and I gingerly pick it up with a paper towel and watch it swirl around until it flushes all the way down the toilet.

Just for the record, I love animals and normally wouldn't kill anything. Spiders are welcome to make a happy home in my apartment, and a beetle or something benign will be calmly relocated outside. But roaches really are unsanitary and for the sake of my mental health, not acceptable roommates.

Choosing to believe that was the only one, as there are no others visible at the moment, I relax a little bit more and make a list of what I need to check on Damon's wi-fi. Technically, my phone would work for most of it, but it's nearing the end of the month, and my data plan is running low.

The pounding of feet on the stairs tells me Damon is returning to his apartment. I wait five minutes for him to get settled in out of courtesy. On a whim, I bring my chips and guac; nothing wrong with being neighborly.

Damon ushers me in. His apartment is uncannily similar to how mine will be once my stuff arrives. Posters of metal bands, some in cheap frames, as if he made an attempt at this whole adulting thing. I look at him again, wondering how old he is, and I bet he's around my age. I walk over to the fake fireplace and peruse his collection of used concert tickets over the mantle. Even though I'm not that into metal, a lot of the bands look familiar, and I even like a few myself.

Damon opens a cardboard container and gets two plates out of the cabinet. "I bet you've never had a *real* taco, so I brought you a couple," he says.

"You might be right about that. Thanks." I lift my bag. "I brought chips and guacamole."

"Uncanny," he chuckles.

We sit at his table, and he watches me as I take a bite of the taco. The spiciness of the pico de gallo, the juicy beef, and the shredded cheese delight my tastebuds. In this moment, my decision to move to Texas is reaffirmed.

"Holy crap, this is freaking delicious!"

Damon grins. "I told you."

He's really cute when he smiles and crinkle lines appear next to his eyes. Conversation with Damon is surprisingly easy. I learn that he is a server admin at a tech company, and marvel at the fact that in Austin, a metalhead IT guy is totally normal. Just from my observations in the grocery store, the ratio of alternative to non-alternative looking people is much different than in my hometown.

A twinge of conflict about my resolution to become a closet goth surfaces, but maybe with Damon I can be a hybrid. If we are going to be friends, which is all I'm looking for right now, he'll see my fully decorated apartment, and my after-work attire. It's different anyway, because being a closet goth is about changing my life's story, not just about physical appearance.

After dinner, he puts the wi-fi password into my laptop, and I get to work on my list. At nine, he turns on a local cable access channel talk show where the host interviews celebrities and interesting members of the central Texas community.

I half-listen while typing on my laptop. After a long list of thanks to local sponsors, the host introduces his first guest, some pop psychologist I've never heard of. I look over at Damon, wondering why he likes this stupid show, but he's looking at his phone. Maybe he just keeps the TV on for company, out of habit. I do that sometimes, too.

The guest starts blabbing on about keeping a gratitude journal or some nonsense and how we all need to find the positive in life, blah, blah, blah.

"Stupid fucker," I mumble to myself. It's like when someone tells me to smile; it makes me want to punch them in the face and then say something witty like, "Who's smiling now?" as they blot their bloody nose.

Damon whips his head up from his phone, his eyebrow raised.

"Sorry! Not you. This jackass on TV," I explain.

Damon glances at the TV and it's obvious he hadn't been listening to the show at all. "Dr. Nicolas Stone? Never heard of him. What did he do to you?"

I can't explain my knee-jerk negative reaction without explaining my complicated mental history, so I drop it. But as Nicolas Stone continues to awkwardly propose his easy ways to improve your mood in five minutes a day, I seethe in silence. If only it were that easy.

Thirty minutes later, I thank Damon for his hospitality and return to my apartment. Walking down the stairs, I'm already dreading entering the living room for fear of what miniature monsters might lie in wait. To my relief, all is still inside.

It's early for sleep, so I pull out my Kindle and continue reading. I love fantasy novels, with magic, witches, and fairies, anything that provides me an escape from this mundane reality. Since my bed isn't here yet, I set a folded blanket on the floor and put out two pillows. I immediately feel disgusted and freaked out by shadows that seem to move from the corner of my eye, but there is nothing to be done about it. Eventually I fall asleep reading but toss and turn all night long.

The following day is all about getting shit ready to start work on Monday. Things start off rough, with the movers running late. Then one of my table lamps doesn't work but it's not obviously broken. Ugh. It's my favorite piece, a rare find from Goodwill, with a bronze base and a burgundy bell-shaped shade with fringe, just like you would see in a tarot card reading shop. Maybe I can figure out how to fix it later, so for now I set it down on my Victorian-style black lace doily.

My spiderweb coasters go on the black metallic coffee table, and my purple crystal skull and pewter cat candlesticks rest on the mantle above the fake fireplace. It cracks me up that this apartment has such a thing with the mild winters, but assume it's supposed to make it feel homier, and it does in a Hallmark sort of way.

Just having my bed makes the apartment feel more like my new home and I can't wait to get a proper night's sleep. My purple velour couch with black satin cushions is ready for watching movies and eating popcorn. The wi-fi is connected now. I unwrap my kitchen items from their newspaper packing and stack them in the dishwasher. Of course, the machine doesn't turn on. Back to the management office for me and the lady says she'll get someone out to look at it on Monday.

Long-term depression tends to make one less resilient, like I'm already world weary and every minor inconvenience takes a larger toll on me than someone without mood problems. When seemingly small things like a broken dishwasher pop up, I have to deal with them right away, because otherwise a hundred tiny things pile up on me and crush me until I can't breathe. The funny thing is, from the outside, I probably look highly efficient and task oriented. But it's really just self-preservation.

One thing on my to-do list is to go clothes shopping. My new life in Texas, my closet goth life, requires a new professional wardrobe.

There was no point in hauling a bunch of new clothes across the country, plus I'll need more warm weather clothes; easier to shop here.

I wonder if there are goths in Texas and how they dress in the 100-degree summer heat, imagining their black eyeliner running down their sweaty faces. I'll find out soon enough; it's already March and summer is just around the corner.

As my phone directs me to the nearest Kohls, I try not to obsess about work. I've had quite a few jobs for someone my age, but now that I'm striking out on my own, far away from my friends and family, I really need this one to stick.

Moving through the store, I collect a cart full of neutral clothing for work. Gray and beige, plain and boring, and most importantly, inexpensive. No one will be talking about my clothes, unless to say they are drab, but most likely no one will waste any energy commenting on them. Underneath there will still be black lace bras and panties, so I always know the real me is there, hiding just beneath the surface, at all times. Like my special powers are derived from my hidden gothness.

I've heard of people wearing a superhero outfit under their clothes and that doesn't sound weird at all. Goth is my superpower. And like Clark Kent, I am going to be a mild-mannered office worker by day, and something else entirely by night.

Looking at my shopping cart I have second thoughts. If I'm really going to be a closet goth, shouldn't Katie wear some color? Back through the racks of clothing for me, replacing two of the neutral tops with one light pink and one in cerulean blue with a ruffle along the collar, and heck, I even throw in a burgundy top with a floral pattern. Now we have Katie settled.

My first Saturday night is spent writing a to-do list for the next day and for my first day of work, planning out exactly what to wear, and double-checking the directions and timing with traffic, which I've heard is terrible here. I want to have everything unpacked and a fridge full of healthy food ready to go. Monday is my first chance to be a new person, and I don't want anything to mess it up. Wishful thinking on my part. What's that saying about the road to hell?

3

Despite all that planning, Monday gets off to a rough start. My stomach is upset, so even though I wake up on time, I have to rush to get ready. Traffic is even worse than what the navigation program had predicted yesterday; apparently there was an accident on the highway this morning and there aren't many alternate routes.

At 8:10 a.m., I arrive at the office complex. Four enormous glass buildings loom over me. At least there is plenty of parking available or I would be screwed. In front of each building a large stone sign with metal plates lists the tenants. Purple Cactus PR is embossed in gold on the top right. My stomach lurches...here I go.

According to the directory, Purple Cactus is on the third floor, so I find the elevators. They are mirrored inside, and my reflection, or rather *Katie's* reflection, startles me, staring back with her gray slacks, pink blouse, and gray tweed blazer, like a Sears advertisement from fifteen years ago.

The reception area inside Suite 306 is dark. I pull on the handle anyway, but the door is locked. It's 8:15 a.m. now and not an employee in sight. Technically, the HR person didn't make it clear what time the office opened; she just told me the start date. My stomach gurgles as I imagine a dozen worst-case scenarios, ranging from the company went bankrupt over the past week, to everyone in the office contracted the plague.

Standing there like a fool, unsure what to do, there really is no choice but to wait. At least I'm not late after all, it seems. Hah—Dr.

Nicolas Stone would applaud me for looking on the bright side, that dumbass.

At 8:30 a.m., a sharp-dressed woman with super tall high heels and fluffy blonde hair exits the elevator and walks towards me. Good thing I bought brand new clothes but still in no way competitive with this woman's polished style. She probably didn't buy her outfit at Kohls. Even her perfume smells sophisticated, softly floral with a note of spice, and only strong enough to give a hint of mystery, not bowl me over like how some people wear it.

"Early bird, huh darlin'?" she says.

I smile because what else is there to do, but where I came from 8 a.m. was the normal starting hour. In my defense, I mumble, "I wasn't sure what time to be here."

As she unlocks the double glass doors, she says, "I open the doors at 8:30, but most of the staff doesn't get here until closer to 9." She puts her purse on the reception desk and turns to me. "I'm Amber. You're Katherine, right?"

I shake the hand she offers. "You can call me Katie." And that's it, I have officially started my new career as a closet goth. Katie is going to be the super stable, superstar of Purple Cactus PR.

Amber shows me to my new cubicle, and I log in according to the instructions IT left on the desk. I take some HR training and go over my benefits package. The health insurance plan from my previous job expires at the end of the month, so it's critical that there are no delays starting my new one. I can't afford my meds without it. Not to mention seeing a doctor who will keep prescribing them for me.

The breakroom has a Keurig, filtered water, and a machine that apparently will make soda in five different flavors. Fancy. My previous company in New Jersey was fairly upscale because our clients expected it, but it was a little more traditional. I get the impression that Austin runs on its own terms and has to be a certain level of hip to keep young people engaged.

Killing time until my boss makes an appearance, I poke through the cabinets. There are stacks of tea boxes, and that sounds nice right now. Jasmine is soothing, so I grab a mug and make myself a cup. As I turn to head back to my cubicle, this woman sprints around the corner out of nowhere like a cheetah and my tea spills down her front as we collide.

"Oh shit! I'm so sorry," I say.

"What the hell?" she barks. I quickly grab some paper towels, and she starts dabbing her black shirt and her red plaid, pleated miniskirt. "That's fucking hot! I think you scalded me."

This can't be happening on my first day. "I'm so sorry—you came around the corner so fast, I didn't see you."

Her eyes narrow at me, pissed that I'm making this out to be her fault, which it was. "Just watch where you're going next time. We can't have you spilling drinks on clients," she says with a snark, the silver chain cuff earring she's sporting shaking with fury.

I stand back, hoping her anger dissipates, and take a moment to admire her style. Her hair is shaved to fuzz on the same side as her earring, and the rest of her hair, streaked with aquamarine, is flipped over to the opposite side like a short curtain, ending at her cheek.

Before she can say anything else, an older, gray-haired woman enters, accompanied by a fresh-faced young man with glasses.

"Katherine," she says, "so great to meet you in person. We spoke on the phone, I'm the owner of Purple Cactus, Gloria Wickersham. I see you've met Roxy already." Roxy glares at me, knowing Gloria can't see from her angle.

"Yes, I have," I say weakly, and then remember it is my first day and I have to set things up right. "You can call me Katie."

"Alright, Katie. Roxy is one of our graphic artists, so you'll be working closely together. And this is Ben, our college intern."

Ben and I exchange our greetings, and Roxy pushes past me to get to the Keurig, jabbing me in the side, so obviously not accidentally.

Gloria doesn't seem to notice but Ben apparently does because he raises his eyebrow in question. I respond with a subtle shrug.

I have to fix this situation fast; sounds like I'm going to need Roxy on my side to be successful. This is the first job where I'm going to take the lead with clients. At my previous company I was always the second in charge on projects and still doing a lot of the production work myself, so it was an exciting opportunity when Purple Cactus offered me a lead position. I'm ready to move up, even hungry, for a challenge. Not to mention I just moved here and I'm all on my own with no friends, family, or safety net, and a meager amount of savings.

Gloria rearranges her chartreuse scarf around her neck. You have to be powerful and confident to wear that shade of green. Maybe my preference for goth clothing taints my perspective, but it looks like something a lizard would vomit up. Her overall style says I own a fucking company, bitches, emphasized by the giant dragon brooch on her suit jacket. She's intimidating but I'm looking forward to her mentorship.

She tells me my first staff meeting is at 11 a.m. in the big conference room and to get acquainted with our previous campaigns and clients until then. She volunteers Roxy to show me where the recent and current projects are stored. I see Roxy scowl out of the corner of my eye. She might as well bare her teeth like a dog with the aggression coming from her direction. Gloria makes herself some coffee and then Ben follows her out of the room.

I give up on tea and stick with water; seems safer for now. When I get back to my cubicle Roxy is already settled in her space, which is the one next to mine. Of course.

Wanting to give her time to get settled in and maybe get over the little accident, I root through the server like an armadillo (which I saw yesterday for the first time at the apartment complex) thinking maybe I can figure out their system myself. I can't. Project folders are assigned numbers and letters that don't seem to correspond to time in any way, nor are they alphabetical by client. Randomly clicking on folders, there are various public relations plans, graphics, and links to former client websites. They have a varied client base, no major household names, but minor entertainers, athletes, authors, a few nonprofits, local and regional businesses, and a couple of small colleges.

Roxy slurps her coffee, and an irritating tapping sound tells me she's kicking something with her foot. She still seems angry, so I'll wait until after lunch to approach her. The staff meeting is in fifteen anyway.

Gloria is the last to enter, no doubt on purpose, as she seems to enjoy her place at the top. She really is badass, but when I spoke with her during my interview, she came across as tough but fair and genuinely interested in mentoring young professionals.

I gaze around the shiny black conference room table. The view from the glass windows is unfortunate; six lanes of highway with a noise wall shielding neighborhoods on the other side. It's still nice to have the bright light and let the Texas sunshine in for a while.

Gloria introduces me to the group and asks me to say a bit about myself. Luckily, I practiced this for my interview.

"I'm Katie. I have a bachelor's degree in English and a master's in communications. I just moved here from New Jersey, where I worked at Cornwall and Kline. I'm really excited to be here and looking forward to working with all of you."

Mentioning my former company gets another scowl from Roxy, and a few nods from some of the others. Cornwall and Kline has several branches across the country, including one in Dallas, and is fairly well known in the PR industry. It tells them that I'm not just some new girl with no experience.

Gloria calls on staff members to give updates on their projects and any needs they have, then she concludes with a "go get 'em tiger" pep talk. Her meetings are short and sweet, just my style. She doesn't talk just for the sake of talking.

As people trickle out, they stop to shake my hand and welcome me, and I feel a little better. Gloria pulls me aside and apologizes. She usually takes new staff to lunch but is taking a client out today, so she offers a raincheck. She also tells me that by the end of the day she expects to have a signed contract for a new project, and that will be my very first assignment at Purple Cactus.

It's thrilling to be able to jump in feet first. I was worried about tagging on to half-done projects, scared to interject my opinions, not knowing what ideas had been previously discussed, everyone else knowing more about the client than me. But this is perfect. I can immediately become the expert on the client and start spinning ideas straight away.

Since Roxy is still giving off stay the hell away from me vibes, I find Ben the intern and ask him about the folder structure. He points me to a system that logs all the clients and cross indexes multiple projects relating to the same client. It's also sortable by contract open and close date, so I can search to see our current clients, as well as recently closed projects. Thank goodness for Ben or I would have floundered around all day summoning up the courage to approach Roxy.

I grab a sandwich at the coffee shop in the lobby of the building and eat lunch alone in the courtyard. At least they saved some large trees when they built this complex, and the sounds of birds chirping away soothes me.

A slow train of staff start to trickle out around 5 p.m., even though I know they didn't come in until 9 this morning. But if it's anything like my old company, people put in some time at home, and work tends to come in frenzied waves; you learn to take advantage of the slow times. Gloria stops by on her way out.

"How was your first day?" she says.

Rough. "Great! I looked through some of your recent projects and it was all impressive. I definitely came to the right place."

Gloria beams and it's obvious she is proud of the company she built. "Glad to hear it. Sorry again about lunch. Let's try for tomorrow, but no promises."

"Sounds good," I say. As stressful as lunch with the boss is, I am anxious to build a relationship with Gloria and learn as much as possible from her.

"Oh, and check your e-mail; I just sent the signed contract for your first project. We can discuss tomorrow. Have a good night."

"Thanks, you too!"

As soon as Gloria leaves, a sound emerges from Roxy's cubicle, as if she leapt out of her chair so fast it tumped over. I roll my eyes. Roxy seems like the kind of person who waits for her boss to leave so she can get credit for staying late then sneaks out immediately after. She passes my cubicle, and I make another attempt at amends.

"Goodnight, Roxy. I'm really sorry about this morning."

She stops and glowers at me. "This stain had better come out of my skirt, or you owe me forty bucks."

I don't think so, lady. Plus, jasmine tea barely has any color anyway. Not like it is a white skirt. "I'm sure it will," I say.

Roxy spins and stomps off towards the exit. I shake my head at her whole attitude. She can't be much younger than me, too old to behave like a bratty child. But still, my success is tied to her cooperation, so hopefully she gets over it soon.

Waking my computer back up, I anxiously click on the e-mail from Gloria, open the attached contract and start scanning.

My jaw drops to the floor. You have to be fucking kidding me.

4

The contract is with a publisher. The publisher for Nicolas Stone's new book about positive psychology. That asswipe from the talk show. I can't believe my bad luck. My first client is selling a product I despise. Telling people to look on the bright side when pain is very real seems to me as bad as torturing puppies. How can I support the image of a person I already loathe with all my being?

But I have no choice. This is my job, my livelihood, and frankly I'm counting the days until my first paycheck, because the move used up a lot of my savings.

This isn't how I had hoped things would go at Purple Cactus. I have to deal with a bitchy coworker who sits right next to me and now I have Nicolas Stone as a client. I shut down my computer and storm out of the office.

It's hard to see the road while trying to hold back the tears welling up in my eyes, and that's dangerous in this horrific bumper to bumper traffic. Who would have thought commuting in Austin would be as bad as it was in New Jersey?

Damon is sitting on his balcony drinking a beer when I arrive at the apartment complex, the operatic heavy metal voice of Bruce Dickinson bleeding out from his open glass patio doors.

He leans over the railing. "How was your first day?"

I shake my head but don't reply. If I start talking to him, I might cry, and Katie doesn't cry. Even Kat tries not to cry for risk of spiraling into serious introspection about her future, which never turns into a good thing.

"That bad?" says Damon but I can't see him anymore. I'm halfway into my apartment. All I want to do is flop on my bed and listen to Bauhaus until I fall asleep. Maybe I'll let myself do that as long as I promise not to cry.

Noooo! Bad Katie. I know how this plays out. If I retreat into slumber at 6 p.m., I'll awaken in the wee hours of the morning, the loneliest time, when everyone else is asleep and the world is silent and dark. I'll lie there staring at the ceiling, wondering how I got here and wishing I could fall back asleep, but I won't be able to, and I'll end up exhausted for my second day of work.

Instead, I go to my dresser and change into workout clothes. I hate exercise almost as much as being forced to listen to "Baby Shark Dance" on repeat, but it's a necessary component of my mood management. Even as important as the pills I take, working out makes a huge difference. Part of the reason I picked this apartment complex was the small gym they have for residents. I just have to do thirty minutes of cardio, and after that I can allow myself to watch tv until bedtime.

The smell of sweat and funky old socks hits me when I open the door with my keycard. There is one woman inside, running swiftly on the treadmill, but she doesn't look over. I take the exercise bike with a view of a bird feeder, nature's television. Soon, my upbeat goth mix penetrates my brain, and the burning in my leg muscles distracts me from reviewing the day's events. My heart rate soars, and I'm forced to revert focus to basic functions like trying to breathe. That's the magic of exercise, as much as it is obviously the invention of Satan himself.

After a quick shower, I put on my favorite black leggings and an oversized, faded Killing Joke concert tee. Still trying not to think about the shitshow called my life, as represented by my fourth day in Texas, I start streaming *The Nightmare Before Christmas*. I relate to Sally, made up of spare parts, badly sewn together, and always hoping there is something more out there for me. But instead of my maker holding me back, the darkness is my overlord.

A knock on the door startles me. I peer through the peephole and see Damon. Of course, it's him because I don't know anyone else here.

"Are you lactose intolerant?" Damon asks when I open the door.

I shake my head, wondering what this is about.

"Put on your shoes, I'm cheering you up."

"Where are we going?"

"You'll see. I promise you won't regret it. I'm about to introduce you to one of Austin's greatest treasures."

My hand grips the doorknob. Part of me doesn't like Damon assuming I'm free to run off with him, but I also don't want to sit alone in my apartment and have a pity party. Actually, I really do, but that isn't necessarily what's best for me. And he was right about the tacos. I slip on my boots, and grab my purse.

When he turns the ignition key, Motorhead starts blaring from the speakers and Damon turns the volume down for my benefit. He's as passionate about his metal as I am about my music, and I find that attractive, even if I'm not a huge Motorhead fan.

Fifteen minutes later we pull up to a shopping center. There's a cute playground with a green slide where a couple of kids are playing, next to yellow and blue painted metal tables and benches. A vivid pink sign on the side of the building reads, "Amy's Ice Cream." I chuckle to myself because only in Texas are people eating ice cream outside in March. Damon is watching my expression, and his shoulders relax when he sees I'm happy to be here.

Inside, each wall is painted a different color, pastel blue, yellow, lime green, and purple, like a set of Easter eggs. A chalkboard behind the counter has a dozen or more flavors, scrawled in artsy handwritten chalk fonts, some with little drawings. They have standard flavors like vanilla and chocolate, but then they have some inventive ones like Red Hatch Chile and Trifle.

A punk-looking woman with a nose ring and tattooed arms greets me. "Would you like to sample anything?" she asks.

"Maple bacon?"

"It's amazing, not what you imagine, for sure." She hands me a tiny spoonful to try.

The flavor is incredible, the sweetness of maple syrup and the savory crisp bacon. But maybe not for me as an ice cream. "It's interesting. But I think I'll take a small coffee amaretto."

Damon orders a sweet cream with Heath bar crush ins, and we watch as the woman smashes the candy into the ice cream with a metal crusher, then flips it over and over, finally catching it in the cup. The family behind us claps. It's a pretty good show.

"It's my treat," says Damon as I take out my card to pay.

"Thanks. I'll get the tip," and I stuff a fiver in the tip jar; this place is awesome.

As we sit outside eating, I keep expecting him to inquire about why my first day was so awful, but he doesn't. He seems like someone who respects privacy, and I like that.

Damon kicks the bottom of my foot gently. "What do you think?"

"This is the best fucking ice cream I've had in my entire life."

"Hell yeah! I told you so. Stick with me, Katie, I know all the best stuff in Austin."

"You are two for two so far, I'll admit." In that moment, I feel fortunate that Damon turned out to be my neighbor. He has been the best part of Austin so far. But that scares me, because I know the dangers of having the best thing in your life be a person. If that person leaves, you're screwed.

For now, I focus on enjoying my dessert.

He tells me his dream is to have a side business screen printing t-shirts for local bands. He has a friend who plans to sell his equipment in the next few months and Damon is thinking about buying it.

"You'll see, like every person you meet here is in a band," he says.

"Are you?"

"I wish. I have zero musical talent. But there are some badass musicians here and I want to help them grow. They make more money from merch than admission."

"I didn't know that."

"Yeah. You should come see my friends in Flaming Goathead sometime."

Is he asking me on a date, or just trying to get his pals a new fan? I'm open to checking them out, although I suspect with a name like that, they are heavier than what I usually listen to. Not that I've sworn off all music other than goth, it's just that I know what I like.

"Sure, maybe," I say. He looks happy and those cute crinkles appear on his face again when he smiles and something in me pings. Down girl! I am serious about not getting involved in a romantic relationship anytime soon. I need to get settled first.

My stomach is sated with sugary contentment, and I feel calm and sleepy. I steal a glance at Damon as he drives us back and I can't help imagining what it would be like if he were my boyfriend. Which reminds me that I don't even know if he's single.

He pauses at the bottom of the stairs that lead up to his apartment.

"Thanks for taking me out, Damon, I really needed that. You're a sweet guy."

Without warning, he leans in and kisses me.

5

His lips are sweet with the taste of ice cream, which is kind of sexy. I kiss him back and relish feeling his warm body pressed so close to me. It's been a while since I last felt someone's touch and my skin has heightened sensitivity. I flinch slightly as he pulls me closer, his cold hand on my back, under my shirt. His tongue touches mine and my legs feel like they are going to give way beneath me, my spine tingling with desire.

Then I remember my situation and push him away.

He looks confused. "Shit. Did I misread this?" he says, embarrassed.

"No, it's not that. You seem awesome, but I just moved here. I can't do this right now. My life is complicated."

His expression says he doesn't believe me and thinks I'm just making an excuse, but I don't owe him any additional explanation.

"Friends?" I say hopefully. It would be great to be friends with a neighbor.

"Yeah, sure," he says. "Goodnight, Katie." Damon turns and scrambles up the stairs without turning to look back.

I storm into my apartment. Shit, shit, shit. This has been the worst day. Roxy being a total bitch to me for no reason, or at least a completely accidental reason that was her fault in the first place. My first assignment is working with Mr. Positive, the one person in the universe I can't possibly relate to. And now, the first friend I thought I had made probably just wanted to sleep with me. I'm such a loser. Why did I think things would be different here? Just because the sun shines brighter? That doesn't change the fundamental truth that people are horrible. They were horrible in New Jersey and they're still horrible here.

The tears come on like a dam bursting and I crawl under my midnight blue moon and stars comforter and hide. I tried so hard to keep it together today, but I just can't. I cry out all the stress of the move and Roxy and Damon and work and money and my past and my life. I cry until my pillow is soaking wet and my chest is sore from heaving sobs. My eyes are dry, red, and puffy, and I curse that I'm going to look like shit for my second day. Maybe I can tell Gloria I got food poisoning or something. I shake my head, knowing that isn't a real possibility.

I have to live a regimented lifestyle, treating myself like a drill sergeant. Because if I wake up and call in sick to work, then one day becomes two days, two days become three, and then an entire week. Then I have to pretend I was really sick with the flu, then I have no PTO, then the next thing I know I'm jobless. It's happened before. That's not going to happen to Katie. Not in Texas.

Sitting up in bed, I start *The Nightmare Before Christmas* streaming where I left off, and hug my stuffed toy animal, a tiger named Saffron. I've had him since I was a little girl, and he moves everywhere with me. I don't care how silly and childish it is, Saffron is good company, and he never asks anything of me.

My head is pounding now, as it often does when I cry too much. I force myself to get up and drink an entire glass of water because hydration helps. While I'm there I wet a washcloth with warm water and use it as a compress over my eyes to reduce the puffiness. Jack Skellington sings on about how something is missing in his life, and I get where he is coming from. He doesn't belong there. Where do I belong? Will I belong in Austin someday? Will I belong anywhere?

Eventually I must have fallen asleep, because now the birds are chirping. I look at my phone, it's 5:30 a.m. I want to return to slumber, but then I remember...Dr. Nicolas Stone. I spring up straight in my bed. I'm already behind. What if Gloria wants to talk about Nicolas first thing? I should have spent last night researching him instead of weeping and wailing. I grab my laptop and get to work.

When I type in "Nicolas Stone," the first entry that pops up is a crappy, amateurish website he obviously made himself using a template. The telltale signs are a hard to read font, a format that doesn't reflow cleanly to mobile, which I confirm on my phone, and way too much text.

I click on his bio.

Dr. Nicolas Stone holds a PhD in Psychology and is a premier researcher in the field of positive psychology. Dr. Stone has presented over one hundred seminars promoting his new positive psychology model. He is the youngest member to ever receive the American Psychology Consortium Award for Special Contributions to the Advancement of Psychological Research.

I frown. I guess he isn't the hack I thought he was, at least from an education standpoint. But just because he sat in some ivory tower for a few years doesn't mean he understands the practicality of living with depression every day of your life. And how patronizing it feels to be told to just try harder, find your own light. It would be like telling a diabetic to just make sugar her friend.

The shower fills with hot steam, fogging the mirror, and I hope it will rescue my face from looking like I partied too hard on a Monday night. I put drops in my eyes and plead with my makeup to work extra hard for me today.

I arrive at exactly 8:30 a.m. "Good morning, Amber."

"Morning, darlin'. Back again? We must not have scared you off," she replies. I bet she makes that joke with every new employee.

"Not yet," I say with forced enthusiasm.

Sure enough, Gloria sweeps in like a tidal wave at 9. Her energy is palpable, clearly the driving force of the agency. She pauses as she passes my cubicle.

"Katie. I have to miss our lunch again, another client," she says with an apologetic shrug.

"I understand. Clients first."

She agrees, glad I get how this all works. "Did you get a chance to look over the contract?"

Ugh, this is going to be the acting role of a lifetime, trying to market this arrogant know-it-all and pretend I'm honored to do so. "Yes, it sounds like a great project," I say, with what I hope is a cheerleader smile.

"Any initial thoughts?"

Shit. She's testing me. I was right that she expected me to do research sometime between 5 p.m. yesterday and this morning. So lucky those chirpy birds woke me up early.

"I looked over his website," I say. "It certainly needs an overhaul. No real branding, no personality. I'm not sure who he really is."

Gloria waves her hand. "That's an understatement. Dr. Stone doesn't know it yet, but he's just about to go primetime and we're going to take him there. That's what we do."

Even though I dread working with him, Gloria's enthusiasm is infectious, and I suddenly do want to make Nicolas Stone the most successful psychologist swindler in the world.

"You know what? I have meetings all day, so why don't we talk in my office right now. Walk with me."

Gloria leads me first to the kitchen where she tells me about the time she had the best cappuccino in Rome, while she makes her morning coffee. I'm gun-shy about hot drinks since my incident with Roxy, so I brought my aluminum water bottle today.

Waiting patiently in her office with my notepad and pen in my lap as Gloria sips her coffee, I take in the scene. Apparently, she loves Italy, because her office is decorated with stunning Tuscan landscapes, professionally matted and framed. The room is dotted with plants, peace lilies and twisted bamboo in ceramic pots of swirling blues and greens.

"Here at Purple Cactus, we like to take an immersive approach to our projects. If we are working with a usable product, we test it ourselves, not just once, but make it a part of our everyday routine, so we can understand how it would be used by an average consumer."

This is not a new concept to me, and we employed a similar method at my previous company, but I'm not about to say so.

"First we need to define the product," she continues. "So...?" She looks at me expectantly. I guess she wants me to define the project. She's testing me again and sweat starts to form on the back of my neck.

"The client is the publisher, and their product is Nicolas Stone's new book," I start, and see a flash of disappointment in Gloria's eyes, "but, for this type of book, consumers aren't just buying a self-help book, they are trusting that the author can help them. For that reason, Dr. Stone is the product. The publisher made a good choice in hiring a full-service PR firm as opposed to solely a digital marketing firm."

Gloria breaks into a smile, and I can tell that was the right answer. "I knew we hired a superstar," she says.

Suddenly yesterday seems a million years away and I'm flying high that I'm starting off on the right foot with my new boss and mentor. I just sit there with a dumb grin on my face.

"Since Nicolas is our product, and immersion is the name of the game here, there is only one obvious first step," she says.

My fist clenches as I dread what she is going to say next.

"Pack your bags, because we're sending you to follow Dr. Nicolas Stone on his Texas lecture tour, starting Thursday."

Fuck.

6

Damon is hanging over his balcony when I get home. "Hey Katie," he yells.

"Hey," I reply.

"Hold on, I'm coming down." He disappears and reappears clambering down the steps until he stops in front of me. "I'm sorry about yesterday," he says.

"You didn't really do anything wrong," I say.

"No, I'm pretty sure I acted like a dick. I swear that's not me. I'm totally down with being friends if you still want that. That was not the Texas hospitality you deserve."

Things suddenly feel lighter, like I was carrying a backpack full of bricks, and it dropped to the floor. "Thanks. I *would* like that."

Having a friendly neighbor is a boon, especially to someone like me. I already feel like I could ask Damon to hang out if I didn't want to be alone. At least now that he apologized, and romance is off the table. I'm not at all upset that he kissed me, but it's true he didn't handle the rejection that well.

"Cool. Let me make it up to you tomorrow night. There's another place I want to show you."

"I don't know, I have to travel for work Thursday, so I can't be out late."

"We won't be. Oh yeah, was your second day any better?"

"It was, mostly." Roxy was out so I didn't see her all day, and Gloria seemed pleased with me, so not much to complain about, other than learning I have to follow Dr. Nicolas Stone around like a groupie.

We chat for a bit, but I need to pee, so I cut it short. Before I close my door, he shouts, "You'll need comfortable shoes!" I wonder where we're going tomorrow.

I change into my workout clothes and do my dutiful thirty minutes, this time on a treadmill. I'm serious about the regimented lifestyle and worry about how my travel with Nicolas might throw me off. I never imagined myself as someone who would use a hotel gym, but now I get it. If only I didn't have to travel while I'm still getting settled in here, but that's life.

A quick shower and a healthy dinner later, I've ticked every box on my depression management checklist. Now I get to relax. I flip on *Edwards Scissorhands* to stream in the background while I begin cyberstalking Nicolas Stone. I reason that I'm just doing my job, right? But I am also nervous traveling with a total stranger. It's weird and bound to be uncomfortable. The more I can learn about him the better it will be. He could be an axe murderer. It's always the nice ones, they say.

He's smart enough to use social media only in a professional capacity, either that or he has no social life to speak of. That's great because otherwise we might have a lot to clean up, PR-wise, but sucks because I can't find anything personal on him, only what he wanted to share, which is not much. His Twitter posts are mostly daily affirmations, Facebook mostly links to studies and workshops, and Instagram is all travel photos, scenic vistas or landmarks without any people in them. Does he have friends, parents, a girlfriend, cats, an iguana? Does he like any sports teams, does he even eat?

His social media is so dry that my first instinct says we're going to need to humanize this guy because he doesn't share anything personal, not even breakfast, and he comes across like a brainy academic robot programmed with a cheerful mindset. If he is so great at helping people be happy, I want to see *him* being happy so I can believe he has the answers.

"Good morning, Amber."

"Morning, darlin'."

It's only workday three and I feel like greeting Amber is part of my daily ritual. Today I brave making tea, but I poke my head around the corner first holding the cup awkwardly behind me, lest Roxy storms at me like a bull again. The coast is clear, and I make it to my cubicle with a full cup. Progress.

I start brainstorming the Nicolas Stone campaign. He's supposed to give me an advance copy of his book when I meet with him, so that is on my to-do list, but I need to learn more about the market he is competing in. One of the things I love about my job is the chance to become so engrossed in my research that hours pass by unnoticed. That initial phase where I'm learning as much as I can, filing the interesting pieces away, making notes, and an infinite world of possible approaches exists before I narrow it one by one to what will work for this particular client. I'm going to figure you out, Dr. Stone.

"You're going on tour with Nicolas Stone?" Roxy practically spits at me, breaking my concentration. I hadn't even noticed when she came in this morning.

I spin around and see her accusatory face staring at me. You would think I ran over her grandmother or something, the way she seems to hate me in a deeply personal way. But I know a trick for handling highly emotional people like her, and I answer in only facts with no hyperbole, explanation, or apology.

"Yes, I am, starting tomorrow," I say.

Roxy's face is like borscht; she's going to go up in flames any moment now out of anger or resentment or jealousy, whatever this is. "I can't believe this," she says.

"Can't believe what?" I ask, still without emotion, which is probably making her more indignant.

"That Gloria is trusting you with this project. You've been here like *a minute*," she says, punctuating the last two words with a pointy finger.

Wow. She doesn't hold back. I admire her honesty, and she obviously has some passion. "Look Roxy, I'm just doing my job. It's not up to me how Gloria hands out assignments. I hope you'll work with me on this, because Gloria said you are the best graphic artist." I'm not sucking up to her, I'm just repeating what Gloria said.

She twitches her mouth to the side. "Of course. I'm a professional, you know."

Ummm. Not really, I didn't know by the way she is behaving but I'm going to have to trust that she is ambitious enough that she can't purposely do poor work just to throw me under the bus. Mutual success or mutual destruction is as far as trust will go in our relationship for now.

I turn back to my computer, and she doesn't say another word.

My sneakers on, and clothed in my least worn workout top, I knock on Damon's door. "Is this going to count as my daily workout?"

He laughs, but I'm serious. "I think so," he says. "Are you ready?"

"Sure."

Backpack in tow, he leads me to his car again and we are on our way. A quick trip down the highway, and soon we're climbing up a steep hill, winding around curve after curve, houses of stone on either side, beautifully landscaped with terraces and retaining walls holding in plants I'm learning are common natives, yuccas and mountain laurels.

We keep climbing, passing high-end gated homes, until we reach an area where a wall of rock forms on the left side. Damon parks the car, and we walk to the bottom of a stone staircase set into a rocky, treed hillside. The sign reads, "Covert Park at Mount Bonnell."

I stand at the bottom and all I see looking up are endless stairs until the view is obscured by trees. Now I get why he mentioned the comfortable shoes.

Damon turns and raises his eyebrows mischievously. "Ready?"

We start walking up and now I'm glad I work out, because even so, my quads start burning after the first twenty steps, so I can't imagine what it would be like if I didn't.

"How many steps are there?" I say breathlessly.

"One hundred and two."

I have no idea if that is a lot or not, since none of my gyms have been fancy enough to have a Stairmaster, so I focus on one step at a time. Damon doesn't even seem winded.

We finally reach the top and there is a giant rock carved with a dedication, declaring our arrival at the peak, and behind that there's a semi-shaded overlook with rock columns holding up wooden slats. I walk towards the railing and look down at the river below, reflecting the dusk sky. I breathe in and savor the vista.

It's beautiful. Streaks of bronze and copper melt into the hills, the last of the sun's rays meeting the dark blue of the looming night. I glance at Damon, and he is mesmerized by the view, even though he has probably seen it many times. He's a real puzzle, this one, a metalhead who loves ice cream and sunset walks. He would be boyfriend material if I were in the market. Which I'm not. But a part of me still expects him to slip his hand into mine with this romantic setup.

Instead, he grabs my arm. "Come over here for a real view," he says and leads me down the path to the left and beckons me to climb up on a large stone table.

"Whoa," I mumble as the Austin skyline appears before me, the twinkling of the city skyscrapers whispering welcome to the evening stars.

This is my new home. I can hardly believe I've been here only a week. With Damon standing beside me, in this perfect moment, I feel content.

If only I didn't have to leave tomorrow to babysit Mr. Positive.

A Lyft car drops me off at the office around 9 a.m. I greet Amber and just finish dragging my business travel suitcase into the office when Gloria appears.

"Are you all set?" she asks.

"I think so."

Gloria gives me an encouraging smile. "You'll be great. Do you have the list of questions we discussed?"

"I do." Part of my job is getting to know the real Nicolas Stone and that can't be done by grilling him with a set of questions, but I know Gloria just needs me to walk away from this with a plan for the man.

"And Amber set you up with the expense card, right?"

"Yes, I've got it." I pat my purse on the desk.

"Okay. Call me if you get stuck or need any advice. And write everything down."

"I will. Thanks!"

It makes me a little nervous that Gloria seems on edge. I figured she trusted me, since she gave me this assignment, but I remind myself that trust is earned over time and not just from reading a resume.

The minute Gloria is down the hall, Roxy creeps into my cubicle and props her butt on my desk. I can see a tattoo sneaking out from under her sleeve. A snake, I think. "Are you worried?" she asks with a fake sweetness.

"About what?"

"Messing up your first assignment."

She's actually trying to play mind games with me. It's almost funny. If she applied as much energy to her work as she is to messing with me, she'd be better off. Of course I'm worried about messing up my first assignment. Who wouldn't be? And what kind of nasty person would point that out? Roxy.

I shrug like it couldn't matter less to me. "It's my first assignment *here*," I say, "but I've been doing this for a while now."

Roxy frowns. She was hoping to get more of a rise out of me. She changes tactics. "Nicolas is cute, huh? I mean in an uptight sort of Katie way. Not my style of course," she runs her hand through her swept over blue hair.

"I guess he is." I have to keep reminding myself that Roxy thinks she knows who Katie is, and yes, Katie might go for a Nicolas Stone type, but Kat digs long-haired, edgier types who aren't good for her.

She smirks like she caught me in a trap. "Well keep it in your pants, missy! I wouldn't want you to get fired in your first week."

I roll my eyes and shake my head. It's not even worth a response, and before I can even think of one, Amber is outside the cubicle.

"There's a gentleman here for you, darlin'," Amber says.

I swallow. Nicolas Stone has entered the building. Or the office lobby, presumably. "Thanks Amber. Can you get Gloria? She wanted to meet him before we head out."

I wait for Gloria, and we walk to the front together. Nicolas stands up from the armchair. He's taller in real life.

Gloria reaches out her hand "Dr. Stone, I'm Gloria, the founder of Purple Cactus PR. So wonderful to meet you."

He has the firm, confident handshake of a man who spends his life interacting with people, at workshops and seminars, in the classroom, and at university events. "Wonderful to meet you as well," he says. "I look forward to working with you." He is as stiff and formal as his online presence. I wonder if he's like this in his seminars and classes, and if so, how he got a book deal. Maybe he is that brilliant of a mind.

"And this is Katie," Gloria says.

I shake his hand. It's smooth and soft. This is a man who probably isn't shy about buying beauty products like expensive hand lotions. A GQ model man, with his gray British-style button down vest over a crisp white long-sleeved shirt. His sandy blonde hair has a Clark Kent side part, giving him an old-fashioned look. Thirty going on fifty-five.

Roxy is wrong; he isn't my type at all. But objectively, few would argue that he is handsome in a conventional way. "Pleased to meet you, Dr. Stone."

"Please call me Nick," he says.

"Of course, Nick." It's showtime, and professional Katie is on the clock. "I'm excited to hear your seminar today. I've been reading all about your work, fascinating stuff," I say. Not exactly a lie, it *is* interesting, even if I think it's all garbage and gives people false hope.

"I hope you enjoy it," he says and then glances down at his watch. "In fact, we should probably get going."

Gloria throws her violet scarf around her neck. That seems to be a habit of hers, playing with her scarves. I bet it has some deep psychological root. Something I can ask Nicolas, I mean Nick, about later. "Have a safe trip," says Gloria. "We will set up a strategy meeting next week with you and your publisher. But feel free to reach out to me personally if you have any questions before then." She hands Nick a card.

I run down the hall to grab my suitcase and laptop and catch Roxy trying to get a glimpse of Mr. Positive.

"I told you he's cute," she says and gives me an exaggerated wink before retreating to the break room.

Grow up, Roxy.

Nick holds all the doors for me and lets me out of the elevator first, unerringly courteous. Soon we are settled in his car.

"Mind if I put on some music?" he says.

"Not at all," I reply, even though the chance that he is going to put on anything I'm remotely going to want to hear is small. But it's his car and he's driving and I'm just a guest. Plus, a little background music is a great conversational lubricant for two strangers alone for the first time.

He taps on his phone and the first song is unrecognizable to me, but it sounds like it could be from the sixties. He puts on his Ray-Ban sunglasses, and I do the same with my cheap ones from Kohls.

We drive silently as he heads towards the interstate that takes us to San Antonio. The second song sounds like early hip hop, I think, and the third song is definitely modern country, but none of it sounds familiar. "This is quite an eclectic mix," I say.

"It's a channel I found that plays all styles of music, all decades, but nothing overly popular."

That's bizarre. "I didn't know such a thing existed."

"Before my lectures I like to be exposed to new stimuli, and the other stations play the same songs over and over."

"Interesting. So, no tried and true pump up mix for you, then?"

"No, not for me," he says. "New experiences, new stimuli increase dopamine levels in the brain."

"And that's why people love to try new things?"

"Partly, yes."

"Do you make most of your life decisions based on psychology?"

Nick's face hardens. Shit. We're only twenty minutes in and I already hit a nerve. I better try and backtrack. I'm not an investigative journalist, after all. "Sorry," I say. "I didn't mean it to come out like that. I mean, you study the human mind for a living, surely that colors the choices you make."

"No, it's a fair question. It is possible, and in fact, happens quite often, that people ignore the very truths they have unearthed themselves, in order to live the lives they always imagined. But for me, I formulate and test theories and study and re-formulate and test again, searching for ways to make people's lives better. And if I find something I believe will do that, wouldn't it be insanity if I didn't do that thing myself?"

Yeesh. Things got heavy fast. I think of my mental checklist for managing my depression, like my thirty minutes of daily cardio, and I know Nick and I are the same in that way, when something works, neither of us can ignore it. "Yes, I suppose it would," I say, and focus on staring out the window before I say anything else that might offend him within our first hour together. We have three days for that.

8

Sitting in the back of the small auditorium, I watch as people trickle in to hear Nick's lecture. I'm armed with my pen and notepad because this doesn't seem the place for click clacking on a laptop. Surprisingly, the audience is on the young side, college-aged, or early thirties. I always imagined self-help seminars filled with middle-agers trying to figure out where their lives went off-track.

Maybe I was wrong about what this is. Based on my online research, self-help workshops can run anywhere from hundreds to thousands of dollars, based on the number of hours and the fame of the speaker. This event probably doesn't count as a seminar at all, it's really more of a ticketed lecture, at twenty-four bucks a ticket for two hours.

I'm still trying to figure him out. His clothes are high quality, but his car isn't flashy or new, and he just doesn't seem like someone trying to make it rich. Hopefully seeing him lecture in person will clear it all up for me. It would be awesome if he turned out not to be a scam artist that I have to abet in order to keep my brand-new job.

The lights dim and Nick makes his way to the stage. He clicks the remote and the screen lights up.

"Hi!" he says, then pauses, which makes the crowd giggle with discomfort. "Who is having a fantastic day, filled with wonder and gratitude?"

There are a few mumbles and chuckles, but no one raises their hand or leaps up in affirmation.

"Are you sure?"

The audience shifts uncomfortably in their seats.

"What if I told you that you probably *are* having a fantastic day, and you just haven't realized it yet?"

I scan the room and see some skeptical, some curious, faces.

"Let me prove it to you. Who here didn't wake up today?"

That gets a chuckle.

"Fantastic start! Who got in a fatal car accident on the way over?" He pauses. "No one? That's great! How many of you ate something today?" A few people raise their hands or murmur affirmatively. "Isn't that great? Most of you had food available to you, that you could afford, and you ate it."

"I'm Dr. Nicolas Stone, and I'm going to share some of the latest research in positive psychology. My goal is, by the end of this lecture, you will realize how fantastic this day really is, and why that does *not* mean blissful happiness every second of every day."

I can see that he has the audience now; they hope he can really do that for them, and I find myself hoping the same for me. I'm already relieved that he isn't promising infinite joy.

"Happiness. What is it?" he says, and the screen fills with people smiling and laughing. The audience waits in silence for the answer. "No, I'm really asking you, just shout it out."

The audience starts throwing out ideas—family, money, health, a promotion at work, a beach vacation, a million dollars, a puppy, fame, winning a medal, having a baby, being in love.

He forwards to the next slide and the photo montage is an uncanny representation of what the audience shouted out, even the cute puppy, and a couple on the beach.

"Something like this, right?" The audience laughs because it's accurate to a fault.

"Those are things that we have collectively, as a society, in this country, associated with happiness. But that isn't happiness. In fact, it doesn't really exist. Happiness is just a construct we invented. So how can we study it? How can we figure out what interventions make our lives better?"

Dr. Stone launches into a brief but somehow digestible history of positive psychology and I scramble to write down the key names, Martin Seligman, Mihaly Csikszentmihalyi, Angela Duckworth, Laurie Santos, but soon there are too many to write down. I had no idea this many people were studying positive psychology or even what it is, or that there are programs at several top universities focused on this field.

He explains some current theories and how what we think of as happiness is actually several pieces, and only one of them is represented by the person smiling and laughing. I feel the audience following along as I am, and I'm entranced by his enthusiasm. Nicolas is an entirely different person when he is talking about psychology, and I can tell he is deeply invested.

After describing some of the best studied techniques, which include practicing gratitude, he asks the audience for some examples of things that have gone well for them today.

I remember the whole gratitude thing is what made me balk when I first saw him on the local access talk show. I thought why should I be fucking grateful that my brain is cursed with this never-ending darkness? What do I have to be grateful for?

But now I see it was out of context; it's just one small part of a wide range of ideas in positive psychology. Ugh, why am I so jaded? Now I see I have a ton to be grateful for: this freaking job, for one, Damon, and Amy's Ice Cream is a new one for me, but it's on the list now. And tacos!

The audience has now changed their tune and are shouting out things like, "I didn't get hit by a truck this morning/The bus was on time/These seats are really comfortable/This caramel latte/I got to hear this lecture."

"And I'm glad you got to hear it," Nick says to the last one. He tells the audience he is grateful that he could share his passion with them, and he hopes it changes their lives, and they share their newfound understanding with others.

As he wraps up, I'm shocked that he doesn't mention his upcoming book. We're going to have to discuss that. These lectures are the best marketing tool he has, and he didn't even take advantage of it.

I wait while he talks with person after person, one woman even getting teary eyed thanking him, and another asking if she can give him a hug. He says yes and it makes her day. It doesn't hurt that he is pretty cute. Damn it, Kat! I don't know what is going on with me lately, between the kiss from Damon, and Roxy's snarky comment, even though I'm professional, I'm not above finding a man empirically hot, even if I don't plan to do anything about it. It's just human nature.

It's been over a year since I last went on a date. It's just too much. My college boyfriend point blank told me it was too hard to deal with my depression, I was too difficult to please. He just wanted to have fun and enjoy life. Join the club, buddy. I want that too—sorry I was dragging you down. But in earnest, I understand. I'm not the easiest person to be around and not everyone is equipped to handle this level of emotional baggage. I barely hold any resentment towards him, just a smidge, maybe.

As a result, I don't actively try to date. My mom wishes I would, because she could worry about me less if I had someone else looking after me. She doesn't understand the whole concept undermines my independence. I need to know I can be on my own; I don't want my boyfriend to be my caretaker.

The kiss with Damon, that was a mistake, a sexy, hot mistake that felt pretty great in the moment, but still a mistake. And anything with Nick would be not just a mistake, but a disaster. As my client, he is strictly off limits.

The line of audience members waiting to talk with him thins, and he makes his way towards me. I like him infinitely more than I did yesterday, which is my fault for being so judgmental, but even though I've gotten to a point where I can generally manage my problems, that doesn't mean I'm perfect. The whole reason I invented Katie was to try and stop seeing everything from jaded ole Kat's point of view.

"What did you think?" he says.

He seems to genuinely care about my opinion. I need to be careful to answer from my professional view as a consultant, not as a twenty-six-year-old depressed woman who needed to hear everything he just said. Oops. Now I've waited too long to speak.

"That bad, huh?" he says.

"Aack—no! I was just trying to find the right words. You really move people, Nick. Do you know that?"

He blushes and looks at the ceiling, avoiding my eyes. "I just want to help as many people as I can."

"I think it's incredible," I say, catching his eyes and holding the gaze, but then the moment suddenly feels intimate, so I add, "but why aren't you promoting the book?"

He stiffens and he is back to the Nick from the office lobby and the car. "People already paid to hear the lecture; if at the end it seems like the whole thing was just an advertisement for the book, it might negate all the positives they took from it."

I furrow my brows. I'm struggling to understand his perspective. Is it just my years working in PR and marketing that has made me lose sight of the evils of commodifying everything?

"Or...," I say slowly, "they could use your book to reinforce everything you said. Isn't the book to help people too?"

He sighs like he doesn't know what he wants. "Yes, of course. That's why I wrote it. But I guess I think of it for people who can't come hear me talk or take a positive psychology class in college."

"But how will those people know the book exists if you don't promote it? And isn't your publisher counting on you using your lectures and social media presence to sell books? They're in the Dr. Stone business now."

His face contorts like he is in pain, and he is practically wringing his hands. Oh, sweet siouxsie sioux, is this what I do? Take perfectly happy people and ruin them? What is wrong with me?

"Honestly Katie, I don't know. I mean, yes, of course they are expecting that, but I don't know how to do this, how to manage any of this. I just want to teach people what we know and give them the tools to improve their lives. I'm not a book promoter, I'm a psychologist. Maybe it was all a mistake."

Without thinking, I pat his arm in sympathy. He clearly is conflicted. "It's okay, Nick. Maybe I can help you sort through some of this. Why don't we go get some lunch before we head to Houston?"

"Good idea. I know just the spot."

Nick and I walk along a typical city street towards his recommended lunch spot. I follow him down a staircase hidden in a corner, and we descend into a Venetian retreat. The River Walk is a secret, subterranean world nestled beneath the city. The emerald river snakes between hotels and restaurants and arched masonry bridges allow tourist-filled riverboats to pass beneath them. It's still early spring and cypress trees are just beginning to leaf, and the landscapes of ferns, roses, fuchsia, lavender, and golden wildflowers are just beginning to bloom and blossom.

Around the corner, umbrellas in bright red, blue, green, and yellow shade the tables cozied up next to the river, the whole scene like a painting by Renoir.

"Would you like to sit outside?" he asks as we approach the restaurant.

"Sure," I say. It's a gorgeous day, so why not?

Minutes later I sit with a view of the water, iced tea in hand. Nick has a faraway look. I sip my drink, wondering if he's thinking about the book launch.

"This takes me back," he says.

"You've been here before?" I ask. I thought he was from California, at least that's where he taught at a university, according to my online research.

"Yes. I lived in Texas as a child. My parents used to take us here at least once a year."

I wonder who "us" is, but I don't ask. I'm not one to pry much into other people's pasts, because I don't really want to talk about mine.

"That sounds like a nice memory," I say.

His face contorts for just a split second before a forced evenness replaces it. "It was...is. Have you been to the River Walk before?" He says, not subtle about his changing the subject. This is going to be tough if neither of us want to be the focus of attention. In fairness to me, I'm specifically being paid to learn about him and not the other way around.

I shake my head. "I've only lived in Texas for one week. I just moved here from New Jersey."

Nick's eyes widen. "And they sent you out of town so soon? You must not even be settled in yet."

"Eh, I don't mind. Purple Cactus is a big career opportunity for me, so I'm willing to do whatever they need." Before he starts asking me why I moved, as people tend to do, I turn it around again. "So, what made you become a psychologist?"

His eyelids flutter before his cool composure comes back, but it's too late, because I saw that momentary panic. What is his deal?

"I've always been fascinated by the human mind, I suppose," he says.

That's not a real answer and we both know it, but it's good enough for now. Surely, he gets that question all the time. I make a mental note that we will need to work on more personable answers to common questions the media or public might ask him when the book launches.

"Who isn't these days? It's like every podcast now is about what led some mild-mannered soccer mom to commit murder," I say.

He chuckles. We are back on safe ground again. "It does seem that way."

That leads seamlessly into a discussion of our favorite tv shows. Surprise, surprise, we have little in common. I love shows with magic and whimsy, supernatural, or dark but hopeful alternate realities. TV-14 is the right level of darkness and violence for me.

Nick watches travel shows and PBS series and British mysteries. Stories rooted in reality and based on facts.

"But you spend most of your life buried in research and statistics—I would think you'd want your entertainment to be something different, dreamy, imaginative."

"I like what I like," he says.

I can't argue with that.

After lunch, we start the drive to Houston. He asks if I mind if he puts on an audio book from a fellow psychologist he has been meaning to check out. I don't mind at all; it saves me from worrying so much about what to say and how I'm going to learn what I need to learn to help him without pushing him away.

When we get to the hotel, he asks me if I'd like to meet later for dinner. I'm exhausted so I decline. I'm still full from lunch, but truthfully I want to use the hotel gym. Especially in this new and stressful situation, traveling after moving, a new job, a new client—something needs to be routine.

Before we leave for our separate rooms, he pulls a book out of his bag.

"An advance copy," he says.

"Thanks. I'll start reading it this evening."

"You don't have to do that," he says.

"I do, it's my job." I think he has temporarily forgotten why I'm here, as have I. It was a nice afternoon at the River Walk, and even though we had some awkward moments, I enjoyed it.

"Of course, I just meant...never mind. Meet in the lobby in the morning at eight?"

"Perfect," I say.

I change quickly and head for the gym. With my upbeat goth mix blasting in my ears, I feel at peace again. No matter where I am, New Jersey, Austin, or Houston, apartment gym or hotel, I'm in the same place when my body is working and sweating and the music pulses through my veins. Just thirty minutes, as always, the Rx complete, I wipe off the machine and turn around to throw my towel in the basket. I freeze.

Nick is standing in the doorway, in gray basketball shorts and a fitted cobalt shirt that hugs his muscled arms, which I hadn't noticed until just now. We both look startled and embarrassed. The last thing I want is my first client seeing me sweaty in a form fitting tank top and spandex capris, my hair matted to my forehead, my face flushed with exertion.

He looks away after, but I already caught him giving me the onceover. I can't blame him, because I did the same, and hope so badly he didn't register my eyes undressing him, imagining his toned body beneath his clothes. He quickly says, "Guess we had the same idea," as he tries to look anywhere but at me.

"We did!" I say with a cheerful enthusiasm that sounds ridiculous in my head. "Goodnight!" I yelp and tear out of the gym like I'm being chased by a herd of running bulls.

Back in my room, I take a shower and think about Nick. Since I moved to Texas, my libido has been on an upswing, which is not necessarily a bad thing, given the common side effects of my daily medications. I think of Damon's kiss, and now Nick's torso. Geez, Kat, get a room. I laugh at myself, since I'm already in a room, but I'm alone, and I prefer it that way, for now.

I slip into bed with Nick's book, reminding myself that this is work, and I need to focus and concentrate on understanding the message so we can formulate a strategy for the launch. After reading the first three chapters, I'm happy to report that the book is compelling. It shouldn't be hard to promote this; it has heart.

I worried that it would be filled with history, theory, statistics, and research, but thankfully it isn't. It distills the basic concepts and provides relatable examples. The first section is mostly background, so I haven't hit the real meat about how to apply this knowledge, but it's a good start.

My eyelids start to droop, and I'm forced to admit I can't read another word. Before I drift off to slumberland, Nick's face appears before me, but not the one at the gym, not the one with the sexy body that made me momentarily think of unprofessional conduct. Instead, I see the troubled face, the fleeting look he tried to hide under his analytical, pragmatically cheerful persona.

10

The hotel lobby is bustling with visitors checking out or returning from the breakfast buffet. Nick is sitting in an armchair, flipping through a newspaper, but he rushes to stand up when he sees me, like I'm the Queen of England and not a hired PR junior client manager.

"Good morning," he says, with a smile that shows his perfectly white teeth. I should have expected the positive psychologist to be chipper in the morning, and he is.

I remember our interaction at the gym and my cheeks get warm. Pushing that thought aside, I attempt to match his expression and say, "What's the plan for today? Your lecture isn't until this afternoon, right?"

"Right. Since you're new to Texas, I thought we might do something touristy this morning, if you're up for it."

My job right now is to understand who he is, and what better way than by watching him experience something he chose to do. "Sure, what did you have in mind?"

"The Space Center?" He tilts his head like a puppy who is worried he did something wrong by eating your slipper.

Not necessarily what I would pick for myself, but I'm open to anything, and Nick did teach me that novel experiences increase dopamine, and who am I to argue with that? "Let's go!" I say with a little bit too much force.

He narrows his eyes at me. "You don't have to pretend to be enthusiastic on my account, you know?"

Ouch! Called out. "Sorry, I guess I just don't want you to see me as negative," I say, and then want to kick myself for sharing something so personal, even though without more context, he'll just assume it's about the moment, and his chosen career. "The Space Center sounds interesting, I swear."

"It's okay. Finish reading the book. No one is saying you have to walk around like it's sunshine and rainbows all the time."

He has no idea. For me, it's more like shadows and graveyards. Some days I want a fucking medal for being as positive as I am, with my natural inclination towards gloom.

The Space Center turns out to be pretty cool. We walk underneath a SpaceX Falcon 9 rocket, take the tram tour, which includes a peek inside the astronaut training facility, and Nick marvels at the historic space suits.

"Isn't it amazing to see these up close? I just finished watching *Chasing the Moon*. It's incredible what humans can accomplish when they put their collective minds together," he says.

Case in point of my gloomy disposition is that while he was reveling in the magnificence of human achievement, I was just wondering if these suits have historic astronaut pee on them. Or worse.

In the Mission Mars exhibit we get to touch an actual rock fragment from the red planet, and they have a virtual landscape projection where we get to see a Martian sunset. I feel like I'm in *The Hitchhiker's Guide to the Galaxy*, just a naïve human learning how incredible and vast the universe really is. Nick doesn't say anything in here, but I can still tell he's in awe as well.

My favorite part of the Space Center is the giftshop. Nick and I wander around looking at the rocket figurines, magnets, patches, and space suit costumes for kids. There's a little plush dog in an astronaut suit, with the name "Laika" on the side, which I find a little morbid. I remember learning how the poor little first dog in space died within a few hours, not that they had planned to bring her back down, anyway. To me, this is a great example of how much humanity sucks.

Determined not to succumb to negative thoughts, I push poor little Laika out of my mind and allow myself to get excited about a pack of glow star stickers, which would look awesome on my apartment ceiling. I used to have those when I was in elementary school, and I remember staring up at them when sleep wouldn't come, and they always kept me company.

Then I spy something even better, and as I reach for the silver foil, Nick's hand does the same and our fingers collide. I drop it and pull back as if I burned myself on a hot stove.

"Pardon me," says Nick, handing me the packet. "Guess we both had the same idea, again."

"Guess so." I hand him a second freeze-dried vanilla ice cream sandwich in return. "This reminds me of going to the planetarium on field trips," I say, waving my imminent purchase. "This was the best part."

"I'm getting that you're not really a space fan," he says.

"*Or* I'm a really big astronaut ice cream fan."

"Fair point."

I can't resist though. "See what I did there? I chose the more positive possibility."

"And the student becomes the master," he says as we head towards the checkout.

Nicolas Stone is confusing. Just when I think he is serious and academic in his passionate pursuit of well-being, like the robot Isaac on *The Orville*, learning what it means to be human, he surprises me with genuine moments of joy and ease.

The lecture in Houston is the same, the crowd similar in makeup. Nicolas still doesn't mention his book, and he once again talks to every single person asking for his attention afterwards. He must really love his work, which I've learned yesterday and today gives him meaning, which is one of the pillars of Seligman's theory of positive psychology.

I wonder if *my* job has meaning. I don't think so, not in the way Nick's job does. He helps people, makes their lives better. What could be more meaningful? I just help people sell more products or become more successful. But is that just my negative interpretation? I'm starting to wonder. I've learned that it's dangerous to know only a little bit about something complex, and psychology definitely falls in the high-risk zone for me.

After the lecture, we head to Dallas. It's already 7 p.m. when we arrive so we are in agreement about eating granola bars out of the vending machine.

This time, before we get to the elevators he says, "Are you hitting the gym? I can wait until you're through if you are."

That's so thoughtful and insightful that I'm taken off guard. I don't want him to tiptoe around me. I reason that if I know he'll be there, and we are two professional adults, it should be fine. Not like I'm wearing a bikini by the pool or something.

"Uh, yes, I was planning to go right now. But don't wait on my account, I'm sure the gym is big enough for both of us."

He eyes me and twitches his mouth, trying to figure out if I'm being fake again, just to be accommodating.

"Really, it's totally okay with me," I assure him.

Fifteen minutes later I'm on the exercise bike, since I like to alternate cardio machines, and Nick walks in and surveys the equipment options. I give him a little wave, point at my headphones to let him know conversation is not needed or possible. He moves towards the free weights that are stacked in the corner and starts lifting.

Honestly, I'm not even into super muscly guys. Scrawny guys are fine, or really, I don't have much preference since it's all about the emotional connection for me. But Nick is a fine specimen of a human male, and I have to force myself to keep my eyes forward, lest he catch me checking him out as he pumps his biceps.

On the other hand, is there any chance he is performing for me? Like a male bird strutting his plumage and singing, "Look at me, look at what a great mate I'd make." Does that make me a female bird in breeding season? It is spring, after all. Geez, Kat, professional much?

I also hate that Roxy was right. Good thing I have her sitting on my shoulder shouting, "Well keep it in your pants, missy!" Just one more day to get through and I won't have to worry that I might jump on Dr. Stone. Of course, I would never, not with a client. That would be a sure sign of self-sabotage, and I'm too careful and constrained for that. Shit. Maybe I'm more like Nick than I thought. Am I the robot? A depressed woman learning what it means to be a "normal" human, imagining a life of joy and positive emotion?

Just focus on work and everything will be fine.

But Nick is my work...

11

In the morning there's a text from Nick, asking if I'm up for another excursion before his afternoon lecture. I say yes and agree to meet him in the lobby at 8:30 a.m.

"Where are we going—wait, I don't want to know. Surprise me," I say when Nick appears with his fresh-faced ever so peppy in the morning smile.

"That must mean you trust me," he says.

"Well...I barely know you, but I enjoyed the River Walk and Space Center, so I don't think you'd steer me wrong."

"I hope you're right. This is somewhere I've never been myself, but have been wanting to, so it will be a new experience for both of us."

"Ahh, morning dopamine boost before your lecture."

"Hopefully," he says with a grin, pleased that he taught me something.

Nick checks his phone occasionally for directions as he leads us through the downtown commercial district of Dallas. My curiosity is peaking as I wonder what could possibly be worth a morning stroll in this part of town.

We cross the street. A plaque on a large concrete planter reads, "Thanks-Giving Square."

I shake my head in disbelief. It's like they built a shrine just for one of the basic tenets of positive psychology.

"I know, right?" Nick says, seeing my wide eyes. "I just had to come and see this place."

"Yes, you certainly did."

Stone steps lead us to a 14-foot-tall hollow golden ring stationed in front of a towering concrete structure topped with three bronze bells.

"The self-guided tour says you're supposed to say out loud something or someone you are grateful for as you stand beneath," he says.

Why does that make me self-conscious? Since I attended Nick's lecture that first day, I've had some time to think about how wrong I was about gratitude, how even if there is an overarching barrier in your life, that doesn't make all of the other things worthless.

But still, expressing gratitude feels personal, embarrassing even. That's certainly something to ponder later. For now, I say, "After you, then."

He stands beneath the ring and says, "I'm grateful that I found positive psychology, that I can use it to help people."

That's on brand for Nick; it's what I expected him to say. I was half-hoping he would mention something non-work related so I could learn a little more about what makes him tick.

Since Nick stuck to work, so will I. "I'm grateful for this wonderful new job that challenges me and brought me to see new places," I say, standing under the ring. And I mean it, because how lucky am I that I'm getting paid to see Texas, eat good meals, and spend time with an attractive man?

We take a moment to stand before a mosaic reproduction of Norman Rockwell's *Golden Rule*, which depicts people of various cultures, ages, races, and ethnicities, united in prayer, with the famous, "Do unto others as you would have them do unto you," written in gold letters. A wall of water rains down into a pool nearby, masking the sounds of a city awakening.

"Shall we go into the chapel?" Nick asks, pointing towards an odd-shaped circular building with two smaller concentric circles stacked above the base.

I tense because my relationship with religion has been somewhat tenuous. Much of my extended family is Catholic, but my parents never pushed Sunday school or church on me, so it didn't stick when my grandparents tried to get me on board by taking me on the most celebratory days, Easter, and Christmas, when the hall was decorated with lilies, wreaths and garlands, and the choir sang joyful hymns. It just never felt quite right, and since my parents weren't religious, it never became a part of me.

"I'm not really religious," I say.

"You don't have to be religious to be thankful, to show gratitude," says Nick. "And I think the message of this place goes beyond denominations, don't you?"

"I guess that's true."

"You can wait out here if you're more comfortable, but I think you'll be missing out."

"Ha! I can't believe you're FOMO-ing me right now."

Nick winks at me and we walk inside, admiring the dove etched in glass above the entrance. When we arrive at the main attraction we stop and look up.

My jaw drops open. I had no expectations, but this is more stunning than I ever could have imagined. The ceiling is a spiral that wraps inward and upward, stretching towards the heavens, adorned by panels of stained glass, in darker shades of blue and red at the bottom, then lightening to yellows and whites as it reaches the top, where it resolves into a peaceful pale light.

As my eyes follow the spiral around and around, a feeling of lightness descends upon me; my petty worries and cares are simply melting away. There is no job, no client, only me. It's slightly euphoric and the walls start spinning around me, the floor falling away.

Nick grabs my hands to steady me as I lean.

"Whoa, you okay, there?" he asks.

His voice brings me back to the room, and I'm staring into his worried eyes. Up close I notice his freshly shaven chin and breathe in his aftershave.

"Yes, I'm better now," I say. Then I realize he is still holding my hands, and his feel soft and warm in mine. He must realize it as well because he releases me and stuffs his hands in his pockets.

"That must be what enlightenment feels like," I say as a way to lighten the mood, but then regret it because it sounded more sarcastic than I meant it. I really did feel something when I was looking at the ceiling, I just don't have any words to describe it.

"Might be," Nick says.

On the way back to the hotel I say, "Thanks for taking me there, it was a really cool place. I would never have found something like that on my own. You're like a gratitude guru."

Nick laughs again and I realize I like hearing that sound; it's like the tinkle of bells at Christmastime. Geez, Thanks-Giving Square really got in my head. Who would ever have thought my day would start out like this?

"My pleasure. Thanks for coming with me. I have more fun experiencing new things with other people."

"Is that a psychology thing?"

"Sort of. It's actually somewhat complicated, as things in psychology tend to be. Whether or not being around other people amplifies an experience in a positive way depends on a number of factors, including how comfortable the people in question are with each other and how lonely they are."

I should have known better than to ask Nick a question about the human psyche and expect a simple answer, but I'm starting to understand that it really is complicated, and that's part of why identifying these basic tenets of positive psychology was such a triumph. Because of all the exceptions and qualifications researchers have to make.

"Oh, that does sound complicated. At least you're aware of what works for you. That reminds me of something random. Gloria always wears scarves, like every single day. And she plays with them and flips them around. Does that mean something?"

Nick shakes his head. "We don't typically give armchair diagnoses, for obvious reasons, and I don't know Gloria at all. All I can say is that sometimes fidgeting, with a pen or hair or clothes, can be a sign of anxiety. But that doesn't mean it is with Gloria. Maybe she just likes the way her scarf feels, or maybe it means nothing at all."

"Hmmm, I see. Sorry for asking, I'm sure that must be annoying when people ask you questions like that."

"Not at all, it comes with the territory. Back to the people being fascinated with the human mind thing. People have asked me much worse."

"Hah. I can't believe Gloria would be anxious or nervous, not around me, her subordinate. She built an entire company from scratch."

"You can't always tell what people are hiding beneath the surface. The ones who seem the most competent may be experiencing a whole other reality in their minds."

That shuts me up fast. My entire goal with Katie and moving to Texas was to be one of those people who appears competent and cheerful, and for no one to see beneath the surface, ever.

12

While I listen to Nick's afternoon lecture, I realize that I haven't had a chance to broach the subject of how to promote the book when he doesn't seem comfortable that he even wrote one.

When we arrive back at the hotel, it's already 5:30 p.m. and we're both famished, so we collectively decide to work out, eat dinner, and stay another night in Dallas before driving back in the morning. I need more time to talk with him if I'm going to feel successful about this trip.

This time we are side by side on treadmills, me walking briskly, while he runs. It's easier this way because I can't see him unless I turn my head, which I purposely don't. Still, I can smell him, like coconut mixed with sweat, and it's not entirely unpleasant.

We meet in the lobby and head towards the nearby Deep Ellum entertainment district for dinner. It's gritty mixed with hipster, brand-new high-rise apartments mixed with old two-story buildings with bars, shops, and restaurants. Murals and street art abound.

"It's a shame," I say, as we pass a mural espousing a plea to save the neighborhood. I've seen it all before in the northeast, the so called "vitalization" of historic neighborhoods, in the name of economic development. And by that, they mean money.

"What is?" says Nick.

I point to the mural. "The way we take places with authentic culture and history and turn them into...that," I say, now pointing to a demoed site encased in construction fencing, with a sign advertising a luxury residential tower.

He considers this and says, "Maybe. But this place used to be crumbling down and now it's seeing new investment."

"Undoubtedly by outsiders," I counter.

"Perhaps. I do see where you're coming from, and gentrification is a real issue, but things change, people change, communities change. The more we try to hold on to the past, the more it slips away, and the unhappier we will be."

"Is that some psychology thing?"

He shakes his head. "No, it's something I've learned from personal experience."

Reminding myself that even though normally it would be okay for two people to have a discussion on a point they disagree on, in this case, he is my client and it's safer to navigate back to less choppy waters. "Where should we eat?"

In only one week, Tex-Mex has become my favorite cuisine, from the first taco that Damon bought me, to the scrumptious enchiladas verdes on the River Walk. Nick asks if I want a margarita, but I have to decline. I'm not supposed to mix alcohol with my meds, and I've confirmed this is a bad idea. I tell him I don't drink on business trips.

This may be my last chance to revisit his feelings around the book launch, and maybe a drink will loosen his lips a little.

After one drink of meaningless chatter, his second arrives and I make my move. "It's our last night and Gloria will be expecting some strategy ideas from me as soon as I get back to the office."

His face immediately droops.

"At risk of messing up my first project, I have to say for a positive psychologist who signed a book deal, you don't seem too jazzed about it. Not excited like when you're lecturing."

Nick gives a sigh deeper than the Grand Canyon. "I don't know," he half-whispers. "Maybe it was a mistake."

This is the second time he has used that word. Mistake.

"Is this about the money aspect? How you didn't want to promote the book at your lectures because you felt uncomfortable charging people to help them? Which is absurd, because psychologists charge patients for therapy, right? And no one expects you to devote your life to studying psychology for free. Everyone understands you have to make a living too."

"You're probably right. But there's more than just that...," he says but doesn't continue.

Now I'm confused. I prompt him, "If it's not about the money, then what?"

Nick takes a deep swig for courage and says, "All I ever wanted to do was help people, but what if it doesn't? What if I'm just another leaf on a tree in a grove of self-help books?"

"So, this is about fear of failure then? You're afraid the book won't sell?"

"No, you're not listening to me. I'm afraid the book won't be enough."

I'm really lost now. "Enough for what?"

We're right on the edge now, I can feel it. Another drink and it would all be out in the open. Drunk people are open books.

Instead, he pushes the remainder of his drink away. "Nothing," he says, suddenly seeming sober. "I'll promote the book to sell it, however you suggest, even at the lectures. It's why I wrote it and why the publisher gave me a contract."

As much as I want to push, I can't. Nick is not my friend, and I have no place digging any deeper. Plus, who is the psychologist in this situation? I'm in no position to help anyone; I'm the only patient I can handle.

We start heading towards the hotel and a group of older teens are coming towards us on the opposite sidewalk. They are dressed in classic goth clothing, dyed black hair, excessive jewelry, lace up boots, dramatic eyeliner. I have a stab of nostalgia, and I wonder where they're heading. Based on what I've seen so far of Deep Ellum, I wouldn't be surprised if the local goth hangout were nearby. I make a mental note to find out what the goth scene is like in Austin. I suddenly miss my people.

"Is it vampire o-clock?" Nick says under his breath. I wince. I haven't heard Nick say anything snarky and it's not a good look on him.

"What?" I say evenly.

"Those goth kids."

My fist clenches at my side. "Do you have something against goth kids?" That look exactly like me at that age? Me before Texas? The real me, Kat?

He looks older, more defeated, somehow, than he did this afternoon. Maybe he's not a good drinker.

"These kids, messing around, while there are real people suffering? People in pain, while they mock the dark side of human nature with their clothes and their music."

My mouth hangs open. I'm dumbfounded by this new side of Nick, and I feel personally attacked. "Why do you assume they aren't in pain? Aren't all teenagers in pain? I would think as a psychologist you would see that."

He stumbles on the uneven pavement, and I steady him. "Is it a cry for help or a show? Is it too many viewings of Twilight or a sign of something deeper? That's the whole problem. We can't know," he slurs.

Now he seems quite drunk again. This is bad, very bad. Luckily, we are almost back at the hotel. I ride the elevator with him to his floor and stick my head around the corner to make sure he finds the right room before I ride back down to mine.

I flop on the bed. What just happened? I'm even more confused about Nick than I was before. On the good side, he agreed to follow whatever strategy I suggest, which will make my job much easier. Look at me, seeing the bright side again.

On the bad side, any attraction I felt for Nick vanished the second I heard those judgmental words come out of his mouth. Or maybe that is also the good side, because I never wanted to be attracted to him in the first place.

I pick up his book again, hoping to find some answers. Flipping to the back inside flap, I read his biography again. I've heard a joke that most psychologists need to see a psychologist. In fact, a lot of them do. Just because they study how our mind works, doesn't mean they have it all figured out. Nick clearly has his own personal issues, but that doesn't mean he can't help others.

Now it's my job to set that knowledge aside and send off the cheerful, positive Nick I have witnessed on a book launch tour. I won't be the first PR person who helped hide the private side of her client and my success on my first assignment depends on it. Ironic that both Nick and I pretend to be someone we're not, at least part of the time. Another thing we have in common.

I flip to the front of the book and this time notice a dedication I had missed before.

Who's *Becca*?

13

We don't talk much on the way back; Nick puts on an audiobook. I think he regrets sharing as much as he did last night and just wants to get back to Austin and pretend it never happened. He drops me off at my apartment and tells me in a formal business way that he looks forward to seeing my strategy plan. I use my most professional voice to tell him I learned a lot from the trip and thank him for inviting me. But it feels cold and weird after the past few days we've spent together.

Pulling my suitcase down the sidewalk towards my unit, I smile when I see Damon on his porch. By now I know he's always out there when the weather's nice, music pounding through the patio screen. It's comforting. After spending all that time with Nick, Damon seems appealingly uncomplicated. But maybe I just don't know him well enough yet.

"She returns!" Damon yells down. "How was your grand tour of Texas?"

"Fine," I say.

"I'm grilling some burgers later with some friends if you want to join."

"Thanks, but I'm exhausted, and I need to get some work done."

"Work? You just got back from work!"

"I know, but my boss will expect me to have a report for her tomorrow."

"All work and no play makes Katie a dull girl," he quips in his best Jack Nicholson impression.

I roll my eyes. "Nice," I respond and keep walking.

Even though I've only lived in my apartment for a week, it's good to be back home, nice that it feels like home. I love my purple velour couch, and Saffron the tiger, and my posters and blacklight ambiance. After spending the past week as Katie, I feel like I'm losing myself. Was this closet goth thing a terrible idea?

So thankful for the internet, because it only takes me three minutes to find out where Austin goths congregate, and as luck would have it, there is a club with an eighties goth music night every Monday, and I decide I'm going. I also find a promising goth clothing store and a vampire lounge that looks like the set of *What We Do in the Shadows*. I'm relieved to find all of these things because it makes me optimistic that I can find some way to fit in here.

What I told Damon wasn't just an excuse though, I'm pretty sure that Gloria is going to pounce on me like a mountain lion first thing in the morning, asking how it went and what brilliant ideas I have, and Roxy will be looking over her shoulder waiting for me to fail. I better get to work.

First, I transcribe all the notes I took during the last four days. Then I write out all the challenges I have identified, and a summary of the competing books and personalities. That's an issue though, is Nick willing to be a personality and not just an author and academic? He can still be successful with the latter, but his book will sell better with the former.

He's going to need media training. He has to be able to explain why he became a psychologist in a compelling way, with a personal story. It doesn't even need to be one hundred percent true, just enough truth that he can tell it convincingly over and over.

Does it bother me to think of a person's image as a commodity? Not really, that's my job, after all. In this case it's even easier because if I can help him sell his book, maybe it really could help people.

Not people like me, but other people.

Voices outside are joking and yelling, must be Damon and his friends. Wow. It's nearly five already. Even before I saw Nick's lectures I knew about the concept of flow. Several years ago, a therapist told me about the movie *Jiro Dreams of Sushi*, about an artisan chef who strives to perfect his sushi making.

That's when I realized maybe I can't be happy per se, as I just don't experience a lot of positive feelings, but I can be deeply engaged in my work. Being in flow is as close as I get to happiness. That's why this job is so important to me, and I don't resent working on a Sunday. There's nothing else I could be doing that would be a better use of my time. Although, hearing Damon and his friends outside makes me jealous, makes me wish I were a person who enjoyed partying and drinking. Maybe I'll make an appearance in a bit. I do want to make friends here, be invited to social events, become part of a community.

I keep at it until I have a neatly formatted draft strategy plan ready for Gloria, complete with ideas for the website, graphics needs (which I'm dreading working with Roxy on), book launch events and promotions, media training, and even some thoughts about the author photo shoot.

I check the clock. It's eight now. Shit—I still have to go to the gym and eat dinner. Five minutes later I'm vaulting out the door in my workout clothes, praying that Damon and his friends aren't outside. Thankfully, they aren't, they've moved back inside, and I smell that distinctly skunky smell wafting from his patio. I shouldn't be surprised, especially in Austin.

Just as well that I didn't hang out with them. A lot of people on anti-depressants smoke weed and seem okay, but I'd rather be vigilant. No alcohol, no smoking, 30 minutes of cardio every day, eight hours of sleep. I'm practically a fucking nun.

Monday morning I'm back at work. Turns out I didn't need to push so hard yesterday, because Gloria isn't even in today, she's traveling for a client event. She sent me a note saying she hopes all went well and an appointment for a meeting with her Tuesday morning.

I guess I can spend today improving the strategy plan and learning more about the resources Purple Cactus has to support my project. Gloria walked me around to meet people on my first day, but so many staff are in and out of the office for offsite meetings that I don't know how it all fits together yet.

Maybe today I'll try to make peace with Roxy.

Right on cue, Roxy rolls in at 9:15 a.m. and says, "How was your getaway with Mr. Positive?" and makes a smooching face.

"Real mature," I say. "It was fine. I learned a lot about positive psychology."

"I bet you did."

I know she's just razzing me, hoping to get a rise out of me, and it's annoying. Ignoring her innuendo, I appeal to her ambitious side. "We're going to need a lot of visuals on this one. Website redesign, promos, branding, all of it. Gloria said I'd be working with you on that. What do you need from me to get started on ideas?"

Roxy looks excited about starting a new project for like two seconds before she remembers she's going to have to work with me, and frowns. "I don't usually work on a new assignment until I get the go ahead from Gloria."

Fair enough. I know what it's like to have multiple bosses and if Gloria prefers to allocate all work, I respect that. "Got it. We're meeting tomorrow morning, so maybe after that."

She raises her eyebrow. "Am *I* on that meeting?"

Shit. I didn't set the meeting, Gloria did. I look at my calendar and exhale in relief. "Yes, you, Ben, and Luis."

That seems to appease her. "In that case, I wouldn't mind looking at whatever notes you have, so I'm not going into the meeting blind."

"Sure, I'll send you what I've drafted so far and some links to his lectures."

"Okay," says Roxy and I think maybe once we actually get into production mode it will be okay.

Eight hours later and I'm done. Not working late today, because it's goth night!

Joy Division blasts from my living room as I rummage through my makeup case and find my lip foundation, the only way to make my favorite dark purple lipstick stay vibrant all night. I put on a dress that laces up the front, with flowy mesh trumpet sleeves, add black fishnets, thigh-high boots, and top it off with a hat with a lace veil like Winona Ryder wore in *Beetlejuice*.

I look in the mirror and twirl around, pleased with my reflection. I know my parents always hated when I wore all black. My grandmother thought it was downright morose. But this has always been when I felt the most beautiful.

This is the real me.

A whistled catcall causes me to whip around on the walkway. Damon waves. "Where are you going all dressed up?"

"Eighties goth night at Revision," I say.

"As a friend, am I allowed to say va va voom?"

I blush, pleased with the compliment. In a weird way, getting that kiss with Damon out of the way up front was a good thing. We don't have to pretend that we don't find each other attractive, but sex is off the table, allowing us to be friends without the 'will we, won't we' tension.

"I don't mind. In fact, say it again if you like." I strike a dramatic pose, the back of my hand to my forehead, my front leg extended.

"Scorching," he says, and makes a sizzling sound. "Have fun tonight. Oh, and maybe you can come with me Friday to see my friends in Flaming Goathead?"

"Maybe," I tell him.

I get a rideshare even though I'm not drinking, just to avoid walking alone in the dark to and from the parking lot. Revision is what I expected, concrete floors sticky with beer, a couple of old booths with torn up vinyl seats in the corner. But it doesn't matter, because the room glows with purple neon and glitterballs, the speakers are belting out The Sisters of Mercy, and people are dancing, in that way only goths dance, movements that make full use of the billowing sleeves, fingers elegantly spread and waving away spiderwebs. Believe me, I know how it looks. But how it *feels*...

Lost in the melodies, the rhythms, the movement, I forget who I am, where I am, and yet I'm with friends, friends I don't have to speak a single word to, just a knowing look says, "I get you." All the stress of the move and Roxy and Gloria and Nicolas Stone melt away as I dance to The Cult and Killing Joke, Fields of the Nephilim and Clan of Xymox, even the kiss with Damon happened in another galaxy. I never lived anywhere but Austin and I don't have a past. Just here, now, dancing.

The night ends too soon, but my ride is waiting, and I have work in the morning. No question that I needed this; it recharged me, renewed me.

The face in my bathroom mirror stares back at me. There you are, Kat, it says. I've been here all along, I whisper. I can't lose myself just because I moved, just because I'm trying to make my darkness the smallest possible part of me. What if my therapist was wrong? What if I am my darkness and my darkness is me? Am I just trying to cut out my own heart?

Ha. I must be goth, so melodramatic. A little makeup remover and suddenly I'm Katie again. She's not so bad. Damon seems to like us both, so he has that going for him. Nicolas Stone would not approve of Kat at all, and I need to make sure they never meet.

14

Roxy, Luis, and I are waiting in the conference room for Gloria. With Luis, who has worked at Purple Cactus for twelve years, in the room, Roxy shows no sign of her combative, immature behavior. She's all business. Maybe that's the trick, to never be alone with her.

Gloria swoops in, wearing a chardonnay pantsuit and a canary yellow scarf. All fashion other than goth eludes me, but I suspect that Gloria's wardrobe is well envied by people in the know. Her shadow, Ben, follows her in. I don't mean that disrespectfully to Ben, as he seems like a sharp guy just trying to soak up all that he can from his internship experience. This is probably his first job in an office, and he still seems a little uncomfortable. I don't blame him because Gloria is a tough cookie, and as much as I want to learn from her, I wouldn't want to spend as much time working directly with her as Ben does.

"Alright, Katie. You spent three days with Dr. Nicolas Stone," says Gloria. "What did you learn?"

Yikes. We are getting right down to it. I share my laptop screen to the conference room system and project my strategy plan on the wall. They'll need to understand what Nick's all about, and for that, they need to understand positive psychology, so I start there.

"Up until the past few decades, psychology was focused on fixing negatives, treating mental illness. But recently, there's been a focus on using psychological techniques to bring greater well-being to everyone, to improve our daily living experience," I say.

Everyone seems to be following along, so I continue explaining the prevailing theory of well-being and what Nick has added to it with his book.

"But we have a few challenges. Onstage, when Nick is in professor mode, he's great, but offstage he can come across as a little mechanical. My gut says that even if Nick's ideas are solid, people need to believe that he holds the secret. Even if the secret is that there is no secret, just simple steps people can follow on their own."

"Hmm," says Gloria. "We've worked with a guru-type before and that all hinges on the persuasiveness of the individual. Is that what we're dealing with?"

"No, he's not like that at all. It's all science, research based. I think we have to push the professorial, expert route. We could make it work with just that, but if we could add in some hint that he personally lives the well-being he touts, then the book could be a major success."

Roxy pipes in, "And does he? Live the well-being?"

I stumble because even though I was paid to spend that time with Nick for the very purpose of strategizing, I feel like he did let me in just a little and I don't want to share every gory detail. "Well...I don't really know, and that's the problem. After all that time with him I'm not sure how happy he really is. And I barely know anything personal about him. He never mentions family or friends, only work. He's a private person."

"Remember when we worked with Sacha Turin?" Luis says to Gloria. "No social media, any discussion of her kids and husband was off limits."

Gloria wraps her scarf around her finger. "I remember. That was a real challenge."

"What did you do then?" asked Roxy.

"We focused the promotion on how the consumer would feel if they followed her diet," said Gloria. "But, Katie, I thought we agreed before your trip that Dr. Stone was the product and not the book?"

My palms are getting sweaty now. "That's true, but after spending time with him, there might be a better approach. In some ways, positive psychology is the client."

Luis frowns. "But why buy this book instead of the competing books?"

"Credentials are critical in the self-help genre, so we can still play up the expert professor side," I say.

"But aren't almost all authors of this type of book a PhD? Why is he special?" asks Roxy.

Crap. This isn't going as well as I'd hoped; maybe I wasn't ready for the big leagues yet. "Yes, typically they are."

Ben looks confused by the discussion, and as he looks up from taking notes, he timidly says, "Sorry if this is a dumb question, but can't we create whatever image of Dr. Stone we want?"

"Yes," says Gloria, "but he has to match that image when he lectures, during the book tour, and at each media appearance. Not everyone can be so consistent."

"Oh, that makes sense," Ben says.

"A little media training can go a long way," says Luis.

"I don't think Nick is going to be comfortable pretending to be someone he's not," I interject. But am I talking about Nick still? Or am I projecting my own internal struggles, my discomfort of having Kat and Katie fighting for my time? In the end, Nick did tell me he would do whatever is best for book sales. And he may already be pretending anyway, so what's the difference?

Gloria waves me off. "Helping a client put his best foot forward while in the public eye is just smart, not fake. We can work within the confines of what he is willing to share. He's trying to sell a book; it's all just business."

Not to Nick it's not. I know this book is personal to him, even if I don't know exactly why that is. But everyone nods in agreement, and Gloria declares that we will meet with Nick and the publisher a week from Wednesday to walk them through some initial ideas.

I have mixed feelings about seeing him again after how things ended, but work comes first. He should understand because his life seems to revolve around his career.

The next few days are a blur of work, cardio, dinner, sleep, rinse, repeat. Thursday night Damon asks me again to come to his friend's show the following night and I agree. I throw on some black jeans and boots, and a plain black t-shirt. I figure it's metal enough to fit in.

Damon drives us downtown to the Red River Cultural District, where several of the nightclubs in Austin are concentrated. It's actually where Revision was, but I wasn't paying much attention at the time since I was dropped off at the door.

We park several blocks away and navigate down the side streets past homeless people sleeping or asking for money or just living their lives. When we reach Red River, it's brimming with partygoers hungry for the weekend, floating in and out of clubs, already an air of piss and stale beer, cigarettes and weed forming.

Flaming Goathead doesn't go on until later, so we loiter outside the club for a while, and Damon keeps seeing people he knows from the metal scene. He introduces me to an endless parade of long-haired dudes, and a couple of fierce-looking women. I wonder if I'll ever feel like part of a community in Austin, and if it will be Katie or Kat, or both, or neither.

Inside, a decent crowd is gathered, drinking beer and banging heads until the opening band finishes their set and Flaming Goathead takes the stage. As I expected, it's a little heavy for my taste, but the bassist is all over the fretboard and I can't keep my eyes off his fingers as they fly. The drummer is pounding like he has a vendetta against the universe and for a moment I get it, because it matches that undercurrent of wrath that I constantly tame back. For a split second I consider maybe I can release this anger by joining in, letting my head thrash with the others, but something holds me back.

Damon is rocking out and having a blast and I enjoy seeing him in his element, his luxurious long hair swinging in his face. After their set is done, he introduces me to the band. They are a nice bunch of guys, nothing like how they were on stage, and they offer us a joint. Damon looks at me and something in my face makes him say, nah, he's driving, but thanks anyway.

He seems chill in that way; I don't think he'd ever care that I don't smoke. He glides down a lazy river, meandering where the stream takes him. If he didn't have a professional job in tech, I would think he was a shiftless pothead, but that would be wrong. It's different here in Austin, not such a sharp division between successful and loser, straight edge and wild; there's more of a gray area, and I appreciate that.

"Do you want a slice of pizza?" he asks as we pass a takeout window.

"No thanks," I say, having already eaten my healthy supper, and it being close to my bedtime to get my eight hours in.

Damon buys two slices but then ends up giving the second one to a homeless man on the way back to the car.

"You're a nice guy," I say as I climb in.

"Nah. Sometimes you just see someone who looks like they are on the edge and if you're holding two slices of pizza, what are you going to do?"

I look at him again with fresh eyes. Maybe he's not as uncomplicated as I thought. Or maybe he is simply a nice guy who knows who he is, unlike me.

15

"These are really good," I say over the cubicle wall, then realize that sounded like I was surprised, which is insulting. Roxy just sent me some ideas for graphics for the Nicolas Stone project, and it's the first time I've seen her work.

She pokes her head around the partition. "I know," she says with a smug look.

Damn, she makes it hard to like her. But I give credit where it's due no matter what, plus, this can be my kindness for the day. "You really captured the concept of well-being, all the parts that feed into the whole." It seemed so abstract, yet somehow, Roxy made it tangible.

For the first time since I started working at Purple Cactus, Roxy smiles at me. "Thanks. You explained it really well, and then I just drew what I saw in my mind. I looked up this positive psychology stuff—it's pretty cool."

"It really is."

She puts her hand on her hip, thinking. "Mr. Positive is dashing and brilliant. Hell, if you don't want your Ken doll, maybe I do," she smirks, "maybe I need to expand my horizons."

Despite my best efforts, I can feel myself blushing and Roxy points at me.

Her lips purse and she says triumphantly, "You do like him! I knew it." So much smugness today I can't bear it. But you know what they say about protesting too much, so I just let it go and hope it dissipates into the atmosphere before anyone else in the office gets any wrong ideas about my trip with Nick.

Setting aside Roxy's ribbing, I'm relieved that she isn't going to sabotage my first project. I'm nervous enough just seeing Nick again on a personal level, much less presenting the strategy plan to him and his publisher in front of Gloria.

The truth is, Nick has been on my mind since Dallas. Up until that night in Deep Ellum, I felt like the real Nick, the one buried beneath this need to help and educate people, might be someone I could connect with. But he didn't really let me in, after all, and then the side I saw of him on that last night was far from appealing.

I feel stupid, since it's like every male I meet I'm thinking of in terms of sex and dating, but I can't help it. Maybe it's moving to a new place and being all alone, but first Damon, and now Nick. I really need to make some friends I'm not attracted to.

Amber lets me know that Nick and his publisher have arrived, and she's seated them in the conference room.

I wait for Gloria to reach my cubicle. She seems to like making a grand entrance and I know she'll want to greet the publisher first.

Right on cue, Gloria is here, dressed in turquoise, with a rusty brown scarf. "It's showtime, Katie. Are you ready?"

Faking confidence, I say, "Born ready," and Gloria flashes a smile.

I follow her down the hallway, and as I expected, she waltzes into the conference room and extends her hand to the publisher. Gloria has a way of making people feel like they are the ones lucky to be in her orbit, even though they are paying us good money.

While Gloria is cementing her relationship with the publisher, Nick rises to greet me. He looks pleased to see me, and maybe I'm imagining that his face seems to light up when I enter. But then he awkwardly shakes my hand, says it's nice to see me again, and sits back down and fiddles with a paperclip.

The presentation goes well. Nick states again that he is open to whatever we suggest, and the publisher loves the idea of media training for their future star author. Nick agrees to add some promotional slides into his lecture tour materials. I'm glad I had planted that seed in his mind; he seems less resistant to the idea now. We talk through some ideas for the main book launch event, but don't land on the perfect one and decide to circle back with additional concepts.

After the meeting, Nick asks me to walk out with him. His publisher has a plane to catch, so he runs off with a wave, leaving us alone in the building lobby.

"Did you have questions about the strategy plan?" I ask, wondering why he led me here.

"No, but great job up there, I hope Gloria is happy with your work."

"Thanks." I stand there waiting while Nick looks uncomfortable.

Finally, he says, "I felt a little weird about how our trip ended."

I decide to feign innocence. "Oh?"

"I shouldn't have said those things at dinner and on the walk home, I wasn't in my right mind. That's why I shouldn't drink."

"You don't owe me any explanation, but in my experience, the words that come out when people drink are the truth."

"I won't deny that, but they don't always include the whole context, either."

I wait to see if he plans on providing that context right now, but he doesn't say anything else. All I know is he basically said he looks down on Kat, the real me, the goth, without knowing it, of course. But maybe he's trying to tell me there is more to the story, something I don't understand, only that doesn't help me if he won't share what it is.

It doesn't matter because he is my client and that is all he will ever be. There's really no reason for us to try and become friends.

"Don't worry about it," I tell him. "It's water under the bridge."

"Okay," he says, but doesn't look convinced. I almost feel bad for him. Why does he even care what I think? But he obviously does, so I throw him a bone.

"I finished reading your book. It's great," I say.

The shiny glow I saw when he was lecturing returns to his face, and I'm delighted to see it. His entire aura transforms when he talks about positive psychology, like he magically sports an angel halo. "I'm glad you think so."

"I even started doing one of the daily exercises."

He's practically luminescent now. "Really, which one?"

"Trying to do something kind for someone else each day."

"That's a great one, my favorite," he says.

"And I decided to start volunteering at the animal shelter. There's an orientation this week."

"Wow—that's wonderful. I love animals," he says. "My dog Pepper was my best friend growing up. I used to volunteer at a shelter during college, and I would love to start again but I travel too much to be consistent."

"I love them too. I had a dog and a cat growing up, Lily and Dude."

"The cat was named Dude?" he says.

"He sure was."

"Ha! Well, I'm glad my book is bringing about positive changes in your life," he says.

Without thinking, I blurt out, "It's not the book that did that."

"No?"

I take a deep breath in and confess, "It was being with you, listening to your lecture three times. Seeing those people inspired and encouraged because of not just words you said and the culmination of years of study and research, but also because you love your work, and you wanting to help people, that's contagious. You made me want to help others. Although in my case, I'm more comfortable with animals than people."

Nick stands there, letting the sentiment wash over him before he speaks. "That means a lot to me, Katie."

"Well, it's true. I'd better get back to work now."

"Hey wait—a friend of mine is doing a book reading and signing at BookPeople on Friday. Do you want to come with me?"

I freeze. "Is this a date? Because you're my client, and I can't date clients."

He stiffens. "Oh no, of course not," he assures me. "Not a date, just two business associates attending a book launch event. For research."

"Oh, okay. Sorry if I misunderstood," I say, even though I don't think I did. "I guess a little research wouldn't hurt. Is it another psychologist?"

"Yes and no," he says. "He is an old classmate from my psychology program, but he writes sci-fi, alien encounter type stuff."

"Huh. No offense, but that sounds more fun."

"Fair enough. I'll meet you there, it starts at 7 o'clock," he says with a sparkle in his eyes. Very sparkly for someone who is *not* going on a date.

"Looking forward to it," I say. And I really am.

16

When I get back from the gym, Damon is on his porch, per usual. Everyone in my life is apparently going to see me sweaty, in workout clothes, so it's a good thing I'm not too vain or self-conscious.

"You're like a machine," he says from the balcony.

"Habit," I say. "It's easier to do something every day without fail, than once in a while."

He considers this but dismisses it with a shrug. That concept clashes with his lazy river lifestyle. "Feel like grabbing some pizza and watching a movie tonight?"

I've been working hard this week, and a little break with a friend would be nice. "Okay. See you in an hour."

Quick shower, and I change into my home goth uniform of black leggings and a concert tee. Part of me cringes at skipping the healthy dinner waiting in the fridge for me, but as much as the disciplined ritual is important, I also have to be flexible enough to actually live. I'll make Damon put veggies on my half of the pizza, I reason.

Damon offers me a beer, but I decline, accepting a Dr. Pepper instead. As he hands it to me, he says, "You know Dr. Pepper was invented in Waco? Just an hour and a half north of Austin."

"Waco? Isn't that where that cult was?"

"Yep."

"Lucky they have Dr. Pepper to balance it out."

He shakes his head. "That's somehow dark and cheerful at the same time."

"That's me," I say.

"I'm learning that. So, how was your big presentation?" he asks while we wait for the pizza to be delivered.

It's sweet that Damon remembers, although I did complain about being stressed over it a few times over the past week. "It went pretty well."

"Mr. Positive liked it? Is he even allowed to say if he hated it, if he's supposed to be that positive?"

I nearly snort soda out of my nose. I never thought of that aspect. What pressure Nick must feel to always look on the bright side. "It doesn't work like that. He explains it better in the book, it's not about being happy all the time. You should read it. Everyone should."

He wags his finger at me. "Tsk, tsk, Katie, don't you fall into your own cult."

I throw a cardboard coaster at him. The Cult of Positive Psychology. I wonder how that would work? It's got the rituals and the meditation, but no gurus or tithes, so I think I'm safe.

The pizza arrives, and I take out my wallet to pay for half.

Damon shoos my hand away, "No worries, it was free, I only paid the tip," he says. "They give you a free pizza in the month of your birthday."

"When is your birthday?"

"Last Saturday."

"Shit, Damon, why didn't you say anything? I would have taken you to Amy's!"

He makes a puppy dog face. "Well now I'm sorry I didn't. I don't like to make a big deal about it. Not like it's a landmark year."

"How old are you?" I ask.

"Twenty-nine," he says.

"Old man," I chuckle.

He fakes a frown. "Oh yeah, how old are you?"

"I'm about to be twenty-seven, in two weeks."

Damon gazes towards the window and dramatically declares, "I remember that age, to be so young and innocent," then turns to me and shoves pizza into his face. This guy cracks me up.

"It's just a number," I say.

Then he turns to me in all seriousness and says, "Not twenty-seven, Katie, you know about the 27 Club, right?"

I do, and I try not to think about it. So many iconic musicians died in their twenty-seventh year, Jimi Hendrix, Janis Joplin, Jim Morrison, Kurt Cobain, Amy Winehouse, to name a few. What does it matter? I'm not a famous musician. But the superstitious, goth side of me whispers, what if this is the year your darkness catches up with you?

I laugh it off. "Yeah, but it's not real, people just see patterns where they want to see them."

"Yeah, I'm sure that's all it is. Anyway, I'm right upstairs if you need anything."

"That's sweet. I'm glad you turned out to be my neighbor."

He grins. "Me too. And you can still buy me a belated Amy's Ice Cream anytime."

"Deal."

Damon announces we are watching *Tenacious D in The Pick of Destiny*, which I've never seen but I'm a big Jack Black fan, so why not. The movie seems fun and chill, just like Damon. I sink back into his couch with my veggie pizza and my Dr. Pepper, appreciating how comfortable I feel here, with him.

I wonder if two weeks ago I would have thought to appreciate moments like these, before I met Nicolas Stone. Then I curse myself for letting thoughts of him invade my private life outside of work. He's just a colleague, and Damon is just a friend. I'm trying to build a life here, not live a rom-com.

The movie is a triumphant, ridiculous ride, and I can see why it didn't do great in the box office but is becoming a cult classic. And it made Damon happy and sharing that with him made me like the movie even more. I wonder how it feels, to love something as much as he loves metal, but to have not one iota of musical talent, according to him, to worship something from afar like that. I'm not sure I'm that passionate about anything.

When the credits roll, neither of us seem to want the night to end, so we talk music, finding the overlap between goth and metal. Suddenly he leaps up.

"You know who's coming to town?" he says, grabbing his cell phone. "Paradise Lost, do you know them?"

I shake my head.

"What? How is that possible? You'd like them." He swipes his phone and soon a heavy guitar riff is blasting through the room, assaulting me out of my relaxed state. "Wait, not that one," he says, and switches to a different song with more of a darkwave synth feel, and more melodic vocals. Music that I can fall back into, swirling like oil on water.

"I like it."

He smiles. "I knew it. They're coming to Houston; you should come with me—it would be fun."

What the heck, it does sound fun. "Alright, let's do it!"

Now he looks really jazzed. Damon makes me feel good to be around, his casual stroll through life makes me want to walk next to him and hitch that ride. Plus, it's flattering that he wants to share his favorite things with me.

"Yaaaas! Tickets go on sale next week; I'll get them, and you can pay me back later."

"Cool."

It's getting late and I need to get my requisite hours of sleep in to be the bright-eyed business Katie in the morning. I pick up my soda can and plate and move to the kitchen to clean up. After I deposit them in his recycling bin and sink, a light catches my eye from the window. The moon is nearly full, glowing like a spotlight. For a moment, I forget where I am and only see the shining white disc, reflecting light off the sun. Maybe I'm the moon. Maybe I need to surround myself with suns, so I can reflect their energy.

Damon moving behind me snaps me back to the room and I spin around, colliding with him as he closes the refrigerator. I trip back into the counter, hitting the small of my back, and Damon reaches out to my shoulder to steady me. The moon is reflected in his eyes and suddenly I want to kiss him terribly. For a split second I think I will but just as I move towards him, he abruptly turns away.

"It's getting late," he says, even though I know for a fact he stays up until two in the morning most nights. He felt it too, the gravitational pull between us. Maybe he is trying to respect my wishes to be friends. Maybe he needs a friend too.

"Yeah, goodnight. Thanks for the pizza," I say, with nonchalance that no one would believe.

Back in my apartment I lie on my bed, thinking of Damon just upstairs, just one flight of steps away, while we both sleep alone.

17

This was inevitable since I ignored her last call, and now she says she's worried about me. My parents try their best, they really do, but they simply don't understand me or my darkness. They only care if I can hold a job, and if so, I'm fine, and if not, then that needs to be addressed stat.

They might be the last generation that thinks work is work, you have kids, you grow old, you die, and what's all this fuss about fulfillment? My friends and I want meaning, depth, not to be pushed up the hill and over the cliff like lemmings.

If gratitude is indeed so important to well-being, then today I'm grateful that Gloria values me and tells me so. To be valued by your employer is a treasure. If I didn't get some fulfillment from work this would really be a shitshow. It's not that Gloria can replace the approval that I seek from my parents, but it does make up for it a little.

Maybe I will call her back after I exercise and eat dinner. I need to build up as much fortitude and positive energy as I can before then.

In the gym, I crank up my music a little louder, and pedal a little harder, in an effort to force all negative predictions of the upcoming conversation out of my mind. My heart is thumping and I'm pushing myself so hard that my breath is heaving and the woman on the treadmill glances over in concern. I don't care, I'm zooming down a mountain, the wind hitting my face as Twin Tribes guides me with their relentless beat. My shirt is soaked with sweat and I'm almost sad when the program switches to cool down mode. Almost.

Shower first, then pick at my grilled chicken salad second. The stress of talking to my parents makes me lose my appetite, but I force myself to eat some of it and shove the rest back in the fridge. Better get it over with.

"There she is. We've been worried," my mom says, the accusation poking into my ear canal.

"Sorry, just been busy getting settled in."

"Running away, you mean."

Ughhh! She was never on board with me moving to Texas, so far away, out of reach. But that was part of the point. To stand apart, to be independent. Why she doesn't understand that is beyond me. She and my dad grew up within twenty miles of where they live in New Jersey, so not too surprising that they view my move as drastic.

My peers are more fluid, we rent so we can take advantage of whatever opportunities might present themselves, no reason to be tied to one place with a complicated mortgage, not that any of us can afford one. None of my closest friends from high school still live around my hometown; they all scattered across the country, or even further.

Don't engage, Kat. I change the subject. "Things are going well so far. My boss is great and I'm learning a lot from her."

"That's something, at least," my mom says. "It's not like you can pop over here if you need a good meal or to save money on laundry."

She acts like I'm still in college and not a professional, several years into a legit career. "I make enough money to eat, mom. And the apartment came with a washer and dryer," I say in defense, even though I know it's not about money, it's about her not being able to check up on me all the time, which is part of why I moved away.

"Okay, okay. I get it, you don't need us anymore. That's all we ever wanted for you, Katherine."

My parents are the only ones who call me Katherine. They say that's the name they put on my birth certificate, not Kat. It just sounds so formal and New England-ish, like Lady Katherine—who even calls a child Katherine? They do.

"I know. You should be happy I'm successful and not living at home." I say that knowing her best friend and neighbor's son, who went to my high school, just moved back in at age twenty-six. But no, her priorities are completely different from mine.

"At least Paula's son tried to start a family."

"He just got divorced!" I shout. "How is that a good thing?"

"At least he put himself out there. I just don't want you to be alone, and now you're so far away from your family. We just want to know that someone will take care of you when we're dead and buried."

No wonder my mind is all dark and muddled, hearing things like that all my life, I'm going to end up alone, that's the worst possible fate in life. Not to mention the morbid language my mom uses regarding her own mortality.

"You're only fifty!"

"I know that. But by the time I was your age, I had a husband and a toddler."

I never had the heart to tell her I'm not having children. No way would I burden them with my genes. How could I bring a child into the world, knowing it might suffer from the same crushing darkness? Even a chance I would curse my baby to live this regimented life or face the consequences is untenable. Plus, I am ill-equipped to deal with that kind of trauma myself, a hurting child, when I'm dealing with my own problems. No, kids are one hundred percent off the table.

Sometimes I feel bad that I'm robbing her of the experience of being a grandmother, but that doesn't change the reality of the situation.

"Let me live my life, please!" I beg her.

"Fine, but don't blame me when you call crying for us to come take you home."

"That will never happen in a million years," I say. "I have to go now."

I hang up as she's trying to say her goodbye.

Why do I let her get to me? It's confusing because I can't figure out if she wants me to be happy and well or if she secretly wants me to fail and run into her arms so she can pair me off with the neighbor's divorced son.

I turn on *What We Do in the Shadows*, the series, not the movie. But even with the distraction, I start to ruminate. Even these awful vampires have a family, have romance that lasts hundreds of years, and all I ever had were a couple of short-lived flings and an ex who essentially determined I was unlovable in my flawed state. That's why I try to hide my darkness from new people as much as possible. Even Damon, who sees my goth clothes, doesn't know the whole me, only the fun me.

Maybe my mom's right and I'll always be alone. My obsessive thoughts circle like vultures over my future, and suddenly I'm eighty, in a decrepit nursing home, no kids to visit me, parents long gone, unloved, alone, my only interactions are with people who are paid to be nice to me. Fucking bleak, I know, but now it's there, in my head. How can I escape it?

I hug Saffron to me, turn off the television, and hide under the covers from the swirling cloud of darkness that looms over me like a storm, threatening my very survival.

18

Thursday is a whirlwind. Gloria gives me a new assignment; now that the Nicolas Stone project is moving forward, and each little bee is working on his part leading up to the big launch, I have more time to focus on something else. That's my favorite part about this job; if I don't like a client or assignment, I just have to wait for something new to replace it. Not that I don't like Nicolas Stone...

Sure, we have long-term clients and sometimes they are difficult, but we also have product launches, or publicity cleanups when a company makes a stupid move because they didn't recognize the change in the mood of consumers.

My new assignment is rebranding a perfume company, a classic situation where the eldest child inherits the business, she thinks her dad was out of touch and wants to bring things forward to this century. She wants to make a grand entrance as the new face of the company. This is a delicate situation because we don't want to accidentally become part of the downfall of a brand that has been successful for decades.

That's where being in my twenties is helpful. Gloria works hard to stay in the know about what young people like and how the world is changing, but she recognizes it's a necessity to have a staff with a wide range of personal experiences who can represent various age groups. That's why I think she's a good leader and why Purple Cactus has been successful, because Gloria surrounds herself with smart and talented people who excel in her areas of weakness. Although saying Gloria has any weaknesses might be a stretch.

My favorite part of the job is getting to immerse myself in a new market, and I spend the day learning everything I can about perfume, the company's competitors, what their ad campaigns look like, what Allure writes about them, all of that. I get to be in flow again, digging into the depths of the internet like an archeologist, only my greatest finds are those key glimpses that something is missing, and our new perfume queen can fill that gap. I'm lucky I get paid to do this.

As per usual, Roxy can't help raining on my parade.

"Gloria gave you the Faraci account?" she says as I steep some tea in the breakroom. She must have followed me in here when I went past her cubicle.

Is she going to question every assignment I get? She understands that I work here now, right? "Yep," I say.

"I'm surprised. She usually keeps a tight grip on our wealthier clients. She doesn't trust her junior staff to hobnob with the elite. And it's not like you're... you know," she says as she gestures at my outfit.

That is an interesting fact—if it's true, since I trust Roxy as far as I can throw her. Gloria does seem to try to present herself as near-royalty, even though I don't think she really comes from money, I think she's a woman who worked hard to build a business and is now enjoying the fruits of her success. But this time, Roxy gets to me, and I start to worry about our pitch meeting with the client and what if I come across as someone who could never understand the world of perfume and high fashion, what with my thirty-dollar outfit from Kohls.

"Well, it seems she trusts *me*, since she gave me the campaign," I say, causing Roxy's eyes to narrow at me before she turns and struts away. I hate that I stooped to her level by being snarky back to her but I'm not a saint.

After she leaves, I realize that Ben is eating his sandwich at the table like a timid mouse in the corner. I was so lost in thinking about work and then Roxy that I didn't even notice him. Sometimes I worry that Gloria keeps him so focused on assisting her that he isn't getting the full experience of working in an office and being on a team.

"She sure gives you a hard time," says Ben softly.

I break into a wide grin. "Thank you," I say.

Ben looks confused. "For what?"

"I was starting to think I was crazy because she's always nice to me in front of other people, especially Gloria."

"Oh, no, you're not crazy, I've noticed it since your first day," says Ben. "Sometimes Roxy scares me. I'm glad she doesn't acknowledge my existence."

I chuckle at the thought. "She can be a little scary, but I'm pretty sure she's a nice person underneath, although, she could also be a serial killer."

Ben almost chokes on his food.

"Shhh, if she hears us, we're both dead," I say but that just makes him laugh harder.

Tonight is the volunteer meeting at the animal shelter, and I'm excited. What I told Nick about him helping me realize I need to focus outside myself was true, but that I like animals better than people is even more true. Cats and dogs, they are blameless, helpless innocents, and they need our support to overcome the impossible situation we humans put them in.

I arrive at the shelter and am directed to the meeting room. They provide an overview of the volunteer opportunities, which include working in the adoption center screening potential owners, assisting with fundraising, or many other office tasks. But I already work in an office, so I want to work directly with the animals. The question is dogs or cats, and I adore both. I decide to walk the dogs and help keep them socialized for adoption.

I never realized how much of a challenge it must be to confine an animal to a cage yet somehow expect it to be cute and friendly when potential adopters come to visit. I can relate to these poor little guys because my darkness feels like a cage, only I walk myself with my cardio and my work ethic and accepting social invitations on principle.

After signing some paperwork and release forms, all the dog volunteers get a tour of the kennels. There are at least twenty animals for adoption in this section, ranging from puppies to seniors, all sorts of breed mixes. The dogs howl and whine, hoping we'll give them the love and attention they crave, or at least a kibble or two. Some of them cower in the corner of their cages, terrified due to past trauma that's hopefully behind them now, but they don't know that yet. It's going to be hard not to adopt them all, but I just can't have one in my apartment right now.

I sign up to volunteer Tuesdays after work, and I can't wait. In some ways, depression is a very inward-focused condition, and I've noticed the more I live in my mind, the worse it is. That's why I focus on my career, so my analytical side can concentrate on clients and campaigns instead of dissecting my past or lamenting my future.

Some nights, lying in bed, looking up at my glow stars, I'm haunted by the ghosts of hundreds of tiny failures, like every mistake I've ever made surrounds me like a dust cloud. Who wouldn't be depressed under this weight? It's the opposite of rose-colored glasses, like watching the world through a dirty windshield, and when I turn the wipers on, it just spreads the muck around instead of offering me a clearer view.

That's why I need work, friends like Damon, cardio, and now, these dogs. Their adorable little faces will keep me from falling too deeply into myself. On the drive home I already feel a new sense of purpose in trying to get these sweeties ready for adoption, helping the innocent creatures find the happiness they deserve. I also feel good about me and my progress. I'm building a life here, little by little.

When I get home, there's a message from my mom asking me to call her back. Ugh—figures something would happen to put my rare upbeat momentum to a halting stop.

19

I awake in a sweat from wrapping the covers so tightly around me, and I gasp for air, releasing my head from under the comforter. It's 6 a.m. and the birds are chirping, and the light is leaking under the bottom of my blackout curtains. My head pounds and I feel so tired, my limbs so leaden I can barely swing my legs over the side of the bed to use the restroom.

My face looks pallid, my eyes tired. I contemplate calling in sick. It's Friday, after all, so maybe I'd feel better by Monday.

Oh, you sly little minx, nice try. I've told myself that once before and the result is an entire weekend of wallowing and sugar binging, and work on Monday grows from a molehill into an insurmountable mountain.

Get your ass moving, I order myself, and my feet obey. Where would I be without my own drill sergeant? Shower, makeup, boring office clothes. Healthy breakfast. Commute to the office.

"Good morning, Amber."

"Morning darlin'," she says.

And that's how it's done. How relentless control keeps me from sliding. I focus on work, longing to fall back into flow, which is harder if you're trying, but eventually I dedicate myself to the task at hand and before I know it, lunchtime.

I take my salad outside to eat under the trees, and I check my texts. Shit. I almost forgot about Nick and the book reading tonight. I don't want to go. I want to race back to my apartment after work and stuff my face full of peanut butter cups. But that's not what is best for me, and one of my many rules is not flaking out on people.

It's so easy to use my depression as an excuse to bail on commitments at the last minute. I did that all the time in college and lost a few friends because of it. I don't want to be that person, so now, once I say I'm doing something, I do it.

I go straight there after work, with traffic I'll be there around six, an hour early, but no time to go home first.

BookPeople is amazing, and I plan on becoming a regular. They have two stories full of books, walls painted in bright colors behind the many bookshelves, and signs, so many signs, pointing to your heart's desires, whether that be the latest TikTok book craze, mysteries, romance, local authors, children's books, you name it. To top it all off there's CoffeePeople, where I grab a Mediterranean style wrap for my dinner.

Once I can't stretch out my eating any longer, I mosey along the bookshelves, stopping to look at back covers of books that catch my eye. I tend to go for fantasy but find my preference changing as I get older, and I've become more interested in real people and their stories. I don't mean non-fiction; I mean fiction that is deeply rooted in the human experience.

My phone vibrates. Nick's here looking for me, so I walk towards the entrance. When I see his sandy blonde hair and his polished vest, I get that familiar ping, like my body trying to alert me there's something I need to take notice of, and it's Nick. Roxy's not wrong that he is fine to look at.

He sees me and there's that wide, Crest Whitestrips smile beaming at me as we walk towards each other.

"This place is great," I say.

"I know, it's a treasure. Not many places like this left anymore."

"I believe it."

"Shall we head upstairs?" he says, and I swear he's about to offer me his arm like in an old movie, but he doesn't. We take our seats for the reading.

Even though I'm not a huge science fiction fan, I enjoy listening to the excerpt, imagining the alien world the author created, and I find myself wondering what happens next. I guess that means he's a good writer. We stand in the signing line, each with our own copies. When we get to the table, Nick introduces me to his former classmate José, and he signs both our books and promises to come find us after the line ends.

"Can I buy you a cup of coffee?" Nick says to me.

"How about a chai?"

"You got it."

We sit at one of the little wooden tables, Nick with his espresso, and me inhaling the heavenly scent of chai. I waft the aroma towards my nostrils and breathe it in without thinking.

Nick smiles as he watches me.

"It just smells so nice," I say.

"I feel the same way about coffee. Sometimes it's nice to savor a moment."

"I remember—you mention savoring in your book."

"I do. Because our brains tend to naturally dwell on the negative things in our lives, but gloss over the positives. We can train ourselves to savor these moments," Nick says as he looks at me, and I swear he is trying to memorize every inch of my face.

I suddenly feel self-conscious because of the way he is looking at me; I wonder if he's talking about the drinks or something else. Time to remind him he is my client, and this is not a date.

"Any lectures coming up?" I ask.

"I have one in two weeks, and after that I'm going to California for a few days."

"You used to live there, right?"

"I went to college and did my research there."

"When did you move back to Texas?"

"Just a year ago."

"Don't get me wrong, I love Austin so far, but California is beautiful too. What made you come back?"

"Ah, let's just say I had some unfinished business. And it's a little more affordable here, although that's changing rapidly. It's a nice place to raise a family."

I almost choke on my chai. He's so private, it never actually occurred to me to wonder if he has a girlfriend or is even married. Wait, that would have come up, right? Who doesn't mention their spouse once in three days? Unless it's on purpose. Oh geez, I'm spiraling now, reign it in.

"Oh. Do you have kids?" I ask because that seems less personal.

"No!" he says quickly. "I mean *eventually* raise a family. I haven't even met the right woman yet."

I nod, but inside I cringe. He wants kids. That automatically means we aren't meant to be together, since I have vowed to be child-free.

"How about you, Katie?"

"How about me what?" I say, being deliberately clueless because I don't want to answer.

"Do you want kids? Are you dating anyone?"

Wow, he went right there, no hesitation. Before I can answer, his author friend appears at our table and the question is left hanging like a punching bag.

"Thanks so much for coming," José says, and sits down next to me so he can face Nick.

"Of course, I wouldn't miss it for the world. It's great to see you," says Nick. "How's the family?"

"Good, Marta's good, Evie and Oscar are growing like weeds."

"He's got twins," Nick says to me, trying to keep me part of the conversation.

"Oh wow," I say, for lack of anything better.

"They are a handful, that's for sure," says José, "but I wouldn't trade them for anything."

I catch Nick making that wistful look I saw once on the lecture tour. I'm starting to think maybe Nick isn't actually much happier than I am. We both get most of our life satisfaction out of our work, but is that enough?

Nick and his friend catch up and reminisce and I just smile and nod like a bobblehead along the way. It's difficult to engage in a conversation about a time I wasn't a part of. Nick excuses himself to use the restroom and there's an awkward silence. Then I realize this is the first person from Nick's past I have ever heard anything about, let alone met. He never mentions his friends or family. I can't resist taking this opportunity to do a little digging.

"So, what was Nick like in college? Was he always so mild mannered, or did he have a wild side?"

José chortles and nearly spits out his latte. "A wild side? Not that I ever saw. But we didn't meet until senior year of undergrad, so by then I think we had already gone through the freshman exploration that comes with suddenly being free from parental guidance."

Geez, he talks just like Nick! Must be a psychologist thing.

He continues, "Nick's a good guy. We bonded right away since we both came to positive psychology after dealing with traumatic experiences."

A chill washes over me and I suddenly feel like garbage for prying into Nick's life like this. José obviously thinks Nick and I are closer than we are, and that I would know what he's referring to, but Nick has been a closed book.

Is it possible to really know someone if you don't know their past? I feel like I know who Nick is today, isn't that all that matters? Neither of us share much about our past, but we freely share our hopes, dreams, and feelings, other than the whole depression thing, and I see Nick interact with other people, which tells me everything I need to know.

Nick returns and they chat for a few more minutes. The store is closing soon, so we all make our way to the parking lot. José thanks us again for coming and buying his book and heads in the other direction.

"Can I walk you to your car?" Nick asks.

The other great thing about BookPeople is they have ample parking right out front. "Sure, but my car is right there," I say, pointing about twenty feet away.

"Hey, I was born in Texas, and here, we walk a lady to her car."

I shake my head, but chivalry doesn't offend me. In fact, I think it's sweet when coming from a place of caring.

When we get to my car Nick says, "I won't always be your client, you know?" and I freeze, my heart fluttering in my chest.

20

I don't ask what that means, because if it means what I think then he's just going to be disappointed when I tell him we just aren't a good fit. I'm a goth who doesn't want children! How much worse a match could we possibly be?

But now that same damn moon from last night is highlighting Nick's strong jaw, and I just want to touch his face, feel the fine stubble that has marred his perfect chin after a long day. What is it with the bewitching moon in Texas?

Instead, I click the remote to unlock the door. "Goodnight, Nick."

His face falls and I turn away, so I don't have to see that I've crushed the hope he just tossed out into the universe with his comment. I feel like he gave me a crimson rose, and I threw it on the ground and stomped the petals into the pavement.

Driving home, my chest feels heavy, and I can't wait for the solace of sleep. Even though I've been determined to be in control of my life, and I chose to reject not one, but two offers from attractive men since I moved here, it doesn't feel that way. It feels like the universe is messing with me, tossing me like a set of bowling pins, rattled by each ball and then I'm the one scrambling to reassemble them after each strike.

Speaking of which, I missed my exercise tonight and the gym is closed now. That makes me uneasy, but I remind myself I have to be able to roll with the river sometimes too. My legs feel antsy and restless as I lie in bed, and I try to fill my mind with images of sweet dogs at the shelter, waiting for my care, and let thoughts of Nick, Damon, and my mother sink to the bottom of the pit.

I decide this weekend needs to be focused on manifesting the life I want here in Austin, with no distractions from men. My goal is to make my tiny patio into a peaceful oasis where I can reset, at least when heavy metal isn't raining down from the floor above.

The nearest nursery is only ten minutes away, but I've heard about this store further out called the Natural Gardener and I want to see it for myself.

Even though I arrive when it first opens, there are already a lot of people shopping, not surprising on a pleasant April morning. I walk around aimlessly, not sure what I'm looking for, but I'll know it when I see it. There's a butterfly garden with bright orange monarchs and yellow swallowtails fluttering from flower to flower, and I wish I could buy the plants that would attract them to my patio but it's not really that sunny. Maybe that's okay, because ever since I learned that most butterflies only live for two weeks, seeing them makes me melancholy, and I hardly need more of that.

As I walk on, I come across an area with goats and chickens. No matter that I personally don't plan on having children, it's always fun to watch little kids when they see a goat. Something about them being on the same eye level makes it seem like they are kindred spirits. A little boy giggles as one goat propels itself off another goat's behind. The chickens do their funky dance, sticking their necks out and pecking at the ground, and the kid imitates their movements with surprising accuracy.

The herb garden section gives me some ideas. The abundance of fragrance fills my nostrils, lavender, lemon grass, rosemary, thyme, and sage, like a mix of floral perfume and a Thanksgiving dinner all rolled into one. I place a mint plant in my cart, imagining sitting on my Adirondack chair with the smell of mint wafting towards me on each breeze. Or adding a sprig to my iced tea sounds refreshing. I must be turning Texan if I'm dreaming of cold tea on a hot day, and I haven't even lived here through summer yet.

I spot the perfect pot for my little patio, a shiny purple glaze with swirls etched beneath the rim. It's pricy, but gorgeous. Decorating my patio is my birthday present to myself, and despite her disapproval of my life choices, my mom will be sending me some money too. I grab a smaller, cheaper plastic dark green pot for my mint, since I remember they tend to take over.

As I turn the corner, movement catches my eye and my heart sings as I spy a calico cat taking a bath in an empty pot. I kneel down next to her, waiting to see if she's friendly. When she decides she's done licking, she stretches her paw out as if to say, I am ready, commence with your adoration. I give her head some scritches, then, as she seems happy, I scratch her cheeks and chin as well, and she purrs.

This place is heaven. But it makes me want a house with a proper yard so I can have a dog and a garden. Maybe someday, who knows? It's not that I'm dead set against the whole marriage, house thing, just not sure it's for me. Maybe house, five dogs, two cats, garden, but no marriage might be more likely.

Now I just need plants to fill my ceramic pot. I tell one of the staff what I'm doing and that my patio is shady, and she finds me some things that will work. What goth could go wrong with something called Heartleaf Skullcap? And it has purple flowers that go with my pot. I also get a periwinkle, which will trail nicely over the edge.

On the way to the cash register I come across a display of windchimes, and I'm mesmerized. The silvery, dulcet sounds whisk me away to another land but not before I notice a black metal crescent moon set that I must have.

It all costs more than I planned, but it is my present to myself, and if I can keep it all alive, my patio will be a haven.

Back at the apartment, Damon is walking out to his car as I pull into the parking lot.

"Need any help?" he asks as I lift a bag of soil.

"I got it. Thanks though."

He walks over and eyes my purchases. "Making the place your own."

"Yep."

He grabs the larger pot with the smaller one nestled inside it despite my refusal of help and walks with me. "Tomorrow a few of us are hiking at Pedernales Falls. You want to join? They thought you were cool."

I guess he means the guys from Flaming Goathead. They seemed nice, and being outdoors and getting exercise checks a lot of boxes for me. But because of the flickering flame between Damon and me it's imperative that I do not build my life around him. That his friends don't become my only friends. I need to get out and make my own friends. And I promised to have a man-free weekend.

"Thanks for the invite but I'm going to take a raincheck on this one."

"Aww, big plans?"

I frown because Damon is not my keeper and I'm sensitive about people nosing in my business.

"Yes, I have plans for some me-time."

He jerks his chin back like I punched him. "Oh," he says. "I guess you enjoy your own company, that's good."

His face doesn't seem like he thinks it's good, but like he doesn't understand at all. I'm not that introverted, but Damon is definitely an extrovert. He doesn't seem to like being alone at all. Personally, I don't think it's good if you can't be alone with yourself and your thoughts. Maybe that's why he smokes so much, to get out of his own head. I guess we all have an inner monologue that needs silencing sometimes.

"You think that's weird?" I demand.

"I don't know...you do you, Katie."

That's not a real answer, but it is an answer of sorts. Damon is chill, but it seems hard for him to understand people who aren't like him.

"I couldn't be anyone else," I say, but then wince at my hypocrisy. Damon is just being Damon, and he was only being friendly by asking me to join him and his buddies. Maybe I'm being a bitch. "Let's hang out this week, though, okay?"

That seems to placate him, and his face relaxes. "Cool. Have fun with your garden. See ya later."

I turn on The Birthday Massacre's latest album and plant my mint, Skullcap, and periwinkle. The dark, fertile soil feels good in my hands, warm and alive. I imagine I'm planting my roots here in Austin and hope that with proper watering I will bloom and thrive.

Twenty minutes later, the black crescent moon hangs from a hook left by the previous tenants. I sink back into my chair, the music washing over me, the smell of mint and fresh earth, and once a breeze blows, the tinkling of the windchimes completes the mood.

This feels like home.

21

Monday, I take extra care getting ready, because we are meeting with the perfume princess. My second client ever at Purple Cactus. Gloria has been happy with my performance on the Nicolas Stone project and I'm anxious to keep this train moving.

As usual, only Amber and I are in the office at 8:30 a.m. That's my routine now, to always be earlier than everyone else, especially Roxy, so I can make my morning drink in peace, without fear of ruining another one of her outfits.

I let out a screech like an owl when something pokes me in the back.

"I caught you," says Roxy with the devil in her eyes.

"Making tea?" I say, confused.

"No. I was walking back from Waterloo Records Friday night and guess what I spied with my little eyes?"

I try to keep my face blank but I'm pretty sure the color drained from my face. "Oh, what was that?"

"Little miss new girl barbie doll on a date with Mr. Positive," she says with a smirk.

Oh shit. If I get defensive that will just fuel the fire, so I try a different approach. "Oh, that?" I say with a wave of my hand. "Nick and I were attending the book release of another psychologist. Purely research for his launch. He was feeling concerned about his big event."

Roxy's eyes narrow at me, and I know she doesn't quite believe me but also hasn't caught me the way she had hoped. "Is that so? Who was the author?"

I tell her, knowing she will no doubt run to her computer and look at BookPeople's event calendar immediately after this conversation. Where she will find the author's name plain and simple.

"Hmmpfh," she says. "I don't know what it is about you, Katie, but you're hiding something and I'm going to find out what it is. And Gloria will not appreciate it if you're sleeping with her clients."

I can't even with this woman. "You have problems," I tell her, "and I have work to do." I push past her, needing to get to the safety of my cubicle.

This is a hot mess. Maybe. So, Roxy saw me with Nick on Friday, big deal. She doesn't have anything to tattle to Gloria about, because nothing has happened between us. However, I realize that I obviously didn't think my closet goth plan through. She could have just as easily seen me decked out head to toe goth, and then she would never let me hear the end of it.

Based on her wardrobe, I'm sure she frequents the Red River area where Revision is, and it's only a matter of time before we run into each other outside of work. Maybe it's not that easy to keep things separate. Just ask Superman, right? I'm juggling too many secrets these days.

Right now, I need to focus on the perfume campaign. What Roxy said about Gloria letting me work with an elite client really freaked me out, but even though I'm in the meeting, Gloria will be doing most of the talking, which is fine by me, so I can watch and learn. I even styled my hair in an updo similar to Gloria today, taking cues from her about matching the style of our clients to build rapport. Perfume princess is wealthy and sophisticated, so I put on long earrings and my ruffled cerulean blue top. It's the best I can do on a limited budget.

Vittoria Faraci is herself elegance in a bottle and perfumery is obviously in her blood. Her style is refined in a way that Gloria probably only dreams; even I know expensive fashion when I see it. But unlike Gloria, Vittoria doesn't need a bright statement scarf to demand attention. In fact, her outfit colors are nearly as drab as what I had initially selected at Kohls, black and dark browns. But the textures and the cut scream high end, the top so silky I have to pin my hands at my sides to keep from touching it. Her heels are even higher than Amber's and still she moves with the grace of a Persian cat.

Gloria is unfazed, having worked with many high-status clients over the years. "Ms. Faraci," says Gloria, her hand extended, "so pleased to meet you." Instead of shaking her hand, Vittoria gently pats Gloria's hand between both of hers, in a feminine, nearly sensual gesture.

Gloria introduces me and we start the presentation. She begins by covering the obvious. The company has been successful under Vittoria's father's governance, and we don't want to risk upsetting that. But we recognize that Vittoria is her own person with her own ideas, and we want the world to know that.

We show images of Faraci perfume ads, the typical ultra white sets, super thin models in scant white flowing dresses. Diamonds and white roses. Women sprawled on a beach, or next to a shirtless male model, with a clear message that the women wearing this perfume can seduce men.

I cyberstalked Vittoria Faraci, which was easy because she's famous enough that the paparazzi follow her at the big social events, both when she is in Italy and in the States. She has an edge to her that her father didn't. Her father was old-school, and it worked for him, so why change it. Vittoria is young and hungry. She isn't afraid to make social statements, especially feminist ones. That's why I pitched my idea to Gloria, and she agreed to run with it.

"With all that in mind," continues Gloria, "we present to you the rebirth of Faraci. Powerful women, dark, mysterious, edgy, sexy for herself, not for a man. Instead of pretending we're in a paradise, Faraci perfume is a rare bird thriving in the dark and complex world we live in." The project shows the yin to her father's conceptual yang, a dark-haired woman with thigh-high leather boots standing fiercely tall, robed in gothic lace, on a black sand beach with storm clouds behind her, the bottle of Faraci perfume set on a glowing Venus clam shell, illuminating the scene. No man in sight.

Vittoria stares at the image and for two minutes Gloria and I hold our breath. Oh fuck. She hates it. I'm so fired. I mentally start updating my resume, wondering if I can just leave this job off entirely and pretend I moved to Austin for other reasons. How many PR firms are there here? Am I going to have to move back home?

Finally, Vittoria turns to us. "I love it! Leave behind all the angelic, Mother Mary bullshit and give me a woman with power and passion. Bravissime!"

The relief that fills me gives way to pride. I'm so killing it at this job, and it feels awesome. This must be what happiness feels like; my brain is fizzy like a shaken soda can releasing foamy dopamine.

Gloria is pleased and she finally takes me to the lunch she promised on my first day, in celebration of our success. She tells me how glad she is that she hired me, and the sky is the limit for me at Purple Cactus PR. I feel like I could burst with glee. I'm so glad I took the chance on this move.

Katie is really kicking ass, although it was Kat who inspired the Faraci rebranding concept. I can't wait to tell Nick when I see him for the media training.

Wait. Why did I think of telling Nick? He's not my boyfriend.

It's just that Nick understands what it's like to get satisfaction from work, to be fueled by mastery, something that Damon doesn't seem to get at all. Well, I'll tell both of them anyway, because they're all I have in Austin so far. Or maybe I'll tell the dogs tomorrow night.

My cardio is less painful today since I'm still on a high from my professional achievement. It's effortless and I cycle faster than normal and don't mind the burning in my legs. My workout mix, set on shuffle, plays Light Asylum, and I'm grooving with their energy, pushing to minute thirty, praying that the good mood chemicals stay with me just a little longer.

Quick shower and a Greek salad later, I decide to see if Damon wants to celebrate with me. I'm a little nervous since I don't usually knock on his door unexpectedly.

It opens with a release of skunky smell and a cloud of smoke. "Oh hey, Katie," he says, and steps outside instead of inviting me in, either embarrassed or just wanting to spare me the stale air.

"Sorry, am I bothering you?" I ask.

"Of course not. I'd invite you in, but I got the impression this isn't your thing," he says, fanning the air.

"It's not."

"I figured."

"But I'm not like against it or anything, and I don't mind being around it," I say quickly. Other than the smell that clings to my clothing, weed is fine with me. It's preferable to cigarettes and alcohol.

"That's cool," he says. "So, what brings you upstairs?"

"I had an awesome day at work, and I wanted to see if you want to celebrate with me; I still owe you birthday Amy's."

"Hell yes, give me one minute and I'll be right down."

"OK. I'll drive," I say firmly since he is obviously impaired right now.

This time I taste test the Frangelico but end up with a scoop of key lime pie in a waffle cone. Damon gets chocolate bourbon. This place is either paradise or the gateway to hell and I'm going to have to limit how often I come here; the ice cream is gloriously rich. I'm trying to find a new balance between my disciplined rigor and allowing moments to enjoy the pleasure this world provides us, like Amy's.

"Tell me what happened at work that brought me such a nice surprise," Damon said, taking a spoonful of ice cream.

I tell him all about Vittoria Faraci and the perfume rebranding.

"That sounds like some made up movie shit," he says.

I pause mid lick and frown. "What do you mean?"

"Uh, nothing, it's just, a perfume heiress? That's a real thing?"

"Why not? Her father built a business, and she took over, it's not unusual."

"I don't know, it just doesn't seem real."

"Well, it is real—she's my client, and it's my job."

He holds up his hand in surrender. "I didn't mean anything by it, it just seems far removed from the life we both live."

Speak for yourself. I'm trying to make something of myself. I knew Damon wouldn't get it. But what's the point in trying to explain it to someone who can't understand why work is important to me? "Don't worry about it," I say, and focus on my dessert, which no one can ruin for me.

"Are you mad right now? I'm a little spaced out. I'm happy for you that your meeting went well."

"I'm not mad," I say. Just disappointed. But he's probably too high to understand that anyway, so best to just drop it.

"Good. I'm glad your job is going well, cause I want you to stay here. I like having you around," he says with an endearing smile.

It's hard to stay annoyed at Damon, he's sweet at heart, and pretty open with his feelings for a metalhead. And right now, he's dripping ice cream on his Flaming Goathead shirt. I hand him a napkin and point.

He looks down and shakes his head. "The dangers of ice cream."

I grin and forget that he just made me mad a few minutes ago.

2 2

On Wednesday I feel the gloom even before I open my eyes. The heaviness, like a weighted blanket is draped over me. The cloudiness in my mind, thoughts are words on a water-soaked page, blurry and incoherent.

Forcing myself to wake up, the pitter patter of raindrops drum on my patio. Ah. Did the gloominess spread from outdoors into my room? Maybe I'm solar charged, and without my blessed sunshine I just don't have the energy to operate.

There's no rhyme or reason. Things went great at work yesterday, so why did I wake up in darkness? I've long since given up trying to solve this ongoing mystery.

It's getting late; I've overslept and I'm going to be stuck in traffic, no doubt worse because of the weather. But what does it matter. Who cares if I get there on time? What's even the point? Why do I spend my days trying to manufacture unrealistic images of people so they can sell more of whatever they're selling? How horribly meaningless. My meaning is derived from helping other people be successful in their meaninglessness.

I hear it, of course. Years of therapy means I can recognize these unhelpful thoughts when my brain announces them. But they feel true. They are true. It's like Nick said, happiness is a construct. Meaning is a construct. Isn't everything? So what if I get together with Damon or with Nick, it won't last forever, so what if I get promoted and achieve career and financial success? It won't fill the bottomless pit of emptiness inside me. Nothing can do that, not drugs, not therapy, not friends or parents, not a lover, not a job.

Acceptance of this state is the best thing for me. Believing there is a permanent cure, a new therapy, a new treatment, only brings new hope and then an even farther fall. Long ago I decided that as shitty as this life could sometimes be, I would rather have a life than not.

For me, the good times are when I'm just *mildly* depressed, which has been most of my time in Austin.

In the past, I'd be *just* mildly depressed, and then things would get really bad, and eventually I'd go back to *merely* mildly depressed again. Apparently, it's acceptable in our culture to be miserable most of the time as long as you aren't suicidal. Being suicidal is totally unacceptable and must be fixed as soon as possible, but once you are stable it's back to the trenches for you, and good luck with your life.

Even I'm confused when I see other people who claim to be depressed, because there is an expectation that they appear sad all the time, be listless, even bed ridden. I was eighteen when Robin Williams died and people couldn't understand how he could seem joyful so much of the time, find so much humor in the world, but still struggle with depression.

But I get it. Damon doesn't even know I'm depressed, nor anyone at work, because I'm not like the lady in the antidepressant commercial, staring out the window listlessly at her child playing in the yard. It's not like that, at least for me, at least not all the time. Sometimes I laugh, sometimes I enjoy eating Amy's Ice Cream with Damon or seeing my favorite band play, and sometimes I just enjoy living a neutral life, for days or even weeks.

And then there are days like today.

The most important thing I've learned is to ignore my brain when it says "You're too depressed to _____" because it's usually not true. Like today. Can I get in the car and drive to work? Probably. My legs are functioning and I'm coherent enough to drive. Will I excel at work today? Probably not. But that's okay. So I force myself out the door.

Today I really have to fake a bright face when Amber greets me. Honestly, I need to give myself a fucking medal for even being here.

I turn on my computer and know that I'm going to spend the day pretending to work. I slouch over, then force myself to sit up straight, trying not to advertise my mood.

It doesn't work because Roxy notices immediately. "What's eating you, today?" she says as she stops at my cubicle.

How can someone like her be so empathic? She might be the first person I ever wished was less so, because it invades my privacy. Am I giving off a cloud of melancholy? I didn't say a word or anything.

"What do you mean?" I say. "I'm just sitting here typing."

"Okay, if you say so. If you're sick, you should go home instead of spreading it around."

And there it is. I don't think it can count as empathy if you can sense people's feelings and then immediately turn it into something selfish. Although she raises a good question. Is darkness contagious? If Nick were here, I could ask him. Surely negative people breed negativity, right? I don't want to be that person, the party-pooper dragging people down.

"I'm not sick," I say, but she's already gone, probably to get some coffee.

I'd better just lay low today. I'm so tired I can barely stay awake anyway.

Fate has other plans for me, because when Gloria blows in like a tornado, she tells me she had a call early this morning from a client on retainer who's in the midst of a PR crisis. She's going to send me some information and I need to drop everything I'm doing and come up with some ideas by this afternoon.

I don't know how I'm going to do this. My brain just isn't working properly today. When the darkness descends it's like instead of things going in an orderly A,B,C, they go A,P,Z,E. My creativity goes down the shitter. This is not good.

A full cup of coffee later, I try to focus on what Gloria sent. Apparently, a regional candy company announced that they were moving their factory, which employed half of a small Texas town, south, across the border. Now there's a whole social media campaign asking for people to boycott.

I don't really see how that's a PR crisis. That was a financial decision that they made, and they obviously thought the savings would justify the bad press. This is the perfect example of how pointless my job is. Why should I help this company? They didn't care about the community that helped make them successful. It's not like people can't live without candy anyway, so who cares if they exist or not?

Because I need a roof over my head is the only answer I can find today. I shake myself to try and wake up my brain. Think, think, think, Kat, I say in my head. Damage control. For them and for me.

But my mind is blank. I have no clue what they should do. Even if they changed their minds and kept the factory open, the damage was already done. They should just move forward and focus on sales. Launch a new product or something.

I slink off my chair like I'm made of liquid mercury and seep my way down to the coffee shop in the lobby. I buy a piece of iced pound cake because my body is insisting that I eat something full of fat and sugar. My brain does that to me, tricks me into making poor choices, and sometimes I go along with it. The sweetness hits my taste buds and for a few seconds I feel good. It's different than when I go to Amy's with Damon. That's a treat, for fun, but this is more like a salve for my pain, one that tantalizes me, telling me to eat more and more, but the benefits are agonizingly temporary.

After lunch, I trudge back upstairs to my cubicle. It's still dark and gloomy out, and I'm so tired. I stare at the computer, trying to come up with solutions to this PR problem, but my eyelids are so heavy.

Bam!!!! A noise right by my head startles me. Oh fuck, I fell asleep. I lift my head off the desk, and Roxy is standing there with her arms crossed and a smug smile.

"Does Gloria know?" I whisper as I wipe slobber off my cheek.

"No. You owe me big time for this. I could get you fired, but I won't, because I'm not that kind of person."

I thought she was that kind of person, but right now I'm grateful I'm wrong.

"Thank you," I say. "I don't know what happened."

Roxy's expression says she knows I'm lying about something, but she doesn't press.

"Just clean yourself up," she says. "I'll make some more coffee."

Wow, is Roxy being nice to me? "Thanks," I mumble, and I'm too frazzled to try and understand this uncharacteristic side of her, so I let it go.

It's nearly three and I don't have any ideas on smoothing over the PR crisis. I down the coffee and head to my meeting with Gloria. I don't know what I'm going to say. This is my first big failure here at Purple Cactus. This day blows.

I'm honest with Gloria upfront, telling her I just couldn't think of anything suitable. She is disappointed in me, but she's actually pretty nice about it. She says we all have bad days when the ideas don't flow, and I will learn how to work under pressure as I get more experience. I thank her for understanding, but I'm crushed that I let her and the company down and now Gloria's going to have to compensate for my failure.

This is the first time since I moved to Austin that my darkness has gotten the better of me, not counting my first day of work and the night I talked with my mom, since those had specific situational triggers.

I force myself to exercise, and it feels like the longest thirty minutes of my existence, and every cell in my body is screaming at me to sleep instead. I get through it, but in compromise, I skip dinner, and allow myself to fall asleep early, because all I long for is the sweet peace of slumber.

23

Even though I feel a little better Thursday, and better still on Friday, I decide that after spending most of the week alone in the apartment, getting outside this weekend is a good idea, especially when the weather is as sunny and beautiful as it is today. I'm unsure how I will fare here once it gets blistering hot, so I need to enjoy spring while it lasts.

There are tons of parks around Austin, greenbelt trails that weave through the city and connect swimming holes and larger recreational spaces. I've seen them online, but I don't feel comfortable going any of those places by myself. Maybe I should have taken Damon up on his offer, but I don't want to rely on him for everything. Until I make some truly platonic friends, I'll have to explore by myself.

There is one place that seems safe, because it is sure to be crowded on a weekend, and that is the hike and bike trail around Lady Bird Lake. It's a little confusing, because the so called "lake" that runs through downtown Austin is actually not a lake at all, but the Colorado River that's been dammed in several places for flood control. To make it even more confusing, it's a different Colorado River than the one that starts in Colorado and ends up in California. I'm learning and will be an Austinite in no time. Hah.

I find out where to park, put some sunscreen, a hat, a granola bar, and my aluminum water bottle in a backpack, and hit the trail. Although I hate my formal thirty minutes of cardio, I usually enjoy a leisurely walk outside in nature. I don't worry about achieving a target heart rate when I walk for recreation; I want to take in everything around me, pause when something catches my eye.

And there's so much to see. I follow the trail along the lake, stopping at the first pier to take in the vista. The water looks turquoise today, and with the sun shining overhead it shimmers like fairies' wings skimming over the water. Directly across from me, the opposite shore is lush with trees and vegetation, and to my left, the city skyline just peeks out from above the trees. I'm headed towards downtown with a growing sense of curiosity.

I reach a section of boardwalk that juts out over the water. From here I spot turtles sunning themselves on the bank, piled up on every rock and log, enjoying the weather as much as I am. Today I feel vindicated that my move to Austin and its abundant sunshine wasn't just a pipe dream, it was a smart move for someone who can't endure the seemingly endless months of gray winter in the northeast.

One thing I appreciate is that all walks of life seem to enjoy this trail, from kids on bikes to groups of seniors, teenagers, families, Austinites and visitors, using the space in different ways, fishing, birdwatching, running, jogging, cycling, spending time with friends.

Closer to downtown there are people kayaking, rowing, and stand-up paddling on the lake, and families picnicking in the pocket parks along the way. There's a woman pushing a Dachshund in a stroller; I guess the poor thing must get tired with his short legs.

I'm wondering where all the 'weird' people are from the city's "Keep Austin Weird" campaign. Sure, there's plenty of people who appear 'alternative,' lots of guys with long hair like Damon, nose rings and other piercings, tons of tattoos, but nothing that unusual. I wonder what counts as weird these days anyway.

Further down the trail, a group of people are taking photos of something in front of them. I'm interested to see what it is and decide to investigate.

"Katie?"

I jerk my head back to the trail in front of me and who do I see, but Nicolas Stone, wearing stonewashed jeans and a plain blue t-shirt. I've noticed Nick wears a lot of blue, but maybe I'm just thinking again about his cobalt shirt in the hotel gym. I think about it way too often.

"Nick! Crazy running into you here." As always, it seems I'm destined for clients and neighbors to see me sweaty and in workout clothes. At least today I'm wearing a modest t-shirt over my sports bra, in an effort to prevent sunburned shoulders.

"I come here most Sundays," he says.

"Nice. This is my first time. It's beautiful."

"In that case, can I show you around? Unless you'd rather be by yourself..."

So much for a weekend free from men. I made it one full day. But it seems like fate that we ran into each other in a city of a million people, and who am I to fight fate?

"I'd like that. What's down there?" I say, pointing to the group taking photos.

"Ah, that's one of Austin's most famous statues. Stevie Ray Vaughan."

"The guitarist, right?"

"Yes...the guitarist, but he's much more than that. If you're going to live in Texas, you have to be aware that he is a state treasure."

"Good to know," I say and make a mental note to listen to a few of his songs for my musical education. We approach the statue, bouquets of fresh flowers resting on the base. Stevie Ray Vaughan clearly means a lot to people here.

Surely not coincidentally, a young man is playing guitar up on the hill in a bluesy style that fits the scene. I'm starting to get the Austin vibe now, nature and music interwoven.

This part of the trail runs by some large open spaces, including a dog park. Since Nick and I both love dogs, we watch for a minute as a spritely border collie leaps in the air, catching a frisbee, then brings it back to his human.

"Wow!" I say. "That was high—five feet in the air, at least."

"That was impressive," Nick agrees.

"Awww, poor thing," I say as a golden retriever walks by using a dog wheelchair.

"Don't feel sorry for her," says the man beside her, "she gets along great. Doesn't even know she's not like the other dogs. Watch. Get it, Ginger—get the ball." Ginger takes off, dragging the wheelchair behind her, fetches the ball, then makes a wide semicircle to loop back in the other direction and returns it to the man.

"Good girl," he says, patting her head. "See?" he says to me.

For some reason that makes me want to cry and my eyes start to water. "I do see," I reply. "She's lucky you found her."

"We're both lucky," the man says.

I turn away from the dog park and Nick follows. "Are you okay?" he asks, as I wipe my eyes with the back of my hand.

"Yes, I'm fine. I can't wait to start working at the shelter. There are so many good dogs out there that need homes, need to find people like that guy."

"You're a kindhearted person," Nick says and pats me on the shoulder.

"Mostly about dogs," I say, and Nick laughs, but I'm serious. Dogs are so much better than people. Cats too. Bunnies, fish, lizards, all animals really, except roaches. I draw the line there.

"How's work going?" Nick asks and I tell him all about Vittoria Faraci. He tells me she sounds like a fascinating client and congratulates me on figuring out the right image for her rebranded perfume company. He says I'm a PR whiz and that cheers me. I knew he would appreciate the importance of my success.

"Have you been walking long?" he says.

"No, just thirty minutes or so before I ran into you, why?"

"Because there is something uniquely Austin that you should really experience, but it doesn't happen until just before sundown."

It's only just barely 4 p.m. and the sun probably doesn't set until after 8. "That's a lot of time to kill," I say.

"True. Maybe some other time," he says, but looks disappointed.

What would I do with the next four hours without Nick? If I hadn't run into him, I probably would have walked around another hour and a half, stopped by H-E-B, and ate alone in my apartment while watching old reruns of *Supernatural*. Which is more appealing—that, or having this dashing man show me around? Easy choice if I put aside the whole issue of him being my client and me being a closet goth.

24

"No, let's do it today," I say, and then realize I don't even know what I've agreed to do. I must really trust him.

Nick's face brightens and it's like the sun coming out from behind cloudy skies. I love his smile, how it includes not just his mouth but his eyes.

"Great! In that case, do you want to walk for a while and then get something to eat?"

"Sure, but I'm not dressed for anywhere nice," I say.

"This is Austin, it's known for being casual. We can find somewhere you'll be comfortable, in fact, I know just the place and it's not far."

"Okay."

I walk with Nick and soon we arrive at a cute food truck park, with a shaded seating area and blue picnic tables. The smells of the various cuisines and smoky grills mix in the air, and I breathe it in, my stomach rumbling with hunger. There are eight trucks to choose from, Thai to gumbo, but I see what I want right away. I've loved every taco I've had since I arrived in Austin, and I doubt I'll ever get sick of them. All those taco-less years to make up for, I guess.

"See anything you want?" Nick asks.

"Oh yeah," I say, pointing to the taco truck.

"Glad you're still enjoying all the great Tex-Mex food here," says Nick. "That sounds good, I'll get some as well."

I order first, then Nick, and I pull out my wallet to pay but Nick says, "Please, let me, I'm the one who highjacked your day."

"But you're my client, remember?"

"Not today. Today we're two friends, and friends can buy each other a ten-dollar dinner."

"I guess so," I say with reticence. "Thank you."

"It's my pleasure."

The al pastor meat is so tender it melts in my mouth, and the tangy sweetness of the pineapple, heat from the chilis, and freshness of the cilantro blend in perfect harmony.

"Mmmm. I'm never going to live anywhere but here," I say after I finish the last bite and lick my lips.

"Glad to hear that's all it takes," says Nick.

"Yep, I guess the way to my heart is through tacos, just never knew it before now."

"I'll keep that in mind," he says.

Is he flirting with me? I know I should stop it, but I don't want to, so I just pretend I didn't hear him.

"What's next?" I say. "It's only 5:30."

"I wouldn't mind relaxing for a while. If we walk back to my car, I can get the picnic blanket I keep in the trunk, and we can find a nice tree to sit under."

This is sounding more and more like a date, but too late now. Anyway, Nick was careful to call us friends earlier, so...

"That sounds good, lead the way."

Thirty minutes later, we're sitting under a huge oak tree, on Nick's blanket. I lie back and look up at the sky through the leaves. There are a few wispy clouds way up high, but other than that it is bright and blue. I glance over and catch Nick looking at me and he quickly turns away, embarrassed.

I sit back up and wrap my arms around my knees, squinting at the shoreline. "Is that a swan?" I say, even though they have an unmistakable shape. I'm just surprised to see one here.

Nick looks over. "Yep. There are usually a few swans around downtown."

"I want to go see."

"They can be pretty mean."

"No, really? They seem so graceful and benevolent."

"Really. I remember one time, a swan bit my...I mean a swan bit me when I was little."

There it is again, Nick censoring himself. I don't push because I'm sure he has his reasons, and it's none of my business. Still, it's odd.

"I'll just stay over here then, shall I?" I joke, hoping to put Nick back at ease. It works because he chuckles.

"It's probably for the best."

We don't talk constantly the whole time, and I even close my eyes for a few minutes, tired from being out in the sun. It's nice that we feel comfortable enough to not have to fill every second with conversation.

As the sun starts to get lower in the sky, Nick says, "We should probably head over there now."

I am intrigued since I still don't know where we're going. We walk to the Congress Avenue Bridge. At the end of this road lies the State Capitol building with its iconic shape. From this vantage point, the city skyline is right in front of me, too close to even be a skyline, complete with construction cranes in the background. I know I'm just one of many people flocking to this place, and it sure is booming.

Nick stops us in front of the bridge railing. Several other people are already assembled and waiting along the street. Down below, people are sitting on towels and blankets on the lawn adjacent to the shoreline.

"What are we doing here?" I ask.

"You'll see," he says mysteriously.

The sun begins to set in a light pink behind us, and in front the sky is turning a dark bluish gray. I wait impatiently as more and more people line the sidewalk. Without the sun overhead, it's kind of chilly near the water and I rub my arms.

Nick unzips his backpack and offers me his sweatshirt.

"Thanks," I say and slip my arms in, then zip it up half-way. I have to keep from closing my eyes and inhaling his scent, that mild coconut again, the smell of Nick, which confuses and delights me.

I'm pulled back into the moment when something flutters out from beneath the bridge. Then another, and another, and a stream of bats fly out from under the beams in an orderly cloud.

"Wow—it's incredible!" I say, as the crowd oohs and aahs in awe of the spectacle.

"I know," says Nick, and I feel the tingle of excitement as much from his body standing so close to mine as I do from the wonder of nature before me.

I'm mesmerized by these tiny creatures, thousands upon thousands of them, flapping their wings with determination as they search for insects to feast upon. It seems like a never-ending stream pouring out over the lawn towards the lake. After a few minutes, there is a soaring river of bats stretching out toward the horizon, and I lose track of their journey as they disappear into the darkening sky.

After forty-five minutes, the exodus seems to have died down and the crowds dissipate.

"Come on," Nick says. "I'll drive you to your car."

We walk through the city streets, and soon we are pulling up where I parked earlier this afternoon.

Nick gets out and walks me to my door. Overhead, the stars are twinkling in the clear night sky. Nick is standing in front of me, and my back is against the car door.

"I'm glad I ran into you," he says, standing so close to me that I can feel the heat radiating from his chest.

"So am I. Thank you for dinner and the show. It really was a sight."

"I enjoyed sharing it with you. Thank you for saying yes."

There's an awkward silence as he gazes into my eyes, and I wonder if he is hoping I'll continue to say yes. He leans in slowly and brushes my hair away from my face, gently grazing my cheek with his hand. I eagerly await his lips meeting mine; I can practically feel his kiss.

"Wait!" I say at the last second.

Nick pulls back and groans in disappointment. He's not the only one. I really want to but can't allow myself to make a terrible mistake that could mess up my future.

"You're still my client, Nick. I could lose my job. You know my career means a lot to me, especially since I just moved here."

"I know that. I'm sorry—you're just so beautiful right now—all the time, really; it's impossible not to want to kiss you."

I can feel my cheeks burning, knowing he feels the electricity between us as much as I do, and also flattered that this gorgeous guy finds me so kissable. I want so badly to throw caution to the wind and pull him close, but before I decide what to do, he intervenes.

"It's okay; I understand," he says. "But I'll say it again...I won't always be your client. I can wait..."

His insinuation sends a shiver of anticipation down my spine.

"Goodnight, Nick," I say firmly.

"Goodnight, Katie."

Driving home, I try not to think about kissing Nick, because him being my client isn't the only reason we can't be together. First there was the goth thing, which is hilarious in this moment, because how goth are bats? We just went *bat* watching! Second, the whole having kids thing, which can't be fixed.

When I get home, I realize I'm still wearing Nick's sweatshirt. I change into shorts and a t-shirt, but right before I crawl into bed, I slip Nick's sweatshirt back on and drink in his scent, imagining his arms are wrapped around me.

25

Monday is a quiet day at the office because Roxy is helping Gloria with an onsite event. I spend my time looking over the latest progress on the Nicolas Stone account but also take advantage of the light workload by surfing the internet. It's been a while since I went dancing at eighties goth night at Revision and with all this focus on my day job, I'm once again feeling that antsy discomfort that comes from drifting too far away from my roots. It's like I'm on a boat without any oars and can no longer see the land. How can I make my way back to shore?

There are still several places I've been meaning to check out in Austin, and I make a list on my phone as I search the web. Maybe I could ask Damon to come out with me tonight; he rarely has anything planned in the evenings. I'm starting to get excited by the prospect of exploring something uniquely Austin again. I mean, the goth side, not to discount everything I saw yesterday downtown, including the bats, which were sort of accidental goth on Nick's part.

As predicted, Damon is up for a drive, and soon we arrive at a small house painted in matte black with a dark red door. As we enter The Glass Coffin, welcomed by a life-sized cut out of Dracula and a sign that reads, "No Biting on Premises," I get that warm fuzzy feeling of being somewhere I belong. The store smells like incense and candles, and the lighting is dark and ambient, like the whole scene is washed in a red filter. Every corner is filled with curiosities, cabinets with glass jars containing long dead specimens, shelves with animal skulls, and a witch's pantry full of herbs for magic work.

In a corner there is a movie poster of *The Lost Boys,* and Damon and I exchange a knowing glance as we take in the Chinese food container with chopsticks sticking out, filled with fake worms. That scene always grosses me out. I love that Damon has seen this eighties classic. I bet Nicolas Stone has never watched *The Lost Boys.*

There is an open room without merchandise that has a coffin with Dracula sleeping inside, and a vintage, high back chair creating a perfect photo op in front of red satin brocade curtains with a beaded scalloped valence across the top.

"If you want to sit down, I'll take your photo," Damon says, and I settle into the back of the throne, feeling like a powerful vampire queen. Instead of smiling, I make my most somber glare.

"This comes too naturally to you, Katie," he says, turning his phone so I can see the image. Looking deadpan is much easier for me than plastering on a fake smile, like I sometimes have to do at work, especially on the days when my mood is low. I ask Damon if he wants a photo too, but he declines; this place isn't really his thing.

There's a back room blocked off with a red rope, that has special pieces in it, and the owner gives us the tour. There is an antique child's coffin, a closet full of creepy old dolls, an old Ouija board, and some vintage horror movie memorabilia.

Even though the store has so many cool things, unfortunately I don't have a lot of extra money to spare since I just moved. Even so, I can't help purchasing a pewter bat necklace, which is going to go awesome with the lowcut satin dress I have that hasn't seen the light of the moon since I moved to Austin.

On the drive back home, Damon says, "You seemed happy in there. You really love the macabre stuff, don't you?"

I grin. "I do, I really do, but the thing is, I don't think of that stuff as macabre." I think back to childhood, finding a dead frog and picking it up with my bare hands and bringing it into the kitchen to look at it in the light. My mom screeched at me to get that dead thing off her counter and looked at me like I was nuts. Death never scared me, never seemed like a thing of gloom and doom; it was just a part of life, nature, existence.

Damon scrunches up his face in thought. "Sometimes I don't get you, Katie."

"What do you mean?" I say, even though I have my suspicions.

"Just the way work Katie and apartment Katie are so different."

And herein lies the problem. I like Damon and want us to be friends. He's been great to me and showed me all around Austin, and I hate lying to him. But I can't explain my reasons for the whole closet goth thing to him without explaining my depression and that isn't any of his business. Not yet anyway. It's too soon and I don't want anything to change the way he sees me, which I think is as a normal, mostly fun, 26-year-old. That's all I was hoping for when I came to Austin is for people not to immediately recognize the constant darkness spinning in my brain.

When I go to places like The Glass Coffin, I'm jealous of the people who advertise their affinity for the dark side without caring what other people think. Goals... maybe someday I can integrate all these parts of me.

"I don't think the two versions of me are that different," I say. "Does clothing matter that much?"

"Of course not," he says defensively, "but do your coworkers know you love Edgar Allen Poe and vampires and deceased things in bottles?"

"They don't need to know any of that because work is about work. My love of Annabel Lee doesn't mean I can't write an apology speech for an actor who insulted his audience, and my love of Victorian corsets doesn't mean I can't advise a client in rebranding her image."

Still, I envy Damon and his uniform metalhead look and persona; he's just himself 24-7. Although I wonder if that is as great as it seems. Maybe it would be nice if people could just take a break from being themselves every so often, just to see how it feels to try on another persona. I guess that is what cosplay, masquerade balls, and Halloween are for.

"Yeah, I guess that's true," he agrees.

I'm keen to change the subject now. "So, Damon, you like heavy metal. Not like there's not a whole lot of dark there, right? I mean the name 'Black Sabbath' says it all."

"Ha ha. True enough, yeah, heavy metal is full of occult references, mythology, human sacrifice, devil worship, especially black metal, but that's not my bag. I love a good song about witches dancing naked in the night, but I'm not into the real hateful, violent stuff, you know?"

"I do. Same with goth music, there's some that's past my level of dark and I just can't listen to it."

"I'm with you. There's a fine line between exploring the evil side of human nature and glorifying it, right?"

"Exactly," I say. Damon and I are on the same page on a lot of important things. Once again, I find myself wondering what Nick would think about all of this. Would he understand why I like my spider-web drink coasters, why dressing witchy on days that are not October 31 feels empowering? Why I love this store filled with curiosities that represent all the mysteries that some of us are so compelled to spend a lifetime trying to understand?

I can imagine Nick there, staring at a mouse skull, then looking at me like I have several screws loose in my head because I find it fascinating. At least with Damon I don't have to worry that he thinks I'm weird. Not that I still get upset when people call me a weird girl, like they did in high school. No, I got over that years ago, yet somehow, I don't think I would like it if Nick thought that. But even I know that you can't hide who you are forever. I just need to hide it until Nick is no longer my client. Then we'll see what the future holds.

26

It's Tuesday and I'm happy to be back at work again, ready for my next assignment. Gloria called me and Roxy into the conference room this morning and we're waiting for her to arrive.

Roxy has a style all her own, one that changes with the wind, unlike me, who has had the same hairstyle since seventh grade. Instead of blue hair, Roxy's is now blonde streaked with bright red, and in place of a traditional suit blazer, she sports one with metal buttons and chains hanging across the breast, paired with black pants studded down the sides.

I've seen Gloria's expression when she sees Roxy's outfit *du jour* and I have mixed feelings. I sense that despite the casual hip vibe here in Austin, Gloria would be reluctant to have Roxy in the room with a client like Vittoria Faraci, and Roxy knows it. I don't think she would want Kat there either, even though it was Kat's idea that knocked it out of the park with Vittoria.

Gloria strides in wearing a moss green belted blazer dress and an ivory cashmere scarf. "My two favorite ladies," she says as she sits at the head of the table. "I have a new assignment, and I want you working together on this. Katie, you've proven your leadership capability on your first two projects, but we need a different perspective on this. Roxy, I appreciate your um, unique style, and we need someone who understands teenagers. Someone a little outside the box."

Roxy looks like a cat who ate a lizard, so pleased that she supposedly has a skill that I don't. Not that being alternative is a skill, but I understand what Gloria is getting at. Plus, Roxy is at most two years younger than me. Whatevs. That's what I get for hiding Kat away on the shelf.

"I'm intrigued," says Roxy.

"Me too—who is it?" I say.

"I'm getting to that. Have either of you heard of Mina Marin?"

I shake my head, but Roxy says, "Sure, she's the next Billie Eilish."

That gives me some context, at least. Gloria doesn't recognize the name.

"So, what trouble did Mina get herself into?" I ask.

"She was offered a contract to appear in the next release of a videogame franchise, but after they made the big announcement, she was caught saying something stupid." Gloria pulls up a video on her laptop and streams it to the conference room system.

An obviously wasted teen, with short, spiky blonde hair tipped with metallic silver, wearing a dress that looks like a short potato sack, striped tights, and Converse is sitting by a pool. She slurs her words as she spouts off about how gamers are losers and they should get some fucking sunlight and a real life.

I shake my head. "Ooof. That was stupid—way to alienate her fans."

"Agreed. What game was it?" Roxy asks.

Gloria looks at her notes. "Black Sunset IV. Obviously, they cancelled her contract."

Roxy rolls her eyes. "What a waste. There are artists who got their entire start on that game soundtrack. It's one of those mega popular post-apocalyptic series. People can't get enough of them. Not just teens, but twenties through fifties."

"Right," says Gloria, pleased that she has the perfect person for the job. "We need to figure out her next move. Even with teen stars, there's a limit to how careless they can be. I've noticed the younger generation has less adoration for celebrities who don't stand for anything, who don't use their platform for change."

"I've noticed that too," I say. "I can't imagine the burden."

"Especially with social media watching your every move," says Roxy.

Gloria flips her notebook shut and looks each of us in the eye in turn. "I want you to work together on this, co-leads, okay? I can't wait to see what you come up with."

I wonder if Gloria knows that Roxy and I got off to a rough start and if she is purposely throwing us together in hopes of team building, or if Gloria doesn't worry at all about such things and just assigned the most qualified staff to the project.

Roxy gives me a glare as Gloria turns to exit. This is going to be tons of fun.

Whatever, I'm not going to let her get to me today because I'm super psyched for my first volunteer session at the shelter. I somehow make it through the rest of the workday without stabbing Roxy, then change into jeans and a t-shirt, and beam the entire ride there, even with the horrendous traffic.

I sign in, then head to the dog kennel and check the list to see which dogs need to be walked next. First up is a black Labrador retriever named Brownie. I get his leash and a tug toy, and we head out to the enclosure.

Brownie is crazy high energy, and I can tell he hates being cooped up in a kennel. He wants to run free. Of course, first I clean up his giant poop that he makes the second we get out there, that's part of the job. I tell him he's a good boy, since it's great that he waited until he was outside instead of going in his kennel. He's housetrained.

I walk him around for a few minutes. He pulls on the leash, so excited to be outside and wanting to explore everything. I reveal the tug toy, and he goes crazy, pulling on it and shaking his head. "Do you want this? You want this toy?" I say as his tail wags.

Finally, I let him win. Part of my purpose here is to socialize the dogs and get them ready to live with a new family, possibly with children. I'm supposed to make note of any aggression or nipping behaviors. But Brownie is a sweetheart. I test his obedience. "Drop it, Brownie," I command.

This angel drops the tug toy right away. I rub his chest and neck and he wags his tail even more. I hope this fine boy finds a forever home soon.

They're not all so easy. One kennel has a note that mixed-breed Julep is aggressive, and they are working with him, so only staff walk him, not volunteers. I hope they can rehabilitate him soon. There's a Chihuahua named Betty who is so shaky and scared that I can barely get her to leave the kennel, then she pees on the floor before we even get outside. In the yard she barks her head off like she enjoys hearing herself. I'm not sure if that's okay or not, but I feel like she deserves to get it out of her system, so I just tell her, "You sing it, sister!"

Last up for my session is an Australian cattle dog, speckled gray with a black head, named Licorice. His kennel card says he likes to run. Poor boy, he's bred to herd animals, not be a city dog. I gear myself up to play hard, and run Licorice around the yard in laps, which I can tell makes him happy as a clam. He'd do great with an owner who runs marathons because this boy just doesn't tire out at all. Meanwhile, I'm exhausted and wonder if Licorice is taking clients as a personal trainer, and if this counts as my daily workout.

I love these dogs with all my heart and hope that I don't see them again. That's the tough part about working in a shelter. If things go well, you won't see the same dogs twice. If you do, then that's not a good thing for their future prospects. All I can do is try and get them ready to charm adopters as best I can.

One workout and a healthy dinner later and I'm listening to Mina Marin while I rummage through my closet. She's passionate with the angst of a seventeen-year-old. The internet told a story of a young lady with a pretty rough childhood, mother died of an overdose when she was twelve, dad seems a little too involved in her career. Not surprising that she is lashing out. If I suddenly had money and fame at that age, I'd be even worse.

Her music, while not really my groove, is more complex than I expected. Her lyrics explore adult issues even I can relate to. I think there is more to her than what was on the drunken video, and I hope we can help her get a second chance. She's too young to throw away her career because of one childish mistake.

Rooting through my closet I wish I had more work clothes, because after four days on the road with Nick, he's seen all my outfits. He's coming to the office tomorrow for his media training session.

I shove the hangars to the side in frustration. What's wrong with me? It's not like Nick is going to notice I wore the same work shirt more than once. But his words, said twice now, "I won't always be your client," have implanted themselves in my brain like an earworm. As much as I know we can't be together, the idea of not seeing him again after the book launch event leaves a lump in my throat.

For a moment I begin to fold up his sweatshirt and put it in my work bag because I really should return it to him tomorrow. But it still has the faint lingering smell of Nick that makes me feel funny in a good way, and I don't want to lose it, so I put it back down. Am I some lovesick teenager from a rom com now?

It's weird moving somewhere new. When you leave your hometown, you're leaving your history, your past, everyone who knew you for eighteen or more years. Leaving the places you spent your youth, and all the associated memories.

Moving presents you with a clean slate. I didn't exist before Austin. None of these places or people held any memory for me a few weeks ago. And because of that, the people I've met, and memories created seem disproportionately important. Outside of work I only know Damon and Nick, so they are an oversized chunk of my life here. Losing Nick from that world would leave a gaping hole.

27

❧

I wake to The Smith's "Unhappy Birthday," because I told myself that would be funny when I set it last night. It isn't. I am not a huge fan of birthdays, least of all my twenty-seventh. Today's a regular workday and none of my colleagues know. Damon knew it was coming up, but I don't expect him to remember the specific day, so I'm not expecting anything except a phone call from my mom. I might buy myself a cupcake at H-E-B on the way home, but that's it.

Since I will see Nick today, I take extra care with my hair and makeup, all for a guy I can't even date. Feeling real mature and well adjusted for my age.

"Good morning, Amber."

"Morning, darlin'. And Happy Birthday!"

I stop in my tracks. "How did you know?" I say.

"I know all the office birthdays," she says. "It's part of my job."

It's on the HR paperwork, but I feel like that should be confidential. Not that I'm mad, she just caught me off guard.

"Oh. Thanks."

After I put my bag in my cubicle, I go to put my lunch in the breakroom fridge. No way. There's a suspicious white box in there. I can't help but pull it out and open it. "Happy Birthday Katie!" it says, and I'm floored. I know Amber does this for everyone, but I'm a little emotional today and it almost makes me cry. It's the little things that make this job special. When Gloria compliments my work, the tea selection in addition to just coffee in the breakroom, Amber's daily warm greeting. It's enough to make a girl drown in gratitude. Nick would be proud that I notice and acknowledge these things now.

I'm even more embarrassed to see a calendar invite for cake after lunch. Sure enough, once Roxy gets in and looks at her calendar, she skulks around the cubicle.

"Birthday girl, huh?"

"Yep."

"How old are you, like thirty-five?"

I'm sure she's trying to make me mad, but I don't think aging is a bad thing, so why would I care. "Twenty-seven."

Her eyes widen for a moment and then she snorts. "Ah, well it was nice knowing you," she says.

I shake my head.

"You know, the 27 Club?" she says.

What a bitch. "Yes, I'm aware."

Roxy smirks and returns to her desk. I'm not really superstitious, but since Damon brought it up and now Roxy, the idea that this year is cursed is seeping into my subconscious. It's completely and utterly ridiculous because most people make it to twenty-eight. I think we'd notice if the population looked like *Logan's Run*.

There aren't any candles, or silly hats in the afternoon, just a nice thirty-minute office get-together where staff can catch up and eat cake. It's not really focused on me, other than the well wishes, and I'm grateful for that also. I don't work with everyone here on a regular basis so it's nice to see some of the less familiar faces again.

Ben tells us about a crazy professor he has at school, Gloria tells us that when she was my age, she was just getting Purple Cactus off the ground. I can't even imagine starting a business right now, I'm still trying to get my shit together.

I'm scheduled to sit in on Nick's media training, even though Luis will be leading it, and my palms are sweating while we wait in the conference room. Why should I be nervous? I'm not in charge of this meeting.

But I know why, I just resent it. I do not want to like Nicolas Stone.

When Amber escorts Nick in, my immediate joyous smile is involuntary, as is his. I stand up to welcome our client and his hand lingers a fraction too long in mine before I remember where we are. I hope Luis doesn't notice, but he's a communications expert, so who knows. Luis says he has to run and get something, and Nick and I are momentarily alone.

"A little bird told me it's your birthday," Nick says.

I shake my head. "Oh, Amber," I say.

"She offered me cake."

I put my head in my hands.

Nick gives me his killer smile and looks into my eyes. "Happy birthday, Katie, I hope you have a fantastic day," he says, and my insides turn to goo. Somehow when he says it, it feels personal, sincere, like he really cares if my birthday is a happy one. He makes me feel special.

Luis returns and we resume our professional posture. Luis begins with interview practice. We've managed to get Nick two spots on regional morning news shows on launch day. Luis teaches him how to enter the room, greet a host, and sit down. Then he walks through some common issues that come up when being interviewed and how to deal with them.

"The most important advice I can give is don't rush to answer," Luis explains. "Take time to think about it. And if you don't have a good answer, tell them what you do know, bring it back around to something you're comfortable with."

Luis and I have prepared a list of questions we expect the interviewers to ask him, such as tell me about the book, how did you become a psychologist, and what is an example from the book of something that can make people happier, among others.

Nick struggles in the practice because he wants to explain the entire complex theory, but there's no time for that during a three-to-five-minute spot. He needs to make people want to buy the book. Sell the dream.

"You'll need to strike a balance between sounding like the expert you are and making you and your book seem accessible to the audience," says Luis.

"I know what you mean, but exactly how do I do that?" says Nick.

"May I?" I ask Luis, unsure if it's okay for me to interrupt. Luis gestures for me to continue, glad for the help.

"During your lectures you asked the audience for examples," I say. "But for this format, give examples from your personal experience. Show that you take your own advice."

"I can do that," says Nick.

"You get the basics now," says Luis, handing him our list, "but I think you will need to prepare answers to these questions and practice them."

"Okay," Nick says, but he doesn't seem sure.

"You'll do just fine," Luis says, as he leaves for another client meeting.

"You okay with all this?" I ask Nick.

He shakes his head. "I don't know. It should be easy, I mean I've taught hundreds of students and given lectures all over the country, but this book thing, it's a lot of pressure. I don't want to let the publisher down. I also worry if I don't do this right, no one will know about it, and it won't help anyone."

"Whoa there," I say as I get up from the other side of the table and take the seat next to him. "Not all of your book's success rides on you answering a few questions live. The publisher has a whole campaign with advertising and free giveaways. Just do the best you can."

"Thanks Katie, I'm glad you're in my corner."

"I am. Let me know if you need anything, I'll be here."

He twitches his lip from one side to the other. "Could you help me practice? After I come up with some answers to all of these questions?"

Nick looks so vulnerable right now it's hard to believe he is a super successful academic. He really is a different person onstage and off. "Sure, I can do that."

"What about Friday, after work?"

"Um, I think I'm free then," I say, pretending to think through my schedule, even though I have zero plans this weekend.

"Why don't you come to my place, and I'll grill something, and I'll throw in a belated birthday dessert."

Oh geez, he's inviting me to his house. If Roxy hears about this...

Despite my misgivings I can't say no, and I don't want to. I want to spend more time with Nick.

"Okay, yes," I say, and hope I'm not making a career ending mistake.

28

As expected, when I check my messages after my commute, the sound of my parents singing the entire birthday song blares from the phone. My mom says she hopes I got the card she sent, which I haven't yet—it seems to take a while for mail to get here from New Jersey. She says she hopes I'm out having fun, and I don't need to call her back today.

It's nice that she believes I've already made friends and am enjoying my special day with good company, but she's wrong. The cake I had at the office was an unexpected and welcome surprise, so I didn't feel the need to buy myself anything on the way home to celebrate further. But now I'm facing a long night alone and it feels hollow. This kind of day makes me really wish I had a cat or dog to keep me company. Imagine how nice it would be to have something warm to snuggle up next to, like sweet little Brownie.

Ugh. What is it about my birthday that makes me feel like a pathetic human being? Is it the way tv shows and movies depict well-loved people surrounded by friends or out to a big family dinner on every birthday? Oh well, that's not for me, at least not this year. I resign myself to watching a movie, put on the 2007 *Sweeny Todd*, because Helena Bonham Carter is a goddess, and stretch out on the couch.

Fifteen minutes into it, there's a knock on the door.

"Happy birthday, Katie!" says Damon.

I can't believe he remembered. Maybe he's not as absentminded as I thought.

"Wow—thank you." Damon hands me a small bag with some tissue paper sticking out. "You didn't have to get me anything," I protest.

"Nah, it's something small, nothing really."

I reach in and pull out a large black pillar candle, which has a little card that says it is supposed to banish negativity. Wait—does Damon think I'm negative? Even with how hard I've been trying to hide my dark side?

"For the big two-seven," he explains, seeing my confused face.

"Ohhh," I say. My secret is safe, he is just really stuck on this 27 Club idea.

"I know you think it's a silly superstition, but why take the chance?"

"That's really sweet, thanks. I'm curious though—when you turned twenty-seven did you do something for luck?"

Damon rubs the back of his neck and looks embarrassed. "My girlfriend at the time was Wiccan, so she did a protection spell for me, but she swore by these candles."

This guy surprises me on a regular basis. "It must have worked, because here you are," I joke.

He says, "Exactly. There's something else in there too."

I'm curious and reach back in the bag and pull out a small plastic container of cinnamon. I raise an eyebrow at Damon.

"You're supposed to blow it across your front door."

"Ah, also learned from the Wiccan girlfriend?"

"Nope, it's something my mom used to do, still does, probably. It's supposed to bring health and prosperity."

"Thanks, I will give it a try." But more likely I will put it on my oatmeal in the morning. I like candles as much as the next goth, but I've never been that into spellcasting. Probably something about my utter helplessness regarding control over my life that made me feel like it would just be another disappointment, sending out energy I really can't spare and getting nothing back in return.

"One final thing," he says, and pulls a cupcake from behind his back complete with a single candle sticking out of the frosting. "You can't miss out on a birthday wish."

Damon is giving me the warm fuzzies with his thoughtfulness today. Remind me again why we're just friends when he's pretty hot and would obviously make a sweet boyfriend?

"Come sit down," I say, "while I find some matches." But Damon has a lighter on him and before I know it, he's singing to me, confirming that he truly does not have any musical talent. But what he lacks in intonation, he makes up with heart.

I have a moment of panic as the song moves along because I don't know what to wish for and there's not much time to think. I've always wondered if what you think subconsciously becomes your real wish, or if only the conscious intent during the moment you extinguish the candle is honored. If it's the former, that could explain why we sometimes think our wish didn't come true. Because the truth is we wanted something different than what our conscious brain told us.

Hold on, Kat, now you're thinking crazy, Damon's superstition must be contagious. I don't even believe in wishes. But nevertheless, as Damon sings the last words, I close my eyes and silently make my wish, *I want Austin to become my true home.*

It might sound silly, given the entire universe of wishes to choose from, but it's what matters to me right now. I feel like I'm on the edge of something and could eventually belong here, after many years of feeling like an outsider in New Jersey.

I offer Damon half the cupcake since I already had cake once today and he accepts. When we're finished eating, Damon stands up.

"Well...I didn't want to take up your whole night, I just wanted you to know I'm happy you moved here, Katie. Happy Birthday."

"Thanks. I'm happy I moved here too."

"Alright. Enjoy the rest of your movie."

"I will. Goodnight," I say, even though I have no intention of watching the movie now.

Once Damon disappears up the stairs and his front door closes, I pull out the cinnamon, pour some into my palm and then blow it across my doorstep. No harm in trying, right?

I find some matches and set the candle on my kitchen table. I may as well make a ritual out of this, and the perfect song pops into my head. "Shadow of Love," by The Damned, meets the moment with references to candles and burning, and aren't I in the shadow of not one, but two potential romances? If I could just reach out my hand without fear, either one would be within my grasp. Maybe instead of twenty-seven being the year of my demise, it could be the start of a new life. Maybe I could open myself up to love and not assume I'm forever cursed because of my propensity for gloom.

The sulfur smell of the matchhead fills the apartment, and I quickly lick my fingers and pinch it for fear of setting off the smoke detectors. The candle flame itself doesn't give off any smoke but flickers now and again, sensitive to my movements. The dancing glow entrances me, and as the wax melts into a pool beneath the wick, I imagine my old life disappearing, evaporating, and being absorbed into the atmosphere, the darkness pixelating into dust.

As the song fades out, I dip the wick of the candle in the wax, suffocating the flame. Perhaps it's my imagination, but I do feel different, lighter, and my apartment seems fresh and renewed, as if I had done a proper spring cleaning. Maybe Damon's ex-girlfriend was on to something with this candle business. I guess I'll know if and when I turn twenty-eight.

29

Roxy sends me an appointment to meet in fifteen minutes even though I'm right next to her. I hit accept. I think she's trying to be more professional, and I sense that it means a lot to Roxy that Gloria gave her this assignment, one that isn't graphics focused. I've seen her face when Gloria compliments me, and it's like one a brother gives his younger sister when it seems mom loves her more. Jealousy is an ugly thing and a competitive industry like PR breeds it. I saw it at my old company, although I was more often the jealous one.

We meet in the smaller conference room, and Roxy is already there when I arrive, laptop plugged into the projector screen, ready to go. She glances at the clock but I'm one minute early, so suck on that. Roxy has no idea that trying to keep from messing up around her is only making me even better at my job.

She dives right in with authority. "I think we need to find Mina a platform," she says, "but it can't be something too political or divisive."

I'm shocked that Roxy and I are on the same page on this one; I was thinking the same thing. "I agree, something that makes her likable again, shows some passion but doesn't offend too many people."

"But what?" she muses.

"We could brainstorm, that always helped at my old company. No wrong answers."

Roxy bristles. "I'm leading this," she snaps.

No, we're co-leading. For the sake of the project, I let it go. Instead, I remain neutral and say, "Okay, then, what do you suggest we do next?"

"Let's categorize possible types of causes and see if we hit on one that will work."

Sounds like brainstorming to me. I'm getting tired of walking on eggshells around this woman just to keep the peace, but I'll play along for today. "Homelessness or hunger?" I say.

Roxy types my ideas into a blank slide. "Nah, she's too rich and privileged for either of those to come off as sincere. Something with children?" she says. "Probably not the elderly, because she's so young."

"There's always environmental issues like saving the polar bear or maybe something about climate change," I say.

She adds those to the list but shakes her head. "Too overdone and too political. Plus, I don't see Mina being taken seriously if she suddenly goes all Greta Thunberg. No one will believe that."

"You're right," I say. "Something with education?"

"Not very hip."

"True."

"Mental health?" Roxy throws out.

I pause at this one; it's topical and a serious issue for teens. "Mental health might be a good choice, but it might give the impression that she is battling her own mental health problems, and she might not like that, even if it's true."

"What makes you think she has mental health problems?" says Roxy.

Ugh. Because I see so much of myself in Mina Marin. Take away the success and fame, and she's just a scared teenager. "You don't? You saw the video—she's sabotaging herself. Plus, have you heard her music?"

"Valid point, she does pour her soul into her songs, and some of it gets pretty real. I feel for her, it's got to be tough at that age, to be in the spotlight with no one looking out for you."

"Without question," I say.

Roxy strikes through 'mental health.' "The last thing we want to do is create more problems for her or make her face her demons in public," she says.

We both stare at the screen, and every line is crossed out. This isn't going well.

I sit back in my chair, out of ideas. "Maybe we need to learn more about her and what would be a natural extension of who she really is. This will be much easier if we find a cause she is genuinely interested in. Like you said, it has to be believable."

"We could check out her social media," Roxy says.

"Great idea."

We start with her TikTok and wade through videos of Mina partying with friends, promoting her tour, showing off new outfits or haircuts, and doting on her miniature Pomeranian. It's all shallow stuff, nothing that shows what she really cares about, if anything. After twenty minutes we are frustrated. There's nothing here we can use.

Roxy closes the window. "Let's check out her Insta."

She scrolls down past more photos of the dog, more outfits, more travel, more selfies.

"Wait—go back," I say, and Roxy scrolls back up. "There, look how happy she is." Mina has none of the angst or look of performing for the camera that she has in the other photos; she has minimal makeup and plain clothes. It's just her and a chestnut horse, and she's grinning as she stands next to it, holding the bridle.

Roxy clicks on the photo. "My best friend Chip," she reads.

"Can you Google Mina and horses?"

She types into the search engine, and we scan the results. "She used to ride in competitions when she was younger," says Roxy.

"Put in Mina plus Chip," I say.

Roxy types and then we look at each other when we see the results. Chip is a rescue horse.

We just found a potential platform for Mina.

A search for horse-related charities shows there are many rescue and rehab places, sanctuaries for abused or mistreated horses. It makes me sick seeing the images. Who could be so cruel to such a majestic and intelligent animal? More proof that people are horrible, and the world has a seedy underbelly.

I know how fickle clients can be, so we come up with two alternative backup platforms to present to Gloria. Roxy presents the ideas as a mutual effort, which may mean she is warming up to me, or that she's smart enough to know that when Gloria expects teamwork, we'd better give it to her. Probably the latter.

Gloria is pleased once again and agrees to pitch the idea at a virtual meeting that Mina is squeezing in while she's on tour.

"Nice work, ladies," says Gloria.

"Thanks," Roxy and I say in unison. I'm relieved that we were able to work so well together and hope this means we can put our shaky beginning behind us.

After Gloria leaves, Roxy turns to me and says, "I could have done this on my own, you know."

Well crap. I guess that was wishful thinking on my part.

"I'm sure you could have," I say, "but sometimes it helps to have another person to bounce ideas around with." I'm being as generous as I can here, when I'd really like to poke her in the eye, but it's utterly selfish because I need Roxy for her graphic arts expertise on my projects. She doesn't need me.

Roxy doesn't respond as she unplugs her laptop and exits the conference room. This woman is really raining on my parade. Forget it. I'm three for three now on major projects, that is if Mina approves our recommendation, and it feels awesome. If I can just get through Nick's book launch without Roxy accusing me of sleeping with a client, and without me actually sleeping with the client, then things will be fine. We're so close to the finish line.

As if on cue, warning me of potential disaster, Nick texts me his address for Friday night and I practically drop the phone. Am I really going to his house? Where we will be all alone, in a place with a couch?

30

I can't remember the last time I took so long to get ready. Can I even pretend I'm not trying to look attractive? That the painstakingly smoothed hair, flawless makeup, and wild raspberry lip gloss aren't for him? The tight jeans and dark purple shirt that shows just a hint of cleavage, and more if I lean over, are not for him?

What's the alternative—trying to look dowdy on purpose? That would be ridiculous. I'm just joining him for a friendly dinner and media practice. It doesn't mean a thing.

His house is a cute Craftsman style complete with a gable and covered front porch, in hunter green with cream borders. Potted plants line the front steps, and a stone walkway leads from the street to the front door.

It's a house that is primed for domestic bliss and two point five children, a good reminder of why Nick and I aren't compatible. At thirty, he needs to find a partner who is on board with having children. A professor's wife type maybe, who he can bring to faculty parties. I think I'm picturing something from the fifties, though. I'm sure Nick would want a smart woman with her own career. Not me, of course, but a different woman with a career.

All that slips away when he opens the door, wearing jeans and a smokey blue t-shirt, and I remember that I still have his sweatshirt and have no plans to give it back. It reminds me of the perfect day we had sightseeing downtown and witnessing the swarming flight of the bats.

He holds the door open and ushers me in. "Thanks for coming."

"Sure, no problem," I say as I take in the living room, wooden floors, brown leather sofa, wooden coffee table, neat and formal, with the only dashes of color a few throw pillows and some framed artwork. I scan the room for more personal items, family photos or heirlooms, but there's nothing like that here. This must be what they mean by bachelor pad.

"Are you hungry?" he asks. "I have some chicken marinating, and grilled vegetables. I know you like to eat healthy just like me."

"That sounds great."

Nick pulls out a bottle of wine. "Drink?" he says.

"No, thanks."

"Right, no drinking while on business, right? Probably just as well so I don't say anything stupid." He takes out a pitcher of iced tea instead.

"That's right," I say, "and we're here to work, aren't we?"

"Yes, of course," he says too quickly. "I really appreciate your help."

"It's no problem."

He pulls the tray of chicken and container of skewered vegetables out of the fridge, and I open the sliding glass patio door for him. His backyard is big, with a giant live oak tree in the middle, and a two-level wooden deck. It would be great for a dog, with plenty of room to run around.

"How is Austin treating you so far?" he says while he gets the food on the grill.

"Not bad at all. Work's been going really well. My second and third clients were a huge success and Gloria told me she is glad she hired me. I finally feel like I'm useful and living up to my potential. It's the best job I've ever had."

"Wow, that's huge! I'm so happy for you. There's nothing like the feeling when you get to put all your skills and knowledge to good use."

I knew Nick would understand how important my work is to me. "That's how you feel with psychology, right?"

"A lot of the time. When I'm teaching students or giving my touring lectures it all comes together. I love the research part too."

"We have that in common. I know a lot of people hate working but it's the best part of my life. Is that weird?"

"No, not at all. Work gives you a sense of achievement and helps you grow. Who thinks that's weird?" he asks.

"No one, really, just my neighbor gives me a hard time, saying I work too much."

"What's right for one person isn't right for another."

I agree, but I still worry. "But all work is probably not healthy, right? Do you have any hobbies?"

"Sure. The regular things, working out, watching TV, reading, cooking, traveling. Nothing out of the ordinary."

"And you're okay with that?"

Nick puts down the tongs and looks at me, head tilted. "I'm not sure I'm following."

"Ugh. I don't know. Sometimes it seems like I'm supposed to have some grand passion, like painting or music, or learning French, or cake decorating."

"And you feel like your life is incomplete because you don't have something like that?"

"Maybe."

"You can't worry about what other people think, or what you could or should do. You seem like a smart and self-realized person who knows what she wants. Stand by that."

I pause a moment to take that in, surprised that he sees me that way. It's weird to see myself reflected back in someone else's eyes. He's right though, I do know what I want. Right now, I want to kiss this man in front of me. Yikes.

After we eat, he leads me to the living room. He pulls out the list of interview questions that Luis told him to practice and hands it to me and we sit on the leather couch. Our knees almost touch and I cross my legs to avoid him.

"Alright. I'm Perky Patsy with KWXN. I'm here today with Dr. Nicolas Stone," I say.

He pulls his spine straighter, as if he is trying to be more authoritative, then says, "Great to be here, Patsy."

"Dr. Stone, tell us about your new book."

Nick recites a memorized statement explaining the format and purpose of the book, but it's hardly compelling. Now I get the concept of over rehearsed.

I put the paper down and look at him. "Take a deep breath in and exhale. Relax. This is not one of your lectures. This is just two friends chatting over coffee. Imagine we're at BookPeople and you're telling José what the book is about."

Nick inhales deeply, and exhales.

"Now try this again," I say. "Tell us about your new book."

This time Nick sounds more natural, conversational.

"That's so much better," I say, patting his hand that is resting on the couch, in a moment of unthinking encouragement. The instant I touch his skin I feel the familiar ping again. I recoil but feel my face reddening. "Sorry," I mutter.

"There's nothing to be sorry about," he says.

"Shall we continue?" I say briskly. "Dr. Stone, what is one thing viewers can do today to become happier people?"

"Well Patsy, it may sound odd, but the most effective thing you can do to make yourself happy is to do something kind for someone else. Rake your elderly neighbor's yard, donate blood, leave your waiter an extra generous tip, say thank you to a friend, the list is endless."

"Great advice, Dr. Stone." I turn to the fake audience and say, "I'm Perky Patsy, and this is your Saturday morning!"

I put the paper on the coffee table and uncross my legs. "I don't think you need much practice; you're going to do fine. You don't need me."

He looks me straight in the eyes and says, "You're wrong. I do need you, Katie." He reaches out and takes my hand into his, warm and tender as he traces circles on my skin.

The intensity in his gaze is melting my resistance. "Nick, I..."

He pulls my hand closer and brings my fingertips to his lips, then brushes them with a gentle kiss, sending a tingling through my body. Nick is hesitant, and so am I, but I've been thinking about this ever since I saw him in his cobalt shirt at the gym, and I don't pull away. I can't help but to run my fingers over his bottom lip.

His eyes meet mine, and in a flash of understanding that we are both volcanoes about to erupt from weeks of denial and false starts and smoke, we collide, lips meeting with the pressure of work and waiting, exploring this feeling, this rightness. The faint smell of coconuts drives me wild, as does his hand on my thigh, and I lift up his shirt to see if his muscles feel as tight as I imagined from afar. They are.

He moans as I caress his pecs, and he grabs my waist and pulls me in his lap, knocking my purse on the floor. We bite and tear at each other, his lips exploring my chin, my neck, the top of my chest, and I lean back to let him. He looks at me with an animal desire and I am melting.

"Come with me," he whispers, and I'd follow him anywhere right now.

As he stands up, his foot slips and he reaches out to balance himself. He stoops down to pick something up off the floor. I freeze. It's the refill I picked up at the pharmacy on the way over. In slow motion, I reach my hand out to grab it, but it's too late. He read it and knows what it is and what it means.

31

“**W**hy didn’t you tell me?” he asks, his eyes swirling with hurt and confusion.

“It didn’t come up,” I say weakly. Which is technically true. Why would I tell him? It’s not something you just casually drop in a conversation with a colleague like, hey—by the way, I’m on two different meds for mental illness, that’s cool, right?

He blinks several times, trying to find his words. “It didn’t come up? For heaven’s sake, every interaction we’ve had was about psychology and well-being, and all this time you didn’t think to mention you were diagnosed with depression?”

“You were—are, my client. And it’s frankly none of your business,” I say.

“You’re right. If I were just a client, it wouldn’t be. Is that all I am?”

I look away, avoiding his penetrating stare. “I don’t know.”

“Two minutes ago, right there on that couch, you knew. You can’t tell me you don’t feel this thing between us. I know you do.”

What a huge mistake that would have been, us being together. I put my hand on my hip. “What do you want me to say? That it’s hard watching you preach on and on about being positive while I spend all my energy trying not to sink into the mud? That I was afraid if you knew you’d see me as damaged, like everyone else?”

He shakes his head. “Give me some credit here. I wouldn’t have seen you like that—you could have trusted me.”

“Look, this thing with us is new. I’m not obligated to tell you my deepest, darkest secrets up front, you know.”

I must have hit on something because his face softens, and he sits back down. "I'm sorry. It's yours to share or not, in your own time. Maybe I just feel stupid that I didn't know. I *should* have known."

"But that's the point, Nick, I'm managing it. I've been managing it since I was a teenager. There's nothing to know. I don't need your help."

"Maybe you don't need *my* help, but you need someone's help. Do you have a good therapist at least?"

Now he's pissing me off. "I'm not seeing one since I left my last job, but that's also none of your business."

"You're not even seeing a therapist? How do you expect to get better if you aren't getting help?" he says, the accusation in his eyes boring a hole into my forehead.

My blood feels like it's about to boil and I will spontaneously combust at any moment. I can't even believe we're having this conversation. I really thought he knew better. I don't hold back at all, years of rage at people who told me to smile releases all at once. "Are you fucking kidding me right now? Unbelievable! You think I'm depressed because I haven't tried hard enough?"

"No, I didn't say that—" he tries to interject but I'm too mad to listen now.

"You think I haven't done years of therapy, dozens of different combinations of anti-depressants, new, old, and everything in between? Hell, I've even done experimental ketamine infusion therapy, and TMS. They just don't work for me, or they only work a little. Would you like to see spreadsheets full of thought logs and mood charts? Would you like to see my medicine cabinet full of pills and supplements I dutifully take every single day just in case they are the difference between surviving and the alternative? I try so hard every fucking single day."

He looks like he wants to crawl into a hole now. Good. He deserves it. In spite of all my shouting, he speaks in an even, measured tone,

"I didn't mean that. I promise. I do understand what you are going through."

"I doubt it," I snarl, tired of people pretending to be empathetic. "You're all 'look how fucking bright and beautiful the world is,' and every day is gratitude this and in the moment that. What could you possibly know about how I feel? How dare you tell me what I need or how I should act?"

Still, he remains calm, which is annoying, and for a minute he doesn't say anything, then he looks down at his shoes.

"When I was nineteen, my little sister killed herself," he says.

I freeze. Oh shit.

I realize I'm the worst, most selfish person in the world, once again assuming no one feels pain but me. All this time never considering that Nick was dealing with his own darkness. What can I even say?

"Nick, I'm so sorry, I didn't know," I whisper and sit down beside him, our arms touching.

"How could you? I never talk about it," he says.

That's true, he didn't open up to me, just like I didn't to him. Maybe we are alike in the way that we put on a front, hiding the dark parts of ourselves. Not because we are ashamed, but because they are private. We are under no obligation to divulge our deepest secrets to others, but can we expect to truly connect with another person if we don't?

I'm still trying to figure out where his lack of understanding comes from if he had this very personal experience with depression, and I have to understand why if there is any chance of a relationship between us.

"Did your sister refuse help? Is that why you were so mad that I'm not seeing a therapist?" I ask.

He puts his head in his hands. "No. Becca had a therapist, and a psychiatrist, and medication, and she was even in the hospital for a while. But none of it was enough. It wasn't like we didn't know she was struggling. We did, we all did, but even so, we couldn't stop it. And it broke all of us. I barely talk to my parents, even all these years later."

"I'm so sorry. There is so much we still don't understand," I say, even though I know there are no words anyone can say that soothe this kind of grief.

"After that I wanted to help people, but I knew I couldn't bear to work with depressed patients, that would be too much—what if I failed them? Then I found positive psychology and it seemed right. Like maybe I'm not the one to save someone who is already drowning, but maybe I can take someone who is just muddling through and make their lives a little brighter."

I lean into him and bump his knee with mine. "That's a really sweet idea. It's a great way to honor your sister, and I know it really helps improve people's lives. You've even helped mine, even with my depression."

"Thanks," he says, turning to look at me. "And for the record, the reason that I care if you are seeing a therapist is that I think I'm falling in love with you."

I blink. This isn't exactly the way I'd want a man to profess his love to me, but it seems right for my life. I don't know what to say, but I know my feelings for him are different than I've felt for anyone else before. Instead of words, I lean over and kiss him gently on his cheek.

He gives me a sad half-smile, and I rest my head on his shoulder. He puts his arm around me as we sink back into the couch. We stay like that for hours, still and silent, as I wonder how this could ever work out between us. Now that he knows about my darkness, won't I always remind him of Becca?

32

I wake up before Nick and gingerly lift his arm from my shoulder. I look at his sleeping face one last time, peaceful and free from the trauma he has lived, and then I sneak out of his house. There is a lot to process and that needs to be done by me, alone in my apartment. Nick and I have both been hiding major secrets from each other, and that is no basis for a good relationship.

Everything is clear now, in the light of the morning; we are doomed. I can't live in the shadow of his dead sister, knowing he is always worrying that I might get worse, that I may endure the same fate. Even if I told him that I'm stable and have been for years, as a psychologist he knows that could always change, and I know that too, thus the militant, ritualistic behaviors I perform to keep myself well.

What would life be with him always asking if I'm okay, always on the lookout for a sign that I'm in trouble? And me, feeling like I have to pretend to be fine all the time, scared that if I ever admit I'm having a bad day it will cause Nick to panic? I can't be the cause of his suffering.

Even worse, what if he views me as his do-over? He couldn't save his sister, even though it was never his job to do so when he was just a teenager, but now what if he wants to save me? I don't want a savior, and I've worked too hard to claim my independence to give it up now.

No, there's only one path forward. I have to tell Nick we are just colleagues. I'll help him through the book launch because that's my job, and then we'll go our separate ways.

In fact, I should tell him right now, right this second, rip off the Band-Aid. What's the use in waiting? I snatch my phone from the side table and type.

Katie: This will never work. Let's keep it professional.

A few seconds later the three dots appear. My hand is trembling as I wait for his response.

Nick: Can we talk about this in person?

I know if I see Nick now, he will convince me I'm wrong, but I'm not.

Katie: No.

I switch the phone to silent and throw it across the room. Smart, Kat, like a broken screen is going to help the situation, but I don't get up to check it.

If that was the right call, why do I feel so monumentally shitty? Like someone poured acid in my heart and my insides are dissolving, and soon I'll be a fizzing pool of blood and tissue staining the carpet. I hug Saffron next to my chest. Will I always be alone for fear of being a burden? Should I adopt five cats and two dogs who will love me unconditionally?

The moment calls for Nine Inch Nails' "Something I can Never Have," and I allow myself a good wallow. For the second time since I moved to Texas, I weep like a geyser, not cute, dainty tears, but a big ugly cry that splotches my face and produces a twelve-inch-high pile of wet tissues on the floor next to me. If it were possible to cry one's guts out, then not only my stomach, but my intestines, kidney, liver, and gallbladder would be keeping me company on the bed.

I've learned it's important to make a distinction between darkness that comes with the territory of depression and actual life events that would upset any average person. Heartbreak is a normal human experience, even if technically I'm the one who called it off. Now I just need to weld the pipeline of my pain shut before it morphs into something else, a downward spiral.

Eight hours is all I'm giving myself. At 5 p.m., I'm putting on my workout clothes and heading to the gym. Stopping any part of my routine could be detrimental.

I fall asleep clutching Saffron and each time I approach waking, I burrow further under the covers, clinging desperately to the dreamworld so I don't have to feel the pain of reality. It just hurts too much; my heart is so constricted I can barely breathe in, and my stomach is twisted in knots.

When I awake it's 7 p.m. and nearly dark outside. So much for my eight-hour cap on sulking. My eyes are practically swollen shut; no way I'm going to the gym. I'm not hungry for dinner either. I get up only to stream *Kiki's Delivery Service*, my go-to movie for when I'm sick. The part where Kiki loses her ability to fly and can't talk with her cat gets me every time.

After that I watch *The Wizard of Oz*, which reminds me of childhood, and how amazing it was when the black and white burst into color, and how Dorothy had big hopes for her journey on the yellow brick road, that the wizard would magically fix everything. I wish I were that child again, before I knew what depression was, knew that I'd have this burden for the rest of my life. Where's my wizard? He would probably say the answer is inside me, the bastard.

Then comes *Miss Peregrine's Home for Peculiar Children*, then *The Last Unicorn*. Now it's the wee hours of the morning but I'm not tired since I slept all day. I rummage through the cabinet and only find healthy foods. I want, no, I need, chocolate.

I don't remember when I fell asleep, but it must have been late because now it's noon and the stupid fucking Texas sun is blazing through the curtains. The first thing I notice is my stomach rumbling. I haven't eaten in over twenty-four hours.

There's nothing I want here, and I just can't face the outside world. From the fetal position and with a sheet over my head like a kid in a play tent, I search my phone for delivery options and come across Tiff's Treats, which claims to deliver warm cookies to your door. I shouldn't eat twelve cookies for lunch. Should I? Fuck it, why not. I place an order for a dozen, half chocolate chip, half snickerdoodle.

They arrive at my door in a little white bag with a rope handle. I get a cup of skim milk and bring the entire box back to bed with me. The smell is incredible, sweet, rich, and chocolatey, mixed with fragrant cinnamon. I take a bite and the warm cookie melts in my mouth. Glorious creation of Elysium. How could something this delicious possibly be bad?

Why can't I enjoy vices like everyone else? Weed, drinking, junk food, sex, the things that make adult life worth living. Why can't they be for me? I have half a mind to run up the stairs and throw myself at Damon; I doubt he'd turn me down. He doesn't seem like the proud type.

Instead, I shove a snickerdoodle in my mouth. Five cookies later, I'm sick to my stomach and in a sugar coma. I set the cookies on the nightstand and hunker down. Movies are my drug of choice, *Return to Oz*, *Hugo*, *The Dark Crystal*, and it's time for dinner cookies.

Now my stomach really hurts but I don't care. It all seems so pointless. Who cares if Mina Marin insults some gamers? Who cares if the perfume heiress makes a million more dollars? Who cares if Nicolas Stone's book sells?

Fresh tears fall as I think of Nick and his book and his sister. Why does everything have to be so complicated? Why do I fall for the one guy who has emotional baggage that mixes with mine in a lethal way?

I should take a shower, but that seems like a lot of effort, so I just lie in bed, waiting for the sun to go down so I can be alone with the darkness again. It doesn't matter. One weekend of cookie binging won't hurt me as long as I get up in the morning and face the world head on, as long as Katie can push this all aside and be her superstar self come Monday morning.

33

My alarm goes off and I can barely move to silence it. I just can't summon the will to get ready for work and face Roxy with her sneer and perfect Amber with her outrageously high heeled shoes, and Gloria with her aged wisdom. I send a quick note to Gloria saying I'm sick and won't be in today. But it's fine, I just need a day off.

The whiny, grating sound of a weed eater wakes me again at 11 a.m. The bed is full of cookie crumbs, which reminds me that there are three left, and I scarf them down. Not as good cold, but still pretty darn tasty. Now I have nothing sweet left to eat, and my stomach hates me for eating only cookies for two days.

I shuffle to the kitchen to get some water and realize I didn't take my meds yesterday. Not good, Kat. I shake my head and swallow them down. No wonder my skull is pounding, and I have a jittery feeling in my legs. I decide I can't wallow in bed any longer and flop face first on the couch. Much better.

After I nearly suffocate in the cushions, I flip over and start watching *Shadow and Bone*. I lie with my arm hanging off the couch for four episodes because I'm too lazy to pick it back up. My stomach groans again and I order a pizza to silence it. No veggies. Just pure cheesy bliss.

Halfway into the pizza there's a knock on the door. My shirt is covered in smashed cookie bits and pizza grease. I haven't brushed my hair in a few days either, so I'm feeling like a supermodel now. Shoving the pizza box to the side, I trudge to the door with leaden legs.

Damon's face appears in the keyhole.

Ugh. Do I want him to see me like this? We're supposed to be friends, but still, I have some pride. Maybe he realized he hasn't seen me in a few days or saw my car still there and wondered why I didn't go to work. He's worried about me. I could use a friend right now.

I run my hands through my hair a few times and wrap a sweatshirt around my mangy tee.

"Hey Ka—" he starts to say but then gives me the onceover and looks concerned. "Are you sick?"

Great, he just confirmed that I must look as bad as I feel. "Um...just a little under the weather."

"Oh no. Can I get you anything? Chicken soup?"

"Nah, it's not that kind of sick."

Damon looks confused but accepts it. "Umm, sorry to bother you, I'll let you get some rest," he says and starts to turn away.

"Wait," I say, not wanting to be alone right now. "Were you coming to ask me something?"

He scratches his head. "It can wait for a better time, no worries."

"No, tell me or it will bug me all day."

"Okay, fine. I was wondering if you wouldn't mind giving up your Paradise Lost ticket. I mean since you didn't even know who they were until a few weeks ago."

Wow. That is not what I was expecting him to say. I can't really argue that I'm not a longtime fan, even though I thought they sounded awesome and was looking forward to seeing them live.

"Sure, I guess that's fine. Who are you taking instead?"

He scratches his head again and then rubs the back of his neck. "Um, well I met this girl, Paige, and she's a big fan."

"Ah. Girlfriend."

"It's new, but yeah, she's pretty cool."

"That's great," I say, forcing my lips to curve upwards into something that doesn't betray my shock. "Sure, give her my ticket and have fun. I have to go now." I close the door in his face before he can see me cry.

Why am I even crying? Am I a total bitch who was keeping Damon on the shelf while I lusted after Nick? Why do I feel like I lost him when I'm not sure if I ever wanted to be with him? I'm the one who insisted we just be friends. Maybe I'm just mad at myself because I wanted him to somehow know I needed help, and I didn't want to be alone right now. My head is a swirling, sludgy mess and I can't think straight when it comes to Damon or Nick.

The one thing I'm sure of is that I'm destined to be alone if I push everyone away. The darkness is isolating, and the one solace is work, where I'm forced to be around people, be on a team. And even knowing that, I called in sick like a dumbass. Classic self-sabotage.

Katie, where are you? I need you.

Tuesday morning, I reason that being out for one day looks suspicious. Who's sick for a single day? No, it's just common sense to call in sick for two days instead. Luckily, Purple Cactus starts people out with three sick days without waiting for them to accrue. It's not lying anyway, because I really am sick, not just in my gloomy head, but this emotional pain has caused my insides to revolt against me and it's hard to even move.

I make an agreement with myself. I can take the day off, but I can't wallow. Instead, it needs to be a true mental health day to get back on track. Exercise, long overdue shower, buy healthy groceries.

Afternoon comes and I haven't done any of those things. Instead, I watched another six hours of television.

Shit! It's Tuesday already. Volunteer night. I hate people right now, especially the happy ones. I hate Damon, perhaps unfairly, for not recognizing that I needed a friend. I hate Nick for the pain I am feeling. I hate Roxy for being a mega bitch since day one.

But I don't hate the dogs, and they need me. The dogs aren't responsible for my misery so they shouldn't be punished. Thinking of Brownie and Betty fills me with purpose, and I feel just energized enough to take a shower and change into fresh clothes.

When I get to the kennels, I'm half sad that Brownie is still there when he's such a good boy, but I'm also glad to see him. He's happy to see me too, or maybe he gets excited to see anyone holding a leash. I prefer to imagine he remembers me. "Hi Brownie! Who wants to go for a walk?"

Brownie goes crazy and I clip the leash on, and we head outside. He is bursting with energy so it's more like jogging than walking, then I take out the tug toy and we have some real fun. Finally, I read on his chart that he knows sit and stay, so I want to practice his training.

"Sit, Brownie!" I say, bringing my hand down parallel to the ground. He shifts his weight but remains standing, but on the second repeat he sits. "Good boy!" I say and give him all the pets. Poor Brownie, he just needs a good home.

I go to find Betty the Chihuahua, but she was adopted. Surprising, since she was ever so skittish, but I hope she found a good home where they will be patient with her. In her spot is Pixie, an elderly beagle whose bark seems outsized for her small frame. Pixie just wants to walk slow, which is fine by me, and she stops to bark and bay at anything and everything that moves outside, birds, squirrels, you name it. I swear she sees ghosts in the corner where I see nothing.

Driving home after my shift, I feel different. I hate that Nick is right about so many things, including how helping others feels so good. I tend to get trapped inside my head, and my world shrinks to just this insignificant body. But in the last two hours it expanded to include the shelter and the dogs, and this highway. I turn into the H-E-B parking lot to grab a few groceries; three and a half days of pizza and cookies doesn't help me any and I know this.

Back at the apartment I eat my chicken wrap on the patio and listen to the windchimes. Guess Damon is out because I don't hear any heavy metal outside. He's probably with his girlfriend, in the honeymoon bliss of a new relationship. A breeze sends the smell of mint my way and I inhale the refreshing fragrance and pat myself on the back for creating this restorative space.

When I first met Nick, he said something about it being insane to not do things that you know make your life better. It's not so simple though. Those things take work, discipline, and motivation, all things depressed people struggle with. My drill sergeant can't always get through the barrier of darkness.

But the thing that gets me the most is that he was right about something else. I do need a therapist. I did plan to get one after my new insurance kicked in, I just hadn't gotten around to it. The insinuation that I wasn't doing everything I could be turned me defensive, but that doesn't make him wrong. Why do I hate him for that?

I grab my laptop and start looking for therapists on my new insurance, because what would really be insane would be if I didn't find one just out of spite, which would only hurt me. It can't hurt Nick because we aren't anything to each other anymore and never will be.

34

❧

"Morning," says Amber, "You feeling better, darlin'?"

"Yes, much," I say with a toothy smile, even though every step feels like a burden and my body longs for my purple velour couch.

My inbox is full of e-mails, but I need a drink, something to sharpen my mind. I don't normally drink coffee, but today the roasted smell in the breakroom seems comforting and I pour myself a cup and add a splash of creamer. I stand there staring blankly while the hot liquid pours down my throat and I imagine it sending energy through my tired body. I remain until I lean the cup back and no more elixir trickles out.

Before I summon the will to sift through my e-mails, Roxy charges around the corner into the breakroom. Proof that it was her fault I spilt my tea on her that first day; she's like a bull and coffee is the red cape waving in the kitchen.

"You're back," she says.

Duh, obviously. "Yep."

"You better not get me sick."

"I won't," I say. "I'm fine."

She eyes me suspiciously and I remember that I do look like someone who's been sick, with red, tired eyes and pale skin.

"Okay," she says. "Did you hear? Mina Marin loved the horse rescue idea."

That perks me up more than the coffee. I knew she would, and that means success number three for me at Purple Cactus. "That's awesome," I say.

I can't wait to tell Nick.

Shit.

Why was that my first thought? I'm not going to be telling Nick anything, anytime soon, at least until the book launch, which I am obligated to attend, since I'm still his project manager.

As if reading my mind, Roxy says, "Your boyfriend is going to be in later today, too."

"What are you talking about?"

"Mr. Positive. He's coming in to sign some releases and approve some display boards. He could have done all this virtually, but he said he didn't mind coming in. I wonder why..." she says with a smirk.

My legs feel wobbly, and I grab the back of a chair to steady myself. I can't see Nick, not today. It's too soon.

Roxy stares at me. "Oh shit. Something really did happen with him!" But her smirk is replaced with something that resembles sympathy crossed with curiosity.

"Fuck off, Roxy," is all I can manage.

This just makes her laugh, and I realize I just confirmed her suspicion.

I assume Gloria will want me at the meeting, since Nick is my client. How can I get out of it? Say I'm still feeling sick after all? I don't want to because being here at Purple Cactus is already making Katie stronger, refueling her spirit, her ambition, and going home will crush that in both of us.

Leaving Roxy feeling proud of herself, I escape to my cubicle and attempt to lose myself in work. My inbox shows the meeting invite for Nick at three, and a long chain of e-mails regarding the production of the draft display boards for the launch, bookstore tour, and lectures. Damn it. I should have been here to review these materials and provide comments instead of getting sick on cookies. Luckily, the team at Purple Cactus was here to pick up my slack and everything appears to be on schedule.

At 9 a.m., Gloria breezes in.

"Katie, welcome back. I was worried about my superstar," she says and for that instant I wish Gloria were my mother. "Are you feeling better?"

"Yes, much better, thanks." And it's true now, because here at work Katie is respected and needed, a valued member of the team, and it feels good.

"Did you hear about Mina?"

"I did—I'm so glad she liked our idea," I say, knowing Roxy is listening to every word from the next cubicle.

"She loved it!" Gloria is beaming; my success is her success. "I know you're still catching up, but we need to go over some details for Dr. Stone's book launch. We're still missing something, a wow factor that will get the media more interested."

I frown. I thought the book launch event was a done deal. I had personally worked with the event planner; venue booked, catering ordered, social media blasts ready to be released into cyberspace.

"What do you mean?" I say.

"I'll know it when I see it," she chuckles. "Something that says Nicolas Stone in a unique way, something different from all the other authors releasing books."

That's not overly helpful, but she's the boss. "I'll try to come up with something."

"Great," says Gloria, washing her hands of the problem.

What is special about Nick? Let me count the ways. He's sensitive and kind. He really wants to help his students and clients, to make people happier. He's smart and inquisitive, determined to find answers to complex psychological questions. He's handsome, with his sandy blonde hair and fitted vests, which I now know cover a chiseled, sexy chest.

Whoa there, Kat. That isn't helpful. Focus.

Is there some part of Nick's book, his strategies for improving lives, that he personifies? What was it he said was his favorite part? Trying to do something kind for someone else each day. Does Nick really do that?

Flipping through my mental rolodex of everything I know about Nick, he just might. He mows his elderly neighbor's lawn. He volunteers his time at the youth center. He makes a point to go to an old classmate's book signing. He's generous to waiters and hotel staff. He talks to every attendee after his lectures.

But what does any of that have to do with a book launch event? Could we partner with some type of nonprofit? But the event is free, and the publisher is expecting to sell books, not donate money. It would have to be something that raises awareness, providing a mutual benefit for both parties, Nick getting the press related to the nonprofit, and the nonprofit getting foot traffic from an audience of people who are going to be inspired that very night to do something positive.

Luckily, Roxy and I just went through this exercise with Mina Marin, so all the possibilities are fresh in my mind. Something with children? Foster care, maybe? No, it's a huge jump from doing something nice each day to the responsibility of caring for a human child.

What if it's not a human child? What if it's a dog or cat? I've seen on the animal shelter's website that they do outreach events, bringing animals to shopping centers and city parks, hoping people will see these sweeties outside of their sad kennels and fall in love.

But would the venue allow it? I'll have to find out. The weather is warm enough that it could be just outside the front door, under the covered front entrance, if needed, forcing attendees to pass by their adorable faces. Who could resist Brownie or Pixie?

I march down to Gloria's office and knock on the open door. Gloria waves me in.

"I think I have something. Nick mentioned he had a dog when he was growing up, and he used to volunteer at the animal shelter. I just started volunteering at the shelter a few weeks ago. What if we have a pet adoption event at the book launch?"

I can see the gears turning in Gloria's mind, probably thinking through the logistics, the pluses and minuses, the media.

"I like it. But how fast could we get the shelter to sign on? We'd need to revise some of the launch materials stat and update the press releases."

"I could go talk with them this afternoon. You don't need me at the meeting with Nick, right?"

Gloria pauses, and a flash of suspicion crosses her eyes, and it looks like she is going to ask a question, then changes her mind. "He is your client, but we are a team here, so I think we can spare you for this."

Did Roxy say something to her? That bitch, she better not be talking about me behind my back to Gloria. If she messes things up for me, she's dead.

Ugh. Who am I kidding? I'm the one who got too involved with a client, kissed a client, almost slept with a client. If Gloria finds out, then I'm the only one to blame. But at least for today, I don't have to see Nick.

35

The shelter is on board once I agree to help coordinate all the logistics. They'll still need volunteers to help out, but they have a list of regulars to tap for that. I call the venue, and they are okay with it as long as it is set up outside. Now I really pray for a sunny Texas day, because even though the entrance is large and covered, a wild and windy thunderstorm would mean trouble.

Back at the apartment, the velour sofa doesn't call to me quite as loud, and I change into my workout clothes straight away. I'm getting back on track. I think of one of my old therapists who encouraged compassionate self-talk, and I congratulate myself for not letting a few days of sulking turn into a soul-crushing pit of despair lasting months like it might have in the past.

Thirty minutes and a gallon of sweat later, I'm done. Next up healthy dinner. Way to go, girl. Of course, since it is apparently the new law that everyone sees me in my workout clothes, post exercise, who is walking back to my apartment but Damon, and he's not alone. This has to be Paige.

She has long bleached blonde hair and a small silver nose ring and she's wearing a Doro t-shirt with black acid washed jean shorts. She and Damon look like quite the pair. And here I am in Lycra and a tank top, bangs plastered to my forehead. This blows.

"Hey Katie. This is Paige," Damon says as we meet on the sidewalk. I take note that he didn't add "my girlfriend," but maybe it's a given, or maybe it's too soon to define the relationship.

"Hi Paige, nice to meet you," I say.

"Ah, this is the Katie I've heard so much about. Thanks for the Paradise Lost ticket. I have been a fan for ages, but I didn't hear they were touring until it was sold out."

I'm so freaking generous; Nick would be proud. Not that I really had a choice in the matter. But it does sound like she appreciated the ticket more than I would have. "Of course, glad to help," I say.

Damon stays quiet, looking a little uncomfortable. He shouldn't be, since we are just friends.

"Hey," says Paige as her face lights up, "my best friend Luna is having an art show tomorrow night. You'd dig it. She uses found objects like crow feathers and rusty screws mixed with pastels. She's really talented."

That does sound kind of interesting, and I am anxious to explore Austin more, find the seedy underbelly of this city, figure out where I fit in. Katie might be a superstar PR project manager, but Kat rules the night. Most of my nights since I've moved here have been spent in my apartment, save for the lecture tour, the goth dance club, and Flaming Goathead, and I'm feeling pent up.

I look at Damon's face and try to figure out if he wants me to decline out of discomfort, or if he would be happy for his friend and girlfriend to get along. I think he'd prefer me to say no.

"Sure, that sounds great!" I say.

"Awesome. I'm helping Luna set up, so you two can meet me there. It's a proper gallery opening, with wine and cheese, so dress up if you like."

Damon looks mortified at the thought but mutters, "Cool," and gives me a bit of a cold stare.

I pretend I don't see it. "Okay, I'd better hit the shower. You two have fun tonight and I'll see you tomorrow, Paige," I say.

Thursday morning Roxy halts at my cubicle on the way in. "Mr. Positive missed you at the meeting yesterday," she says, then watches like a hawk for my reaction.

"Oh?" I say casually. "I was sorting things out at the shelter."

"Good, because he liked that idea. It seems like you two have a lot in common." She lets that drop with a weight of meaning behind it. Of all the people, how is it Roxy who knows my true feelings about Nick? That's just unfair.

"Just doing my job."

"Sure you are. Anyway, he asked about you and Gloria had to assure him you were still committed to this project and are managing the book launch event like it's your baby. It better go well, or..." Roxy makes a throat slitting motion. She's so fucking dramatic.

"It will go perfectly," I assure her.

She purses her lips, knowing she got under my skin and is pleased with herself for it.

Now I am worried, and I go through all my checklists for the launch event, and the schedule of a million tiny tasks that have to happen before then, which just got longer with the addition of the pet adoption.

Roxy is revising some of the media content to include the shelter aspect, and Nick will have to reapprove everything when she's done. Hopefully, he will do that by e-mail. I'm sure he only came in to force me to see him, which I think is kind of manipulative, since he knows this job is important to me.

Just being out for two days made me feel woefully behind, and I kick myself again for falling into bad habits. In addition to finalizing everything for Nick, Gloria gives me a new assignment, doing a social media appraisal for a political candidate. The client isn't actually the candidate, it's a group that finds potential candidates for office that they'd like to support, and they hired us as a sort of pre-screening.

It's back to the thing I love, online research, digging up dirt on this guy, searching for skeletons in the closet. First, I just Google him, seeing what comes up. Nothing much. He's currently a professor of Public Administration at the University of Texas at Austin, and that dominates the results. I check his faculty page. It's likely that someone like him keeps a clean profile, so I don't expect to find much online.

People his age have no idea how lucky they are that their first twenty years of mistakes weren't recorded for posterity.

I find him on Rate My Professors, to see what his students think of him. He has a 4.6 out of 5 with twenty-one ratings, most saying he is tough but fair.

Moving of their own volition, my fingers begin typing "Dr. Nicolas Stone" into the search bar. I'd love to know what his former students said about his classes. Did they find him inspirational? I bet they loved him.

No—bad Katie! I clear the search and shake my head. I must train my brain not to think of Nick any longer and focus on my work.

LinkedIn next, not to see what the candidate says about himself, but to see what kinds of things he posts, what groups he belongs to, and what he likes and comments on. Frankly, it's all boring and professional, specific to public administration. His Facebook is private, good for him, Twitter is same as LinkedIn, but he hasn't posted in months, no Instagram. He's probably too old for TikTok, but I check anyway. YouTube has some school events, graduation ceremonies, but nothing scandalous.

I fill out the form that Purple Cactus PR has created for this very purpose and conclude that he's pretty clean. I recommend if his candidacy moves forward that we create a separate public Facebook page for him as a candidate. Of course, I offer our company's website and social media management package with a 10% discount if they sign up within thirty days. Gloria pointed that out in the example she gave me from a previous client a few months back. I'm killing it at this job.

Gym first, shower, snack, rummage through my closet to find something to wear. What says art opening? I don't want anything too sexy, since I'm going with my friend that I once kissed and his brand-new girlfriend, but I can't help wanting to redeem my image from my post-workout grubbiness.

I settle on a solid black A-line, cold shoulder dress with spaghetti straps, with a lacing corset belt. For color, I put on sheer dark purple tights and layer those with fishnets. I complete the look with a purple cat nestled into a pewter moon around my neck and an oversized garnet ring. And my favorite boots.

Oh wait, maybe this is too sexy. Oh well...

It's too late to change because Damon is knocking on my door.

"Come in, I'll just be a sec," I say. I'm pleased that he can't help but give me the once-over. Am I an evil witch? No, because I would never help someone cheat, so even if we weren't just friends, the fact that he is with Paige now, even if it's still new, means he is strictly off limits. Am I a bitch for wanting to make him wonder what he is missing? Maybe.

I grab my purse from the bedroom and look at my cat-eye liner, thick mascara, and deep scarlet lipstick, one last time. Gothic perfection if I do say so myself. Pulling my light velvet jacket off the back of the chair I say, "Alright, ready."

Before we get to the door, there's a knock. Damon looks at me with a questioning expression. I shrug. Damon is the only one who knows where I live besides Tiff's Treats and the pizza delivery driver. It's probably someone at the wrong apartment. I look out the peephole and gasp.

It's Nicolas Stone.

36

❧

"Oh shit," I say.

"Who is it?" Damon asks.

"Nicolas Stone."

"Who?"

"My client, the positive psychology one that I went on a lecture tour with."

Damon frowns. "What's he doing here at your apartment, at night?" he says. "Wait—are you two together?"

"No!" I bark. "We are not together. But...we did kiss last Friday. But then I called it off."

"Jesus, Katie. You made out with your client? That doesn't seem like you."

"Well, maybe you don't know me that well."

He gives me a look.

"Okay, fine. I don't know. We just had a connection, but it could never work, we're just too different. But I have to work with him through the book launch, it's important to my career."

"Alright, well open the door then. I'll be here."

I turn the knob and brace myself to see Nick. What I forgot was that I'm all decked out in full goth, Kat mode. Shit.

"Katie?" Nick says, his mouth hanging open as he takes in my outfit then scans the room, his eyes growing wider as he registers the glowing blacklights, the Edward Gorey print, the Disintegration poster, the black lace curtains, the candlesticks, and the crystal skull.

"What are you doing here, Nick?" I say, focusing his attention back to me.

"I was worried about you. You missed the meeting, and Gloria said you were out sick the day before."

Damon clears his throat, standing with his arms crossed like an angry, protective dad. "So, this is Mr. Positive?" he says with a bite.

Nick looks at Damon, then turns back to me, and the hurt in his eyes is like a dagger in my chest. "Mr. Positive? Is that what you call me behind my back?"

I shake my head. I want to reach out to him, but it's weird with Damon here. "No, of course not. I mean...yes, but that was before I got to know you and the wonderful things you teach people."

Nick looks crushed. "And what's all this?" he says, waving his hand at my outfit and my apartment.

"Um, this is me...outside of work."

"So, you're goth? The way you were at work and on the lecture tour, that was all a show?"

"No, it's not. That's who I am too. That's just my professional image. Do you remember what you said about those kids in Deep Ellum? I have to dress like that at work because of judgmental people like you."

I didn't mean to hurt Nick, or maybe I did because he is hurting me.

His head jerks back like I punched him. "Wow. Okay. I'm sorry I said those things, I really am, but that's two big things you've lied to me about, Katie. I guess I don't know you at all."

"Wait, Nick, I–"

"I'll see you at the book launch. Have fun with this guy," Nick says, practically spitting at Damon.

I realize he probably thinks Damon and I are together, and I do nothing to persuade him otherwise; it's for the best. Damon takes the hint, stands closer to me, and says, "We'd better get going, we're going to be late."

Nick stares at us for a moment longer like he can't believe what he's seeing, then turns on his heels and storms down the walkway.

"Whoa," says Damon. "I feel like I'm missing something here."

"Don't worry about it," I say.

"Do you still want to go? I can tell Paige you couldn't make it."

"No, I'm going. Damned if I'm going to let Nicolas Stone ruin my night."

"Yeah, fuck that guy," says Damon, and I get the impression that there is jealousy on all sides tonight.

Damon drives us to East Austin, to a gallery in the old warehouse district. Not sure I'd want to go there all alone, and I'm glad he's with me. Paige is happy to see us, and kisses Damon on the mouth as if to mark him, let me know he belongs to her now. But she's super nice to me and is excited to introduce us to her friend, the artist, Luna.

Her artwork is unlike anything I've ever seen, a mix of harsh materials, metal and stone, soft textures like feathers and silk, and mixed medias like acrylics, oils, plaster, clay, in various forms, framed two-dimensional works, 3-d statues on pedestals, and temporary installations under plexiglass boxes that will cease to exist after the show.

Luna herself is a wonder. She makes me fall in love with Austin in a heartbeat, a gorgeous representation of keeping it weird, with a long flowing purple robe, open except for where it is artistically adorned with a geometric pattern of safety pins, layered over a flimsy twenties style slip dress of shimmery gold. She's like a queen, only with brown Ugg boots with plush trim. She wears a twisted paisley scarf as a head band, keeping her unruly long curls out of her eyes. Honestly, I'm having a bit of a crush on this woman right now. She's like an art goddess and practically glows like the moon, her namesake.

Luna is gracious as well.

"I love your work," I tell her after Paige introduces us.

"Oh, thank you," Luna says, "I'm just honored I get to share this evening with my friends."

This room is packed with people, and more overflowing outside into the parking lot; she must have a lot of friends. I wonder how long Luna has lived here, curious as to how people find their community, wondering how long it will take to find mine. I feel a bit desperate, longing to find my place, and jealous of those who have settled into theirs.

I've only been here for a short while, so I need to be patient. But in truth, I never found my place in New Jersey, I didn't have any close friends, and I'm worried the past will repeat itself.

Luna offers me wine, but I decline. "Straight edge, are we?" she says with a knowing look.

"Something like that," I say. "Just need to keep my mind clear."

"Ah, I understand," Luna says. "I don't drink much either. There are better ways to open up to the world's possibilities."

I'm not sure if she's talking about psychedelics, or weed, or something else, but whatever it is, it's not for me. That's okay. I gave up a long time ago expecting to meet people who are artistic and open minded yet also reserved when it comes to drugs and alcohol.

Paige and Damon seem to be having fun, Paige introducing him around to her friends. She hangs on him like a new prize pony. Nothing against Paige, I really do like her, it's just weird to see Damon being fawned over, and clearly, he is enjoying it.

In fact, everyone seems to be enjoying themselves except me. They're all friendly enough, but I feel small and alone, an outsider. Even though these people look like me, I don't know how to talk to them, how to break in. After a while I stand outside looking up at the stars; the night is clear, and the moon is almost new. That fucking Texas moon. Maybe a new moon is a sign for me, that I need to put aside thoughts of romance for a while and focus on other things.

Work is good, and volunteering at the shelter has been a fulfilling addition to my life, but there's still a lot missing. I need to go places where I can make friends. Maybe take a class or something, I don't know. It's not that easy to make friends after college. Roxy is the only woman my age at work, and we're not likely to be besties any time soon.

Damon comes outside to find me and says we can leave soon if I need to get home. I assure him I'm fine, and we can stay as late as he wants. I should have driven myself. Now I'm stuck here, but I don't want to spoil Damon's night. I'm a third wheel.

Three different people outside offer me a drag off their joints, but I decline. I amuse myself by pretending I'm a mouse nibbling on the cubes of cheese and then play solitaire on my phone until Damon is ready to leave.

I say my goodnight to Luna and congratulate her again on her show and thank Paige for inviting me. Paige seems more comfortable with me now, I'm no longer a threat to her, just Damon's neighbor.

Before Damon heads up the stairs to his apartment, he turns to me. "Are you sure you're okay, after the whole thing with Mr. Positive?"

"Yeah, I'm fine. Nick is nothing to me anymore."

"Okay, good. He doesn't deserve you if he can't accept all of who you are. You can do better."

I thank him, and we go our separate ways. Damon is a good guy. Paige is lucky to have him.

37

Things settle back into a routine. Gloria gives me new assign-ments. I lose myself in work, thankful for the opportunity for flow and achievement. Roxy continues to be snide; Amber continues to call me darlin' every morning. Damon and Paige are still hanging out, the Paradise Lost concert came and went without me. I haven't heard a peep from Nick. All the remaining details for the book launch have been coordinated by e-mail, with digital signatures for Nick's approval.

Working at the shelter has been a bright spot in my life, but I can't understand why no one adopts sweet Brownie. He's such a good dog and I wish again I had a house with a yard so I could adopt him myself. Maybe someone will see him at the book launch.

I'm back to my regimented ways, cardio, healthy dinners, eight hours of sleep. No deviation.

I meet with a new therapist, and I have to admit it is nice to have some support navigating life in a new city. She gives me a lot to think about. I accept that I'm someone who will always need help, both meds and therapy and I no longer feel bad about that. It's just like if someone had high blood pressure, they might take medicine to lower it but also have to eat a low sodium diet. It's no different just because one is considered mental and the other a physical affliction.

Time is passing by, and I'm neither particularly depressed nor happy, I just am. Which for me is quite good. My best is like nothing-ness, like lukewarm water that feels the same temperature as the air, so you barely sense it at all. I'm okay, and I'm independent, so maybe Texas was a good move. The sunshine really does make a difference.

Maybe it should be no surprise then, when the next gloomy, rainy day comes I struggle once again. But what I didn't expect was that I would pull into the parking lot late, due to the terrible traffic that happens because people here are dreadful at driving in the rain, only to find Roxy crying in her car.

It was a coincidence that I pulled into the spot next to her, but perhaps it wasn't, perhaps it was fate. Roxy catches my eye, and I can almost taste the sneer she gives me, because it's that sour. She's angry and embarrassed that I caught her being vulnerable. I think back to that terrible workday when I was so depressed that I fell asleep at my desk and how nice Roxy was to me, at least nice for Roxy. She could have used it as an opportunity to bring me down, but she didn't. Now I need to return the favor.

I get out of my car and knock on her passenger window. "Are you okay?" I yell through the glass.

Roxy waves me away. Normally I would respect a person's wishes to be alone when they are upset, but something tells me Roxy needs a friend right now, and I don't think she's much closer with any of our other coworkers. I test the handle, but it's locked, and I stand there while the drizzling rain soaks my clothes and hair.

When she realizes I'm not leaving, she relents, and the door makes a clicking sound. I climb into the passenger side seat.

Roxy's makeup is smudged with tears and her face is splotchy and red. "Are you okay?" I ask again, and hand her a tissue from my purse.

She accepts it and wipes her runny nose. "I'll be fine."

This is a delicate situation. Right now, Roxy is like one of the dogs I work with at the shelter, clearly wanting someone to care, but easily spooked if I don't move slowly enough. "Is there anything I can do to help?" I say, instead of asking her to tell me what's wrong. Sometimes it's possible to help someone without them having to share their personal baggage.

"I don't know," she says. "You wouldn't understand, anyway."

"Why is that?" I ask.

"Because you grew up in a big city, where you could just be yourself."

Ha. That couldn't be further from the truth. I shake my head. "No, I didn't. New York City was a train ride away, but I grew up in a small, suburban town. And it was closer to the rural parts of New Jersey."

"Oh," she says. "I just assumed you were a city girl."

"And I assumed you were from Austin because you seem so at home here. I guess you're not?"

"I'm from a tiny Texas town no one has heard of, and I got out of there as fast as I could."

That must have been tough on Roxy growing up. I caught a lot of shit for being goth, but I had a couple of friends who kept me from being a total outcast.

We sit in silence for a few minutes. Then Roxy wakes up her phone and hands it to me. "Look at this," she says.

It's opened to her text messages and the last one reads, "We think it's best if you don't come to the wedding."

"It's from my father," she says. "My little brother is getting married."

I'm starting to piece things together, but I can't imagine why Roxy's parents wouldn't want her at a family event like that. There's clearly a lot I don't know about her.

"I'm sorry—that must feel awful," is all I can think to say.

She shrugs in defeat. "I should be used to it by now. I'm an adult, with a job and friends far away from them now—Austin saved me. But they still get to me, sometimes."

"I don't think that ever goes away. It's tough not getting acceptance from your parents."

"You're lucky, the perfect daughter. I bet your parents brag about you all the time."

"You'd be surprised," I say. "The last time I talked to my mom I was a mess afterwards."

Roxy looks shocked and I suddenly regret opening up to her. Not like we're friends or anything, and she still seems out to get me some days. "I guess no one has a perfect family," she says.

"Nope. But luckily, we both moved to a cool city where we can make our own family of sorts. Friends are the new family, haven't you heard?"

"Totally and it's a great thing. My friend Ronda has an annual Thanksgiving dinner just for folks with no family to share it with, whatever the reason. I've gone for the last three years and it's better than any holiday I had growing up."

"That sounds awesome," I say.

"I've met some great people here in Austin."

Roxy seems to be a little better now. Her tears have stopped flowing and she dabs at her eyes in the visor mirror. I hand her some more tissues so she can fix her makeup.

"Can I ask you something?" I say.

"Why not," says Roxy.

"That day that I fell asleep at my desk—why didn't you tell Gloria?"

She looks at me. "Oh that. Don't get all sentimental on me. It's not because we're great friends. It's more like when an athlete wins a gold medal but only because his biggest competitor was out with an injury. I want to beat you fair and square."

Wow. That is not what I thought she was going to say, although it is consistent with how Roxy's always behaved around me. I guess she really is that ambitious and competitive. She's really good at her job too, and sometimes I wonder if Gloria needs to see past Roxy's façade. But on the other hand, Roxy's rigid insistence on being Roxy at all times borders on inflexibility. It certainly makes me feel conflicted about my Katie persona. But it's working and who can argue with the results?

"Well thanks anyway, I don't know what would have happened if I lost this job."

"It was nothing. Thanks for checking on me. I'll be up in a few minutes," she says, dismissing me.

I head out into the rain to start my workday.

On the way home I run into Damon. I rarely catch him alone anymore; I miss him. He was such a big part of my first couple of months here, tacos and Amy's Ice Cream, and Mount Bonnell. But now his first priority is Paige, which I totally get. It's as it should be.

"How have you been?" Damon asks.

"Not bad, you?" I say.

"Can't complain."

"How's Paige?" Why did I ask that? I don't care about Paige; I don't want to hear about Paige.

"She's alright."

Huh. Trouble in paradise? What is wrong with you, Kat? Are you wishing for them to break up? For what, so he can be your friend again? That's downright selfish. Paige is a really nice woman, and they are great together.

"We should get Amy's again sometime, now that it's getting warmer," I say.

"You're on. We should definitely hang out soon."

As I move towards my apartment, Damon calls out. "Hey. You have any more trouble with Mr. Positive?"

"Nah. Haven't seen him since that night. The book launch is tomorrow and after that I won't have to work with him anymore."

"That's good."

Is it? And why does Damon care?

38

Book launch day is finally here. I wake up at five, completely wired, even though I barely slept, going through checklists in my mind, worrying about every detail. My team at Purple Cactus has done a great job with all the press and announcements, and the local media covered the event even more than we had anticipated because the shelter is overcrowded with late spring puppies and kittens.

I checked and doublechecked every detail with the event planner and everything is ready to go. Best of all, the weather is sunny and clear, not a rain cloud in sight. I'm excited for this event, the culmination of my first big project at Purple Cactus PR. I have so much riding on this, since Gloria took a real chance hiring me to be a project manager for the first time in my career. I don't want to let her down, and I don't want to disappoint myself, either. And at all costs, I want to deny Roxy any satisfaction she would feel if I failed at my first big event. She still has no idea her competitiveness makes me stronger.

It's not just about my work success though. I'm really rooting for Nick. The fact that we aren't meant to be together doesn't mean his work isn't important. It really is and I sincerely hope the book is a runaway success and helps millions of people like he has helped me. I can't wait to see him do his reading; I miss the way his face lights up when he talks about his passion.

The things I learned from his lectures and his book haven't cured my depression, but the little changes I've made, the simple acts of kindness, an eye towards gratitude, recognizing that engagement and achievement at work are big pieces of my mental health puzzle, have made a difference. And his inappropriate outburst about me needing a therapist was not appreciated at the time, but he wasn't wrong.

The venue is all set up. I tried to make it look more like a cozy living room and less like a lecture hall, with plants and floor lamps, a comfy armchair for the reading up front and the audience chairs curved around it in a semi-circle. A book signing table is to the right, and the catering area is outside in the hall, away from the books, to accommodate mingling after the reading.

The volunteers from the shelter arrive with the animals and a table with information on adoption. I say hello to my favorite friend, Brownie, and he tries to lick my face through the bars. "You're such a good boy," I say. "I wish I could play with you, but I have to do adult things now." He looks at me with enormous, sad anime eyes. "You just be your handsome self and I'm sure someone will snatch you right up."

Glancing around, I still don't see the man of the hour, and I'm double worried, first because what if he's late or something unexpected happens that prevents him from being here. Second because this is his big night, and I don't want to ruin it with awkward tension between us. In an attempt to distract myself, I move to the adoption desk to see if they need anything from me.

They are all set, and when I turn to go back inside the building, there's Nick, looking like a GQ model again, in a fitted suit with one of his signature gray vests and a pale blue shirt. He's talking to Brownie. I can't help moving closer to hear what he's saying.

"Are you a good dog? I bet you're a very good boy," he says in that voice reserved for talking to pets. Now I know what I must have sounded like a few minutes ago. Who could blame us with a dog like that. Brownie looks pleased with the attention, so I guess it's not personal; he likes anyone who likes him.

"He's sweet, isn't he?" I can't help saying as I approach.

Nick turns towards me, startled. "Katie. Hi."

I caught him off guard, which was unfair of me, so I keep it casual. "I work with Brownie at the shelter. He's the best."

Happy to take a 'pretend it never happened' approach to our first encounter since my apartment, he says, "Brownie looks just like—"

"Pepper," I say at the same time as Nick.

His eyes widen. "You remembered the name of my childhood dog?"

"Of course." I probably remember every word Nicolas Stone has ever said to me. I shake off this realization; I need to focus tonight. "Brownie would love to have a yard like yours to run around in," I say.

"Giving me the hard sell—but you know I travel for my lectures."

"So? There are dog sitters, dog walkers. That would be better for Brownie than withering away in the shelter. Trust me, he's miserable there and just wants to be loved."

He shakes his head at my tenacity. "I'll think about it. But maybe he'll find the perfect home tonight. This was a terrific idea—you are really great at your job."

I blush but am pleased that he thinks so, that he's happy with my work, that I was right about who he is and how he would want to be represented. "Thanks," I say, our eyes meeting for a split second too long. I need to be professional Katie right now. "We'd better get inside and go over the schedule."

We leave Brownie and his puppy dog eyes with the volunteers. I show Nick around the facility and go over the event timings. He seems a little nervous, rubbing his hands together like he's trying to warm them.

"You okay?" I ask.

"Sure, just a little nervous. It's really here now, I can't believe the book is actually out after all this waiting. It's just...what if it doesn't help anyone?"

"Oh Nick, it won't save everyone, you know that. But it will help some people—I can say that with one hundred percent confidence, because I'm proof that it helps. This is no different from your regular lectures or classes; you're just sharing what you know. How people use it is up to them."

"I know. It's just this is local, this is my community, my city," he says. "I'm going to see some of these people again. And my name and face are on that book."

"You're going to be great—just remember during the reading to imagine you're talking to a friend over coffee. Maybe imagine you're talking to me."

A tinge of remorse crosses his face, but he pushes it away and brightens. "I will, that helps. Thank you, Katie."

I give his arm a gentle squeeze, then leave him to mentally prepare for the big night ahead. I really wanted to give him a big hug and whisper in his ear that he's an amazing person, but obviously that would be inappropriate, given the circumstances.

Gloria and Roxy arrive, trailed by Ben, who will be wrapping up his internship in just a few weeks when the semester ends. I am going to miss working with him, if for no other reason than he played witness to Roxy's unfair attitude towards me since my first day.

"Everything set?" Gloria asks.

"Yes. Caterers are prepping in the kitchen. I'm sure you saw the shelter volunteers and animals for adoption on the way in. I've tested the mic system and lighting. Nick's already here, the signing table is ready to go with plenty of boxes of books. We are ready for showtime."

Gloria looks around the room with approval, and Roxy gives me a glare.

I pray with all my heart that nothing goes wrong.

39

Watching Nick do his thing makes my heart ache. He's beautiful when he talks about positive psychology, earnestly sharing what he's learned and how we can all use it to live better. His eyes shine when he speaks, and the light he emits when he smiles creates a gnawing feeling in my stomach. I could spend a lifetime watching this man speak and never tire of it.

The place is packed, and all the local media showed up to cover the event, doing a bit outside with the shelter folks, then filming part of Nick's reading, and now getting a few seconds of footage showing the signing line, which wraps around the back of the room.

I breathe a sigh of relief as I step out into the hallway and see smiling guests carrying Nick's book under their arms while holding a glass of punch in another or noshing on a canapé. Other patrons are perusing the community wall, another one of my ideas, a bulletin board with information about local groups that need volunteers. Gloria said Nick adored that idea when she told him about it that day I was coordinating with the shelter.

I peek outside and see people cooing over the puppies and kittens, and the folks at the adoption table handing out info and answering questions. I bet the adoption center will be flooded with appointments next week.

The signing line moves slowly due to Nick's willingness to chat with each person, but because of the atmosphere Nick created during his reading, people seem good natured and patient with the wait.

When the last book is signed, I watch him give a giant exhale. He's glowing and I want more than anything to give him a giant hug. He catches my eye, and I give him two thumbs up instead.

As the last of the guests trickle out, the caterers start to pack up, the shelter volunteers load the animals back in the van, and Gloria comes out and pats me on the shoulder. "You did a fantastic job with this project, Katie. Congratulations."

I grin with glee. "Thanks so much Gloria, but it was a team effort."

"It was, but every team needs a good leader," she says.

Roxy is spying and eavesdropping from the corner, her eyes narrowed. She was hoping I'd fail. Too bad, so sad.

Gloria beckons Roxy and Ben over. "This calls for a celebration. Drinks on me. Juanita's is right down the street."

"Ooh, Juanita's has my favorite queso," says Roxy.

"Queso on me, then," says Gloria.

For once I'm grateful to Roxy because now I can order food instead of sitting there with just a soda. The whole not drinking thing is hard to navigate in social situations, especially work ones.

"Let me go congratulate Nick and I'll meet you there," I say.

Back inside, I wait for Nick's publisher to finish talking to him. The man gives Nick a warm handshake and Nick looks as happy as I probably did when Gloria complimented me. I guess no matter how old we get, approval from someone in authority feels good.

Butterflies swarm my insides as I walk over to Nick. "Congratulations," I say, "that was a great reading. And what a long signing line! You must have a great PR person..."

"That must be it," he says. "This has been an amazing night. You know I was reticent about this book, but seeing all these hopeful faces, knowing I inspired them to make changes, it was awesome. And I have you to thank for it."

"No way, this was all you, Nick."

He turns serious. "No, Katie, if it had been anyone else with me on that lecture tour, I might have bowed out of the book. But you made me realize it's worth it. You inspire me."

I shake my head. "I don't know what to say."

"Can we talk somewhere? I really need to say some things." His eyes are so earnest they melt my heart nearly as much as Brownie's.

"I can't. Gloria is taking the team out for drinks."

"But you don't drink," he says.

"Queso, then. This is the first time we've socialized outside of the office. It's important."

"I get it. But can we talk soon?"

"I don't know."

His face falls. "Please, think about it. Just thirty minutes, that's all I need."

"Okay, I'll think about it. And congrats again. This book is something special."

Juanita's is a loud, crowded bar with lots of neon. I'm surprised it was Gloria's suggestion but then I don't know what she's like outside of work. Maybe she has a private life personality that's as different from her work one as mine is.

Roxy was right, the queso is delicious. Screw healthy eating, I just keep shoving this cheesy, spicy goodness into my mouth with crispy chip after crispy chip. Tacos and queso, that's what life is all about. Gloria orders a strawberry margarita, which arrives in an elegant, salt-rimmed glass with a slice of lime. Ben has a beer, and Roxy has a locally brewed IPA.

Gloria starts off with shop talk, saying again what a great event tonight was and how she has big plans for Purple Cactus. She even embarrasses Ben by surprising him with an offer to continue on as a full-time summer intern, which he gladly accepts. We all drink to Ben, even me with my iced tea, and he looks happy to be part of the team. I bet we hire him on after he graduates too; he is a sharp guy.

Soon, the alcohol loosens lips, except for mine, and conversation turns to other things, movies, television, Gloria evangelizing the air fryer, Roxy lamenting how Austin used to be before all these outsiders moved here. Like me, I'm sure she means.

I'm enjoying being the sober observer, and grateful the discussion never turns to politics, because I'm not sure Gloria and Roxy see eye to eye on things. I sit back in my chair, pleasantly full of queso and iced tea, when a voice surprises me.

"Katie, is that you?"

It's Paige and Luna.

Paige is dressed in her standard heavy metal attire, this time in her must be brand-new Paradise Lost t-shirt, which sends a twinge of resentment through me. Luna is dressed like her grandmother was a teenager in the sixties and kept all her clothes to pass down, a red and yellow patterned shirt that ties into a knot above her belly button, leaving her smooth stomach exposed, with long sleeves that flare past her wrist, a shin-length denim skirt and tan boots with actual fringe on them.

My face immediately burns like I smothered it with tabasco, so I keep my voice cool and calm. "Hi ladies, nice to see you."

"I almost didn't recognize you," says Paige, which makes Roxy's eyebrow raise.

"Lovely to see you again," says Luna, in a ridiculously aristocratic way.

"Good to see you, too," I say, trying to regain my composure. "These are my colleagues, Gloria, Roxy, and Ben."

"A pleasure," says Luna, and Ben steals a glance at her tight stomach and belly button ring. Gloria seems amused as she looks them up and down.

After an awkward silence, Paige takes the hint, and says, "See you around, Katie."

Luna follows her, then turns around and says, "Don't be a stranger..."

I want to cover my face in my hands, but I force myself to look casual.

"I see you've made some interesting friends since you've moved here," says Gloria.

"Um, we're not exactly friends. Paige is dating my neighbor."

"They certainly have that Austin vibe," Gloria says. "Artsy types, I presume."

"Luna is an artist," I say. "I went to a show of hers a few weeks ago. It got a great review in the Chronicle."

Roxy looks impressed. "I think I read that, Luna does the collages with the crow feathers, right?"

Gloria rolls her eyes. "Oh goodness, is that what passes for art these days? Crow feathers? And what does Paige do, is she in a carnival?"

I wince and Roxy looks shocked. "Paige is a pharmacist," I say.

"Really?" Gloria says. "I guess I'm just old and out of touch."

Yes, and yes, I think, but feel guilty. "No, you're not, it's just the world is changing. In the fifties, your pantsuits would have been scandalous in the business world. But it doesn't reveal anything about how competent you are, and neither does a nose ring or blue hair."

Roxy's eyes are opened wide, surprised by how I'm talking to Gloria.

A heavy silence falls over the table as Roxy, Ben, and I hold our breaths, waiting for Gloria's response. She takes a large sip of her margarita, slurping through the straw.

"You're right, of course," says Gloria. "It's just so hard to keep up with things—that's why I have to surround myself with you young folks, to keep me grounded."

The relief at the table is palpable and the conversation returns to lighter topics. When Gloria slurps the last of her margarita, Ben offers to drive her home. I don't know if you can get tipsy from just one, but it was gigantic and Gloria didn't eat anything, so Ben is doing the right thing.

Roxy catches up with me in the parking lot, just before I get in my car. "That was nice how you stood up to Gloria for me," she says.

Shit. Roxy assumed I was talking about her and her punk aesthetic. There are too many lies in my life, and I can't keep any more. "I wasn't. I was standing up for me."

Roxy looks confused. "What do you mean—you're like a brown-haired barbie doll."

I pull out my phone and show her a photo of me in full goth attire. "I'm not as conventional as you think."

Roxy examines the picture, then glares like she's going to spit on me. "So, you're a fucking phony, that's even worse."

40

A burning sensation flows through my torso, and I feel the rage that is always simmering beneath the surface bubble up to my mouth. "What's your fucking problem with me? You've been a total bitch since day one. There's nothing wrong with having a professional persona. You should try it sometime."

Roxy takes a step back like I just slapped her. Believe me, I want to, but she's still my coworker and I don't want to get arrested for assault in the Juanita's parking lot. I'm trying to control my inner volcano, but this woman has been making my life miserable for no good reason and I've had enough. I don't wait for her to answer.

My hand on my hip, feet firm on the ground in a fighting stance, ready for what happens next, I demand, "What do you have against me, anyway?" I expect her to lash out, defend herself, but instead she snorts with laughter.

My shoulders drop and my fuel fizzles out. "Why are you laughing?" I'm helpless now; I've lost the edge because I no longer know what's happening.

"Because," Roxy says with a smirk, "this is the first time you've ever had the balls to say anything real to me."

I blink in confusion. My brain quickly retrieves all the files of our interactions since my first day of work and plays them in superfast motion. This bitch is right. I've been pretty fake with her, all because I was trying to be the new Katie. But I'm still right about the professional image. It's not wrong to dress and behave like you actually care about your career.

Roxy clenches and releases her fist like she's holding an imaginary stress ball. "The truth is, you took my job."

Aaaah. Recognition dawns on me. Roxy applied for this position too. She really did resent me before I even started. But I worked hard at my old company, and I was ready to move up. No way I'm feeling bad about being the better candidate. Except I do feel a twinge of guilt despite my best efforts.

"No," I say, attempting to keep my voice firm but empathetic. "I just applied for a job and won it. It isn't my fault they didn't choose you." I pause, then add, "But if I were in your shoes, I'd probably hate me too."

"I don't hate you," says Roxy. "I hate that you're right. I probably didn't deserve the promotion. I guess I need to decide how much I really want a career."

"I've been there," I say. "I never wanted work to be my whole life. But I like this job and there's nothing wrong with feeling a sense of accomplishment from work even if your whole belief system says you should hate the man." I leave out the part about how I need the external structure of a corporate job in order to keep from falling into a pit of darkness.

"So does Mr. Positive know about your secret life?"

I roll my eyes. "There is nothing going on between me and Nicolas Stone. But yes, he knows. No one else at work."

"Your secret is safe with me. And bullshit on Mr. Positive. I've seen fewer sparks at a fireworks show," she says.

I think about that all the way home. When I'm around Nick, I feel that ping, over and over, like Tinker Bell is throwing fairy dust in my face and saying wake up, wake up. But I can't change the circumstances, his past and my present. Neither of us can go back in time and be honest with one another. There's just no remedy.

On the positive side, the launch event was a smash. Nick is booked on several regional morning shows, and even some smaller national ones. I know he's going to be a great success, and I wish him well.

Maybe I'll even watch a few of his appearances. And I'll definitely check the book rankings, hoping he becomes a best seller.

But that's it. I'm done with Nicolas Stone.

Things are better with Roxy now that we had it out, and I'm looking forward to working with her on the new project Gloria gave us, a tech company that got bad press when they had a data breach that leaked consumer information and need to rebuild goodwill. Not my favorite type of client, because I feel like I'm defending the bad guys, but I choose to view it as a challenge.

Tuesday is shelter night, and I'm looking forward to seeing if the adoption booth at the launch event resulted in any takers. I go to the dog kennels to see my favorite friend, but he's nowhere to be found.

"Hey," I say to one of the staff, "did Brownie get adopted?"

"The lab? Yep, someone saw him at an outreach event over the weekend, and they were approved this morning."

My heart is full of joy for Brownie. I hope he gets a nice home with a huge yard he can run around in, someone who will play tug with him and love him forever. Volunteering here is hard because I get attached so easily; I'm going to miss my first kennel friend fiercely.

No time to wallow; there's a whole list of new dogs to be walked. First up, my little beagle, Pixie, who bays at everything in sight. She's a doll in dog's clothing. Then there's a newbie, a boxer named Hercules, brindle, with white paws and chest. His kennel card says he's not a biter but can get a little carried away when playing so we should use caution.

"Hercules, Hercules, let's go!" I tell him as I latch the leash. He immediately pulls me down the hall, using all of his seventy pounds. I wonder if I'll be able to get him back inside. I practically run after him the whole time and he wears me out, but he needs the exercise. He just has a lot of pent-up energy. I would too if I were stuck in a cage.

Next is Greta, a Dachshund, which is nice because her petite legs can't carry her as fast as Hercules, giving me a little break. Before I leave, I take a flyer for the annual volunteer appreciation picnic. I don't interact much with the volunteers since we're each working one on one with an animal, but maybe my new best friend is someone who works at the shelter. It's a good place to start looking for my kindreds.

Speaking of friendship, Damon and I still haven't hung out alone since he started dating Paige. I wonder if she told him about running into me at Juanita's. It's a good conversation starter.

Post-workout, I knock on his door. It's air conditioner season now, so I don't see him on the porch as often.

"Katie! Come in," he says.

I check inside, hoping I'm not interrupting anything with him and Paige, but he appears to be alone.

"You hungry?" he asks.

"I just ate dinner."

"Room for dessert?"

"I don't think I can manage Amy's today."

"Nah, not Amy's, I had somewhere else in mind. You'll love it. It's light."

I grin because this is the Damon from when I first moved in, showing me the best places in Austin. I missed him. "Let's go," I say.

We pull up at a cute little white building with two yellow-framed windows, and a sign that reads, "Casey's New Orleans Snowballs."

"I feel like I'm cheating on Amy with Casey," I joke.

"They are worlds apart, like comparing puppies with a banana."

"What do puppies have in common with bananas?"

"Nothing, that's my point."

Damon's silliness is part of why I like being around him. He's not so serious, like I am. It's a nice break from my drill sergeant brain.

Leche Canela has cinnamon, cream, and vanilla and tastes like a dream. Damon gets a Rainbow, with pineapple, blue raspberry, and strawberry. After he eats the raspberry part, he opens his mouth like a child, revealing his blue stained tongue.

"Nice," I say.

"This place reminds me of happy summers when I was a kid. Did you have these up north?"

"We had snow cones, but even better, we had Italian ices, usually lemon, during the summer."

"I've had something like that at the State Fair," says Damon. "It's like a frozen lemonade and it's so good when it's ninety-five degrees out."

"Ugh. I can't imagine," I say.

Damon looks at me and snorts. "You know it gets well over a hundred in the summer, right?"

"Yeah, but I just assumed no one moves, they just sit in front of the AC."

"Heh. I'm going to enjoy watching you survive your first summer."

I throw my wadded-up napkin at him in protest. "That's mean," I say.

He makes a *mea culpa* face. "I'll make it up to you. The first weekend it's over one hundred I'm taking you swimming at Barton Springs. It's a cool sixty-eight degrees year-round."

"That doesn't sound so cold," I say.

"I'll remember you said that. Just jump in and you'll see..."

On the way home, I remember to ask him about Juanita's. "Did Paige tell you I ran into her and Luna on Friday after the book launch?"

He shakes his head. "No, she didn't mention it, but we haven't seen each other as much lately."

"Oh. Is everything okay?"

He shrugs in his lazy river way. "Yeah, yeah, we're both just busy."

I nod in agreement, but would be surprised if Damon were really busy, that's just not his style.

He obviously doesn't want to talk about it because he changes the subject. "How did the book launch go?"

"It went great! We got media coverage and a big audience turnout, and a long signing line. My boss was really pleased."

"That's awesome. I know how important work is to you."

I don't need everyone to be like me, and I appreciate that Damon has learned that I love my job, even though he apparently doesn't love his, but I'm still curious to understand what makes him tick.

"What about you, do you hate your job or something?"

"Nah, there's not much to hate. It's just something I do to pay the bills. But I don't aspire to move up and become head of the IT department or anything. Life outside work is much more important. Did I tell you it's a go with that screen printing equipment? I saved up the money and my friend is wrapping up some orders he committed to and then it will be mine," Damon says, with the excitement of a teen getting his first car.

"Wow! That's cool. You'll have to show me how it works; I've never seen someone print t-shirts before."

Now I get it. Damon's day job is nothing to him, but when he talks about band promotion his face lights up the same way Nick's does with positive psychology. I'm curious about one more thing, though.

"I was wondering—you dress like that at work, right?" I say, gesturing towards his black Flaming Goathead t-shirt, boots, and black jeans.

He looks down like he's wondering what could be wrong with it. "Yeah, for the most part. I don't wear the older t-shirts with holes or anything."

That's the subtle difference between Damon trying and not trying to look professional? "And your boss doesn't care what you look like?"

He raises his eyebrows and pulls out his phone. "This is the CEO. He's younger than we are. Does he look like he cares?"

The man in the photo looks like he could be in Green Day, with spiky blonde hair and an eyebrow ring. "Oh, I guess not."

"Does your boss care?"

"Gloria? Yes, maybe...I don't really know, but she seems a little more traditional. Plus, it's PR and not some hip tech start up."

"I guess. It seems silly at this point in time to worry about that kind of thing, but whatever."

That's another thing I like about Damon, he thinks the world should just follow some simple, obvious logic. But it doesn't.

The sun is setting now, and it's a doozy, the kind that looks pink and purple like a Bob Ross painting. Damon and I admire it for a minute before we make the split at the bottom of the stairs.

"Thanks for taking me there," I say. "You're like my Austin guardian angel, you know."

He rubs the back of his neck. "It's my pleasure. I like sharing Austin with someone new, it's like I get to experience the awesome things here for the first time again. Just wait 'til Barton Springs; it's a rite of passage," he says with a devilish grin.

"I can't wait," I say.

41

There's a text message on my phone when I check it back at the apartment. It's Nick. "I miss working with you," is all it says, followed by a sad puppy dog emoji. I can tell he's trying not to nag me about giving him a chance to say his piece, and I appreciate that. In fact, I haven't thought about it at all; I forbid myself to entertain the idea and whenever his face, his voice, his lips pop into my mind I think about work instead.

There just isn't any point because nothing he could possibly say will change the facts of the matter. I don't respond and turn my phone on silent. I lie on the couch watching *Wednesday* on Netflix, but can't silence the voice that nags at me, arguing that with everything Nick and I have been through maybe I owe it to both of us to hear what he has to say. If it's really true that nothing he can say will make a difference, then what's the harm in listening?

Is that me being reasonable, or is it just that I really miss him and want to see him one last time? Before I decide, my thumbs take on a life of their own and text him to come over and have his say but warn him not to expect any miracles. I must be losing it.

Not thirty minutes later, there's a knock at the door. I open it and my jaw drops.

In front of me is Nicolas Stone, wearing black eyeliner, a black silk shirt, and tight black jeans.

My first instinct is to pull him inside, throw him on the couch, rip off my top and press my chest against that soft silk, then cover his mouth with kisses. Who would have thought that a goth version of

Nick would be hot, but it so is, like a sexy gothic Superman. But physical attraction has never been the problem between us. Control yourself, Kat!

Instead, I fold my arms across my chest. "Okay, Nick, what did you want to say to me?" I ask, ignoring that he's obviously trying to make a grand gesture with his attire.

"Thanks for letting me come over. First, I'm so sorry about how I reacted when I saw you and your apartment."

"Thank you, I appreciate that."

"I just want to explain—"

"There's no need, really."

"But I want you to know. When I saw you here with Damon..."

"Damon and I are not together, FYI. He has a girlfriend."

Relief washes over Nick's face. I didn't want to confuse the issue, for him to think Damon is what is standing in the way of Nick and I having a relationship. This has nothing to do with Damon.

"Oh. I'm sorry. When I saw him that night, jealousy took over. It's not about you being goth, I don't care about that and I'm sorry it seemed like I was judging you."

"Bullshit. You were totally judging me," I snap.

"No, I was hurt. I thought I knew you and twice it turned out I didn't. It was embarrassing. And Damon seemed like a better match."

"Why, because he dresses more like me? I dress like you at work. I can't believe you're a psychologist and even you can't see beneath the surface."

"But I can. I see how amazing you are, smart, talented, intuitive. Please give me another chance. I came here like this," says Nick as he points at his eyeliner, "because I want you to know I'm not superficial. I don't care how I dress, or how you dress, or what anyone else thinks of it. I just want to be with you."

Frustration wells up inside me because I long to be with Nick too. It takes every ounce of my willpower not to give in, to put my arms around him and nuzzle his neck, to feel his warmth next to mine, to finish what we started on his couch that night.

"You just don't understand," I say quietly.

"Then help me understand, explain it to me. I'm listening."

"It has nothing to do with the goth thing, it has to do with Becca, with me, with my constant struggle with darkness. I can't deal with making you worry all the time, and you know you will."

He shakes his head. "You think you're protecting me? That's what this is all about? I'm a grown man. You can't decide for me what I can or can't handle. You can't decide for both of us that this will never work."

I put my hand on my hip. "I can and I have. I don't want to be your do-over. I'm taking care of myself just fine, and I don't need a savior. I have a therapist now, so you don't have to worry about me anymore."

"I'm not trying to save you, I swear. This isn't some kind of second chance for me. You're nothing like Becca. Every case is different; every person has different strengths, different weaknesses, different chemistry. I can see that you're doing great, you've figured things out for yourself. I just want to share that with you."

More than anything, I want to believe him, but I just can't. Not that I think he's lying to me, just that he's not being honest with himself about how hard this would be.

"I'm sorry Nick. I just can't. Even if you think you can handle it, *I* can't. The burden of never messing up, never faltering is too much. I make mistakes. Sometimes things get worse despite my best efforts. Sometimes it's hard to get up in the morning. I can't put you through that."

"You wouldn't be putting me through anything. That's just the thing we call life, Katie, and what we call love. You take care of people in their best and worst times. I'm sorry if that hasn't been your experience in the past, but if someone only loves you when you're at your peak then that isn't love."

Could it be true? Am I still traumatized by my college boyfriend rejecting me because he couldn't handle my bad days?

No. This is about me doing what's best for me and for Nick. There's just too much to overcome between us. He needs to find a nice stable girlfriend who wants kids, and that isn't me.

I feel like an ice queen as I say, "I'm sorry Nick. The answer is no. Please go now."

A crestfallen Nick gives me one last look and turns towards the door.

When he's gone, I cry for the third time since I moved to Texas, and the second time because of Nick. Is that what love is? Tears and pain? I think I'll pass. Maybe I'll become celibate. Or maybe just have no-strings-attached flings.

This time, the tears don't drown me. I don't know why. Maybe because I already mourned my loss of Nick when I had my multi-day cookie and pizza binge. Maybe because I know this is for the best and the sooner I put him out of my mind, the better. Mostly I just feel numb, like when you're poked and prodded so much that eventually you don't even feel the pain anymore.

This closure motivates me to do something I should have done before, find events in Austin where I can make new friends. Luckily, there's an easy way to do that and I check *The Austin Chronicle*, a local alternative newspaper that's distributed for free every Thursday. They have a calendar section that lists all the upcoming things to do. It doesn't take me long to hit on the perfect one, an outdoor singalong screening of *The Rocky Horror Picture Show*, and it must be the goddess shining on me because it's showing tomorrow night. This is exactly what I need to take my mind off Nick and focus on moving forward.

I saw *Rocky Horror* in the movie theater twice in New Jersey, once when I was a senior in high school, and once more in college. Both times I dressed as Magenta, which is the easiest costume, because it's basically just a maid. I think I have it here because I packed my entire closet from home, except for the cold weather clothes. I'm excited as I order my ticket and wonder what the audience will be like.

The venue is basically a well-manicured lawn with a large outdoor screen and speakers. There's a food truck with burgers and fries, but I already ate a light dinner. Maybe I'll see if they have any snacks to nosh on during the movie. First, I want to get my blanket set up and stake out my space before it's too crowded. Two informal rows have formed, so I sit in the middle of the third row. Most people are here with at least one other person, which makes me feel a little lonely, but that's the point, to get out and meet people.

The space begins to fill with the chatter of ticket holders, people ordering their food from the truck, and Meat Loaf's greatest hits wailing through the sound system. I get in line to order a strawberry lemonade from the truck. Thankfully at least half the people here are wearing costumes, so I'm not the odd one out. Those of us dressed as Magenta give each other a conspiratorial nod, and it's nice. I think that's why this show has endured since the 1970s, because it is an inclusive community that anyone can be a part of. All you have to do is like the movie and show up.

My drink is perfect for this warm night, and I can't wait for the movie to start. When I get back to my seat, I now have neighbors on both sides. I gulp when I see who is sitting to my right.

It's Paige and Luna.

42

"Katie?" says Paige, who is dressed like Eddie, complete with sleeveless black faux leather jacket, cream scarf, and torn blue jeans. I don't care what Damon thinks, Paige is pretty cool in my book. Now I remember that things between her and Damon might not be going that well, so I figure best not to mention his name first. Plus, the last time I saw Paige and Luna was at Juanita's, and that was a little awkward.

"Hi Paige, Luna. How crazy is this, sitting right next to each other?" I say.

Luna, who is dressed like Columbia, with a sparkly gold top hat and jacket and striped shorts, says, "We absolutely must stop running into each other like this." Then she gives a wide smile. Luna has a movie star quality I can't explain, but I like watching her.

"Good to see you again," says Paige. "I'm getting the food, back in a minute," and she darts over to join the food truck line.

I sit down on my little square of space, next to Luna, her long legs stretched out in front of her.

"I'm sorry if I was weird at the bar the other night. It was the first time I went out with my coworkers," I say.

"Ah, it all makes sense now," says Luna. "You don't like when your work world collides with your private world."

How did she know? It's not just her name that's mysterious, Luna really is a modern mystic of sorts. "Something like that."

She tilts her head up to look at the stars, and her jacket shimmers under the lamps. "I'm lucky, I don't have that conflict. I get to be Luna all the time." She looks back at me.

I'm not sure I believe her. Being Luna all the time looks like it could be exhausting. But I don't really know her, so who am I to say. My tendency to assume people who appear self-actualized are faking it probably comes from my own insecurities about who I am and where I'm going in life.

Paige comes back and soon the movie begins. They include me as part of their group and the three of us have a blast, singing and dancing, and shouting out at all the right bits. I was worried I'd forget what to do, but it all comes back to me effortlessly. It's funny because I've been overwhelmed trying to figure out who Kat, Katie, and Katherine all are, and tonight I'm having the most fun as Magenta.

After the movie ends, we mill around a bit, chatting about this and that. Paige seems like she's torn about saying something, but finally she comes out with it.

"Seen Damon much lately?" Paige asks with a forced casualness.

I panic. What am I supposed to say, yes, we had a nice time getting snow cones? When I hear that in my head it sounds like a date. Or how about how her boyfriend promised to take me swimming? This is all bad. It's true that I'm only friends with Damon and I barely know Paige, but I believe in the girl code, chicks before dicks.

"Just in passing, I've been pretty busy with work lately," I say, which is not the whole truth, but the truth would only hurt her.

She nods and doesn't say anything else about him.

Luna cuts in and says, "I'm having a party, very cazh, to celebrate my thirtieth birthday. You should come."

"You should," seconds Paige. "I'll be there, and some of the people you met at the art show."

That's really sweet of them to try and include me in their group, but I'm not sure if I fit in; I didn't at the art show. "Maybe, thanks for the invite," I say.

Luna isn't letting me get away with such a noncommittal response. "Give me your phone number," she demands.

I do, and she types it into her phone. A few seconds later I get a text from her with her address and the date of the party. "Now you have my contact info," she says. Luna is a gorgeous woman, and she gives off some flirty vibes. I don't want to give her the wrong impression, because I'm already juggling two romantic interests, and what I desperately need is real friends.

But I feel stupid and conceited, and maybe a little disappointed when she adds, "Feel free to bring a plus one, if you like."

I wonder if Paige will bring Damon. Thinking about bringing Nick to a party like this makes me feel weird, which only reinforces my decision. I miss him so much it feels like I swallowed shards of glass, but on the other hand, maybe we live in two different worlds. Or to be more accurate, I live in two worlds, and Nick only exists in one of them.

Both women hug me goodbye and tell me they hope to see me at the party. Driving home, I reflect on what a weird and wonderful night it turned out to be. I just need to stay busy and active and focus on work and building my social life, sans men, and everything will be fine.

Sometimes the universe provides the perfect distraction just when we need it. Gloria is sending Roxy and me for a day trip out of town to meet with an artist who does large-scale temporary installations that comment on modern life.

Gloria said that after her embarrassing comment about Luna and the crow feathers, she had to admit to herself it was time to let her younger proteges shine, particularly on this new project. Gloria wasn't sure if she could pretend to understand the art this guy produces.

Roxy insisted on driving, and I'm enjoying hearing the soundtrack of her life. She's giving me a welcome history lesson on women in punk, the riot grrrl scene, Bikini Kill, Bratmobile, followed by a history of Texas punk, the Butthole Surfers to Pleasure Venom. It just doesn't call to me like goth music, but I appreciate it all the same. Even though I'm frequently angry, I'm more comfortable with melancholy than fury. But it's nice to hear Roxy be so animated about something she's passionate about.

In between her explanations, we talk about this and that; it's the first time we've had a long period to connect outside the office. We have more in common than I thought and she's pretty easy to talk with now that she isn't gunning to get me fired.

"I guess we're Gloria's new go-to duo for anything remotely alternative," I say.

Roxy rolls her eyes. "At least Gloria knows what she doesn't know."

"That's true."

"Someday that's going to be us," says Roxy.

I never thought of that, but now it seems so obvious. "Oh geez, you're right. I'm only twenty-seven and I already don't know what college kids like Ben are talking about."

"Hmph. I never did, even when I was in college, so maybe it won't be such a change for me."

"Maybe we'll keep up only with the pieces that matter to us," I say.

"I doubt it."

"Why?"

"Take punk music, for example," says Roxy. "There's already fifty years of punk for me to listen to. Will I always be looking for the next best punk band? I doubt it."

Hmmm. I think about my goth playlist and she's right. It's a lot from the eighties and nineties, much of it before I was even born, then less from the two-thousands, and even less from the past ten years. It's like the past sorts out the gems from the rabble and only the shiniest survive. But music in the present hasn't stood the trials of time, and there's a lot to wade through to find something that can compete with an old favorite.

"You might be right. Check with me in twenty years," I say, and she snickers.

We arrive at a small farm in the Texas Hill Country, two hours outside Austin. We know we're at the right place because the front field contains old rusty farm equipment that has been welded and piled up to form a larger than life-sized death figure, complete with a rusty old scythe. It actually gives me chills framed against the clear blue Texas sky.

A man walks across the grass to meet us. He's wearing heavy work boots, dark blue jeans, a long-sleeved shirt, and a tan welding apron. He looks to be around fiftyish judging by the gray tendrils framing his face, contrasting with the dark brown of his unruly chin-length curly hair. This man is a mystery, and he knows it.

"Ladies," he says, "welcome to my studio. I am Zulimar."

43

We introduce ourselves and shake hands with the artist known only as Zulimar. Roxy gestures towards the sculpture in the field. "The death figure is quite a surprise after miles of country roads lined with bluebonnets," she says.

"Ah well, there is always death among life, in the city or the countryside. But that sculpture represents the loss of traditional farming methods."

I can't say I know very much about farming, but having the context makes me appreciate the piece more.

"So, Zulimar, how long have you been making art?" I ask.

"Since I was a baby. Everyone makes art instinctively as a child before we're told it is only for the chosen few. But professionally—only four years. I used to be the Chief Financial Officer for a large distribution company."

"Wow, that's a drastic change," I say.

"It was. I sold everything, the Lexus, the McMansion, all of it, and bought this old farm. The barn is perfect for welding and piecing together what's in my mind's eye. I wasn't alive until I came here."

Roxy looks dreamy. "You're making me fantasize about quitting my job," she jokes.

Zulimar gives us a sad smile. "Don't wait two decades to decide you're not kidding," he says. "Life is shorter than you realize."

He offers us a tour of the barn where he does most of his assembly. The space is cavernous, and the back section is cluttered with objects just waiting to complete their transformation from junk to art. Rusted farm equipment, lumber, scrap metal, spray paint, and various tools for which I can only begin to guess their uses.

In the center is a structure made of old fence wire, with thousands of single use plastic coffee pod cups strung like rain chains, with a single cowbell at the bottom of each strand.

"I don't have to ask what this one is about," says Roxy, and I know we are cringing because Gloria buys those pods for the breakroom at Purple Cactus. I vow to never use them again.

"Subtlety is not always best," Zulimar says, "especially when we're running out of time."

"You're right. We see that in marketing and PR too. Be too precious about something and people miss the point all together," I say.

Zulimar leads us over to a workbench where he has a series of sketches laid out.

"This is my baby, my grand vision. Once this appeared in my head, I knew I had to make it happen. But I need help. It won't have any impact if it's installed on my property and people only get to see it in photos. I need a partner; someone who will let me install it where students and commuters and children can see it."

I can tell Roxy is enchanted with the idea. She probably can look at the sketches and see it as Zulimar does. I can see the potential but not a detailed picture of the finished project.

"We know Gloria told you that this is a little different from what we normally do, but I think the principles are the same. We need people to know about you and understand your vision, and then the right partner will come along," I say.

"This installation means everything to me. I could die happy knowing this was in the world's consciousness."

Roxy seems entranced by this man. "This *needs* to be seen," she says as she pours over the sketches.

I'm not quite as moved by the project as Roxy, but it is an exciting challenge and is clearly important to our client. "We will do our best to make your dream come true," I say.

Zulimar's eyes are shimmering. "Thank you, that is all I can ask."

Back in the car, Roxy seems thoughtful and doesn't immediately blast the stereo again. "Zulimar really has it figured out, doesn't he?" she says.

"I don't know. It's all well and good to move out to the country after a long career making loads of cash. He's probably got retirement funds and everything."

Roxy sighs in frustration. "It's not about money, Katie. It's about purpose. Is your purpose to help divas make up for saying dumb shit?"

I wish I could explain the meaning and engagement part of Nick's book better. How can I make her understand that I get so much satisfaction out of the effort I put into each project at Purple Cactus, even for the mouthy diva or the perfume heiress?

Instead, I just say, "I think purpose is wherever you find it."

Roxy rolls her eyes. "You've been hanging out with Mr. Positive too much."

My expression must have changed because she follows up with, "Oh shit, sorry. Did you two break up?"

"I told you we were never together—now please fucking drop it!"

Roxy grimaces. "Sorry. I won't mention him again."

I don't want to backtrack on the progress Roxy and I have made just because she hit a sore spot. "It's alright. It's just complicated."

"If someone looked at me the way he looks at you, there would be nothing complicated about it," she says.

I don't reply.

The weather is a little cooler today and I come home to a familiar scene, Damon hanging off the edge of his balcony, Dream Theater piercing the air. He leans over.

"Hey Katie! Can you come up after your workout?"

"Sure. See you later." I wonder what this is about. If he gets me hooked on one more Austin dessert I might explode.

It's cycling day and I crank up the resistance and put on my most driving goth playlist and think about how next time Roxy and I travel together she's going to listen to my thoughts on goth music. I can't say I have a whole history lesson prepared like she does, I just like what I like and don't worry about subgenres or purity. Like I don't care if Concrete Blonde is not goth, the *Bloodletting* album is in my top ten list.

After dinner, I head upstairs. Damon gestures me in.

"How's it going?" he asks, but not like in a casual way, but like he's really asking. It's strange.

"Fine—good. Normal, I guess?"

"Okay, good," he says. "It's just that I happened to see Nick leaving the other night and I wanted to make sure you're okay."

"Oh that. Yes. He apologized for what happened last time. He thought you and I were together."

Damon's eyes narrow. "And that was an excuse for him to act like a dick?"

"No, that's why he apologized. And he even made a nice gesture by trying to look goth, even wore some eyeliner. It was kind of funny now that I think about it."

"So, you forgave him?"

"Yes."

"And you're back together?"

"No! We were never really together in the first place, and I told him it just wouldn't work out."

Damon looks relieved. "I'm glad to hear that."

"No offense, but why do you care so much? I mean it's nice if you're just worried about a friend, but..."

Damon rubs the back of his neck, which by now I recognize means he's nervous.

"Wait, you're still with Paige, right?" I say.

"Um...no—we broke up."

"Oh, I'm sorry. When did that happen?"

"Last night," he says. "But it kind of fizzled out before that."

"I kind of wondered when you said you both had been too busy."

"Yeah, you probably know I've just been hanging on my porch most nights," he says.

"I may have noticed."

Damon sucks in a deep breath. "The thing is, when I saw Nick, I got pissed. He doesn't deserve someone like you. But then I thought, well do I deserve someone like her? And does Paige deserve someone who has feelings for someone else?"

My heart sinks. Is Damon trying to profess his love for me now? I don't know how I feel about him, and frankly my heart is too broken over Nicolas Stone to think it through right now. I just want some time without any romantic intrigues.

I can't deny that the kiss Damon and I shared was molten because it was. And Damon is showing real emotional maturity by considering Paige in all of this, which shows he is a pretty decent guy. But right now, I wish we could just be friends and he could show me around his favorite places in Austin.

"I hope you didn't break up with her because of me..."

Damon looks away, which answers my question. I didn't ask him to do that, but I feel guilty just the same.

"You're an awesome guy, Damon, and I have fun when I'm with you. But...I just can't right now, maybe someday, I don't know. I need to take a break from men until I find my place here. I'm sorry."

He flops on the couch and throws his hands in the air. "Strike two. When will I learn with you?" he says.

I repeat, "I'm sorry," and leave him there alone. This time I'm not sure we'll continue on as friends, and it sucks.

44

Roxy and I are in the conference room discussing our latest client when I remember something. "I was thinking last night, when Zulimar said, 'I could die happy,' do you think he meant something else?"

She looks at me over the top of her laptop. "Like that he has a terminal illness? 'Life is shorter than you realize,' is what tipped me off."

It's terrible if we're right, but I'm also glad that Roxy saw it too and it wasn't my penchant for the dark side imagining things that weren't really there.

"If it's true, we have to work fast and make this happen for him," I say.

"You're right. We don't know the timeline here, so let's assume worst-case scenario—it's imminent. No pressure."

"Sure, it's only a dying man's last wish; no pressure at all..."

Roxy and I brainstorm about who would own the type of space Zulimar needs for an installation this size. Perhaps it could be in a park through a city or public agency, but the red tape needed to get something like this approved could be longer than Zulimar has. We'd have a better chance with a private entity.

"I'm imagining a large building complex with a covered plaza with columns and wide steps leading up to it. That way it could be sheltered from the weather but still visible from the street," says Roxy.

"Hmmm. I like that idea. Probably does need to be rainproof. But how can we find something like that without spending infinite hours in Google Streetview?"

Roxy frowns. "I don't know yet."

"The other option is to try and find companies who have a corporate message in line with Zulimar's and then look at their buildings to see if any of them are the right fit."

"Great idea," says Roxy. "Let's split up, you start on the company end and I'll see if any of my architect friends have leads on potential sites based on our description."

My phone buzzes and I flip it over. "Shit—it's my dad. He never calls so I better take this."

Roxy takes her laptop back to her cubicle, giving me some privacy.

"Dad? Is everything alright?" I stare out the window at the cars whizzing by on the highway.

"Katherine. Yes, I mean, no. Your mom and I are fine. But your Aunt Cassie was in a car crash."

"Oh my god, is she okay?"

"I'm afraid not."

"You mean she's...dead?"

"She was already gone when the ambulance arrived on the scene. There was nothing they could do."

I'm speechless. I wasn't that close with my Aunt Cassie because she and my mom didn't get along that well, but I liked her. She never chided me about being goth, even told me I looked beautiful in my goth outfits once or twice. Cassie accepted people for who they are. I can't believe my cousin's wedding was the last time I saw her and now I'll never see her again. It doesn't seem real.

"Katherine, are you there?"

"Yes, I'm here."

"I know it's difficult news to hear over the phone. The funeral will be in three days since the rest of the family still lives here; they didn't need much time to travel."

Dad doesn't need to remind me I'm the only one who moved away. All my cousins stayed in New Jersey or moved to New York. They are all still a giant extended family who meet up on the big holidays. I'm the outsider, the one who left, although that only cemented the status I had already been assigned since I was a teenager who didn't join my cousins on ski trips and sat alone in the corner at family gatherings.

"Oh."

"I'll buy you a plane ticket. Your mom needs you."

"Of course. I'll be there."

"Good girl. We miss you."

"Miss you too, dad."

I don't know how to feel right now. I'm in shock over losing Cassie. She was so young.

And I have mixed feelings about going home. I didn't want to go back so soon after leaving. I wanted to be settled in Austin, to feel like my life is here before I returned to a place with so many memories and so much struggle. It's also weird because things with my mom have been tense since she disapproved of my move and generally all my life choices.

But then I feel like an ungrateful piece of shit. My mom just lost her sister, so the least I can do is play the dutiful daughter and support her. Aunt Cassie was widowed, so I'm sure my mom is helping her two sons with the arrangements. It's a lot to handle when you're grieving.

I knock on Gloria's office door and tell her what happened and that I need some time off. I tell her that I will take my laptop and get some work done in between family responsibilities, but she looks at me like I'm crazy. "Don't you dare," she says. "Family comes first. You go and be present with your family. Roxy and I will handle things here."

For some reason, it's Gloria's empathy that makes the first tear fall from my eye. By the time I get near my cubicle, several more tears have fallen, and Roxy jumps up when I pass.

"Oh no, what happened?" says Roxy.

"My aunt died," I say.

"I'm so sorry," she says, and gives me a big hug. After she releases me, she makes a dramatic gesture over wiping my tears off her jacket.

"Sorry about that," I say.

"No worries, you still owe me for that skirt you spilled tea on; I'll add this to the bill."

That makes me chuckle through the tears and I'm grateful that Roxy and I made amends. Only she could lighten the mood with her dry ribbing.

I head home to pack and wait for the plane ticket to arrive in my inbox. At least I have plenty of clothing choices for the funeral, ha ha ha. In fact, for three days no one will even comment on or question my wardrobe. Ironic. For good measure I throw in one of my brighter office outfits; it might cheer my mom up to see the Katie side of me, might make her believe I'm okay on my own.

The ticket is for an early morning flight from Austin to Newark. I'm going to have to wake up well before dawn to find parking and get through airport security tomorrow. Sleep always eludes me when I worry about oversleeping and missing a flight.

Despite Gloria's advice to be present, I take my laptop. Not so much for work, but because I might need it as an escape; if I can't sleep at night, I can stream my favorite shows.

Before I turn out the light, I think of what I'll be leaving behind here. Damon with last night's bomb drop; I didn't really give him a finite response other than that I refused to respond right away, and it feels like a cloud hanging over my head from the apartment above me. Along with Damon is Amy's Ice Cream and Casey's snowballs, Mount Bonnell, and tacos. My hometown in New Jersey does not have good tacos. Not that I knew this before I moved to Texas. I just thought tacos in general were not that good.

Leaving behind Nicolas Stone, who is no longer anything to me, even though I know exactly where he is right now on his book tour. I can't stop myself from following his journey. I tell myself that it's just because he was my first client at Purple Cactus, so I'm invested in his success, but that's a ridiculous lie. Maybe you can care about someone, want them to thrive and be successful, even love them, but still not want to be with them. That seems ridiculous in its own way.

Leaving behind my canine friends at the shelter, my poor little baying Pixie and all the others. My new apartment, that finally feels like me. I hope roaches don't move in while I'm gone because I can't go through that again.

After checking my alarm app twice, I stream the original *Dark Shadows* series, starting when Barnabas Collins is introduced, because that's really when the show gets good. The eerie theme is like a lullaby to my ears, and my eyes feel heavy. As I grow drowsy, I start to wonder, who will I be in New Jersey? Kat, my oldest friend, Katie, my kick-ass business persona, or the well-behaved Katherine my parents long for me to be?

45

For the sake of comfort during my flight, I wear black yoga pants, a long-sleeved black pullover, and black boots. Then I pull out my single favorite piece from the red velvet jewelry box, an onyx crystal, set in pewter, which someone once told me is protective and wards off negativity. Not that I believe in the power of crystals, but they're pretty and what can it hurt? I need all the help I can get.

I defaulted to Kat this morning, fashion-wise, because black clothes make me feel empowered. When the airport security guard looks at me at the checkpoint, I feel like my attire is armor, saying "go ahead and make my day." I don't get picked for a search, which is an auspicious start to the journey.

This look also discourages people from talking to me, which is great. I hate chatting on planes, trying to make myself heard over the roar of the engines.

My seatmate is a woman, maybe fortyish, wearing a burnt orange t-shirt that reads, "Longhorns," which I learned within two seconds of moving to Austin is the local state university's football team. They're a big deal in Austin.

She doesn't get the message from my wardrobe.

"My son plays on the team," she says, tugging on the sleeve of her t-shirt. "He's a running back and he's only a sophomore. Full scholarship."

"Oh, that's cool," I say, trying to be polite since she's obviously very proud, even though I don't follow much college football or any sports, really, and I don't know if that is an impressive achievement or not.

I'm betting she tells this to every person she meets. Nothing wrong with being a proud parent, I'm just not in the mood to talk.

"Where you headed, honey?" she asks me. "You look ready for a funeral."

"Do I? Good," I say, and slip on my noise cancelling headphones to block her and the other passengers' meaningless conversations out by playing Switchblade Symphony's *Serpentine Gallery,* topping it with a black eye mask to complete my defenses.

I can't sleep on planes because I worry that I'll be out when the plane crashes and won't have time to figure out how to get my life-jacket on, even though no one pays more attention to the instructional video than me. I just pretend to sleep so I don't have to deal with the flight attendant asking me if I want a drink, which I don't.

At the airport I text my dad to let him know which terminal I arrived at, because he waits in the cellphone lot instead of circling. After fifteen minutes I finally see his silver Chevy Malibu. He's always considered it his civic duty to buy an American car, even though my mom's all about her Toyota Corolla. He's a little old fashioned in that respect.

He gets out of the car and gives me a hug. "Good to have you home, Katherine," he says as he throws my suitcase in the trunk. "What do you have in here, bricks?" he says.

I don't pack heavy at all, but he still always makes that joke, like he's in a sitcom where the character would look at the camera and shrug, "Women, right?" and the laugh track would kick in.

On the way to my childhood home, my dad turns on the classic rock station. It's funny to me because my parents went to high school in the late eighties/early nineties, but they didn't like any new wave stuff; my dad is the hipper one because he liked Pearl Jam and R.E.M., but my mom listened to Amy Grant and Wilson Phillips. Not that I have anything against those musicians, just that it's a shame I love some of the music from their youth only to find they hated it back then and still do now.

My dad isn't much of a talker, so I'm not that surprised that he doesn't ask how things are going in Austin. I know my mom fills him in on everything I tell her, and he mostly cares that I'm financially secure. Hopefully, she relayed that my job is going great.

Before we get to the house, he slows down.

"Your mom's not handling Cassie's death very well. Be patient with her," he says.

"I will."

My dad's warning didn't prepare me enough, not for my mom's pallid skin and red eyes. She looks years older than when I moved away just months ago. I don't say anything, but instead, put my arms around her.

She whispers in my ear, "I'm glad you're home, Katherine."

I realize now that my leaving was hard on my parents, when their only child purposely moved seventeen hundred miles away, they must have felt abandoned, wondering what they did wrong that made me view my hometown like a prison I had to escape.

It really wasn't like that. The darkness is what I was running from, that and the idea that I needed them. I didn't want to need them, thought it was a sign of weakness and mental illness. But in this moment, I see how wrong that was. Right now, my mom needs me, and it's not weak, it's just the biggest perk of having family, having someone to lean on, unconditionally.

When my mom releases me, I say, "How about I make us some tea?" She loves a fine herbal tea, just like I do.

"That would be nice," she says, and I head to the kitchen. My dad gives me a little half-smile, letting me know he appreciates me, but he doesn't follow us in, so my mom and I can bond in private.

I bring two oversized glass mugs of tea to the table, mine with jasmine, and hers with peach. I wait for her to speak first, because I'm not sure if she wants to talk about Aunt Cassie, but it feels weird to make small talk.

Finally, she says, "Alan and Mark are crushed."

Alan and Mark are Cassie's grown children; of course they're devastated that their mother was killed so suddenly.

She continues, "With their dad gone, all the arrangements fell to the boys. I'm helping as much as I can."

"Let me help, too. You know I'm great at organizing," I say, glad to have a concrete way to show that I do care about this family.

"Thank you. I have a list." She pulls a legal pad from the counter and hands it to me.

Maybe funerals were invented to give the deceased's loved ones something to focus on, to structure their days during this difficult time. The list is surprisingly long, from selecting the flowers and thank you cards, to choosing readings. There's a wake the day before the funeral mass. Then she will be cremated as per her wishes, and her sons will have a private ceremony at the family mausoleum.

An obituary in the local paper with a notice for the wake, food for the funeral reception, gathering photos for display. It's too much like the preparations for a wedding. Why is there even a thank you card? What kind of sadistic person came up with this etiquette that burdens the survivors? But again, I wonder if it's a blessing to keep them busy.

Alan and Mark are coordinating with the church since it is their family parish. My parents aren't particularly religious, really the only ones in the family who aren't. They're not dramatic about it; they simply don't attend church.

I decide to tackle the wake first, so I call the funeral home to check that someone will be there this afternoon. Then I call Alan and let him know I'm here and what tasks I'm taking on. He is grateful for the assistance and sounds completely overwhelmed.

My mom looks a smidge brighter since I've arrived to share some of the weight. She even noshes on some cookies, which is a good sign.

"Are you still glad you moved away?" she asks.

This feels like a loaded question given the circumstances, and I try to gauge if she is asking innocently like am I happy in Austin, or if she's asking like am I still happy to be so far from family now that I have immediate evidence that they won't be around forever?

I don't want to hurt her feelings by saying yes, even though I like the life I am slowly building there, even with the two romantic mishaps.

"It's been interesting, so far; only time will tell," I say, purposely not answering the question. "My job is still going really well."

"That's great, honey. I'm proud of you," she says.

That almost brings a tear to my eye because she doesn't value career much, never understood why I was so ambitious, and it is rare for her to say such things. I'm sure it has everything to do with Cassie. These little squabbles over moving and jobs seem so insignificant now.

46

After taking care of the remaining details for the wake, I can't resist visiting my old haunts. Even though I haven't been gone long, everything feels different, like I don't know this town and it doesn't know me. I drive past my old high school and shudder; that's when the darkness started, not that it's the school's fault. Looking back, I did pretty well, considering. I had a couple of decent friends, wrote for the school newspaper, got good enough grades to go to college. Other than my goth façade, people might not have guessed the torment I was enduring inside my mind.

I pass the town graveyard where we used to hang out on Friday and Saturday nights, and I pull over the car and walk up, memories flooding my mind. Now, especially given Cassie's death, it seems disrespectful, teenagers ignoring the sanctity of a sacred space, but at the time it seemed the only place that felt private and welcoming, that was ours. Such is the fate of suburban youth, I suppose.

This is an old cemetery, hundreds of years since the most recent burial, the kind with fancy tombstones with carvings of skulls with wings, angels, and doves, and the old poems that warned the living not to take life for granted.

From the top of the hill, sheltered by the trees and shadows, we could see Main Street laid out beneath us, a town meant for adults. This was our space. We never hurt anything, we just talked until midnight and occasionally drank small amounts of alcohol someone had stolen from their parents.

Standing in the quiet stillness, I can hear my friend's voices talking about the future, about leaving this town, about getting out of here and never returning.

It might seem weird that this place is a treasured memory, but I felt safe here; maybe it was the sense that I was just a tiny sliver of history, and my pain and sorrow would mean nothing over time. Or maybe I was just a teenager, trying to find her way in a complicated world. I walk back down the hill, realizing this might be the last time I ever come here, so I leave my thanks and say goodbye.

As long as I'm home I may as well eat at my favorite pizza place. They might not have good tacos here, but the pizza is fucking amazing. Yes, so good that it requires a swear to describe. The crust is doughy on the inside and crispy on the outside, just the right amount of sauce and cheese, and cooked to perfection, which for me is when the cheese bubbles up but it's not too browned. It's bliss in a triangle.

When I get back home, my parents are watching television. They are still making their way through *Better Call Saul*. They were late adopters to streaming, and now they're catching up on several years of shows, one channel at a time.

I tell my mom I checked a bunch of things off the list, and she looks more relaxed than she did this afternoon.

"Did you eat anything?" she says.

"Yes, Fiore's."

"We figured," she said, and she and my dad share a smile because they know that's the thing I miss the most about this town, my favorite pizza place.

"If you don't need anything else from me, I'm exhausted from waking up so early," I say.

"Of course, your bed's all ready. Sleep tight," she says.

I'm not really that tired, I just don't want to watch tv right now. A reminder pops up on my phone; Luna's party was tonight. Would I have gone? I can't even say right now with everything that's happened since then. I wonder how Paige feels about me now that Damon broke up with her. I hope she doesn't blame me. Maybe she is as casual as he is about it since they weren't together long. Nothing I can do about it, anyway.

Despite Gloria's insistence that I focus on my family, I pull out my laptop and log into my work e-mail. I just want to see if anything interesting happened. I'm definitely not hoping for a reason that I would have to work with Nicolas Stone again.

Aaaaah—who am I kidding? I miss him so much. There is a Nick-shaped hole in my heart and there's no point in denying it. Even if we can't work together as a couple that doesn't change the feelings I have for him. Against my better judgement I Google him and look at each and every book tour event, newspaper article, social media mention, you name it. Every photo where his face is shining as he talks about his life's passion makes my entire body ache with sadness. Must be what they call lovesickness because it feels like the flu.

I read reviews of his book in small town papers and on bookstore sites, and they are generally favorable. That cheers me a bit because I want Nick to be happy and fulfilled, and this book is helping him meet his lifelong goal to help people. I'm grateful that I could play a small part of that.

There's nothing about him or the book campaign in my work e-mail but I knew there wouldn't be. There is an update from Roxy, who says she is hitting a bunch of dead ends on finding a space for Zulimar. She reached out to her architect friends in a few different cities, hoping they would have a suggestion, but no luck.

That worries me. Faced with the shock of Cassie's unexpectedly short life, I feel even more pressure to help Zulimar find his peace with the world through his final art installation. I start searching the internet for companies that are pioneering environmentally sustainable technology or goods, then check Streetview to see what their main headquarters look like. It's painstaking work, and by midnight, I really am tired and have come up empty. I play Gary Numan's "Absolution" through my headphones and close my eyes.

My dad makes me blueberry pancakes for breakfast. My brain nags me that I can't completely disregard my healthy eating and exercise, so I vow to find some time to take a walk.

Mom gets up later, but she doesn't look like she slept at all. No wonder because the wake is later today. After breakfast I call Alan to see how he's holding up and if he needs anything, but he doesn't, so I will see him at the funeral home.

"Anything I can help with?" I say to my mom, who looks like she's walking in a stupor.

"I don't think so, thanks honey," she says.

"If you want to talk, or anything..."

She just gives me a sad nod and goes to the kitchen to make some tea.

Since it seems she needs some time alone to start her day, I sit out on the back patio and enjoy the cool weather. Cool compared to Texas, I realize. People here think this is practically a heat wave. That makes me snicker to myself. I think of my tiny porch with my wind-chimes and mint plant, and I miss it. And I love that I miss it because it means Austin is truly becoming my home.

I go for a brisk walk around the neighborhood, which keeps my drill sergeant from reporting me to the higher ups. It really is pretty around here, and now I notice the landscaping, comparing it to Texas. The trees are taller, the grass is lusher, like a carpet, even without regular irrigation. Whereas in Austin they use drought resistant plants, here there is an abundance of fuchsia, azaleas, rhododendrons, and showy white flowering dogwoods.

It's funny how moving away makes you notice things you took for granted when you lived in a place. I walk back to the house with a new appreciation for the beauty I grew up surrounded by.

At quarter past three, we pile into the Chevy in our black mourning outfits and drive to the funeral home for the wake. The staff shows us to the room set up to honor Aunt Cassie. I greet Alan and Mark, give them hugs and condolences. Then I walk around the room, examining each photo of Cassie, as a gorgeous bride, at the birth of the twins, with her giant German Shepherd named Millie. I nearly gasp at the next photo.

It's mom and Cassie, in fancy sequined dresses, two stunning, elegant women ready to conquer the world. My mom comes up behind me, tears welling in her eyes. "That was Cassie's senior prom, and my junior prom. We double dated. Wasn't Cassie beautiful?"

"She was stunning," I say. "And so were you."

Before she can say anything else, Cassie's father-in-law appears and offers his condolences, which my mom accepts graciously, as do I. I feel guilty that I didn't know Cassie better. It's not like my mom forbade me from seeing her, I just didn't take the initiative since the two of them were so frosty.

Alan and Mark tell some great stories about Cassie as a mom, how she caught them playing hooky from school on a sunny day, but instead of grounding them, she took them to an amusement park to ride the roller coaster. Her best friend talked about the time she and Cassie went over the border to Canada and ate fresh maple syrup in the snow. Her neighbor said Cassie always helped with her spring garden, on account of her back not allowing her to stoop over for very long.

Aunt Cassie was well loved and will be missed by many people, including me. Three hours was not enough time for people who knew her to share how wonderful she was and how many lives she touched.

Some guests are meeting up at a restaurant where we reserved a side room, but mom says she's tired and wants to go home. Dad looks worried and puts his arm around her as they walk to his car.

She's silent the whole way home, we all are. Once we're inside, I instinctively put on water for tea, and my mom sits down at the table.

"We were best friends back then," she says sadly.

"I know you were. Maybe this isn't the right time to talk about it, or maybe it is, but what happened?"

"I ruined everything," she says, and rests her head in her hands.

47

"Cassie was brave, much stronger than me," my mom continues. "We had big plans, to see the world, to find ourselves and have a grand adventure. She wanted to join the Peace Corps, but that was way outside of my comfort zone. Then she wanted to teach English abroad, in Japan or South Korea. That sounded like enough excitement for me, safer and more predictable."

I can't picture my mom living in South Korea; she's barely left New Jersey. "That's why you studied English in college?"

"Yes, and afterwards I got my TEFL certification, and so did Cassie. We were all set to start our next chapter."

"But you never went?"

"No. We started applying for teaching positions, but then Cassie met Will. Suddenly she didn't want to go anymore. I was so angry that she would give up on our dreams for a guy she'd only been dating a few months."

"She was in love…"

"I know that now, but I hadn't been in love before, not like the kind Cassie had with Will, so I didn't understand. I thought she was being a stupid romantic, not a modern, independent woman like me."

"And you didn't want to go without her?" I said.

"I couldn't. I was only brave with her; it was all her idea in the first place!"

I want to side with my mom here, but how could she blame Cassie for falling in love? "But she couldn't have known that would happen."

"Of course not, I know that now. But at twenty-two I was self-righteous."

"So, you never forgave her?"

"I forgave her! You think your mother is a monster?"

"Of course not. So why were you never close?"

"Cassie and Will, they were all fireworks. Not that Will was a bad guy, just that he was a little wild, irresponsible. After just four months of dating, they left to go backpacking across Eastern Europe, then Thailand. She would send me postcards. I still have them, even one from South Korea."

"Oh gosh, so Cassie did travel the world."

"That's right. She just left me behind in New Jersey."

"That must have hurt after all the years you two had spent planning."

"It did. But when she came back after a year of traveling, she told me something I will never forget."

I was intrigued. "What?"

"She said that when she saw herself reflected in Will's eyes, she was the person she always wanted to be."

I consider this. There's so much emphasis on having common interests or backgrounds, but this makes sense. Maybe real love is when two people bring out the best in each other, help each other become who they are meant to be.

"Wow...that's beautiful," I say. "But that still doesn't explain why you fell out."

"It's complicated. First, let me state without a doubt, that I love your father with all my heart, and having you was my greatest joy, and I don't regret any of my life's decisions."

"Okay..."

"That said, after they came back, Cassie settled into a job teaching ESL. I liked having her back. But Will—he was restless, and after a while he took off again, said he needed to be free. Cassie was heartbroken. I was here to pick up the pieces. Towards the end of the year, we decided to pursue our original dream of teaching abroad. I was excited to get this second chance."

"Oh no," I mumble, knowing this was ill fated.

"Yep. We were all set to go again, assigned to schools and everything, when who do you think shows up?"

I shake my head and say, "Will."

"Nope—your father. This time, *I* fall head over heels and tell Cassie that I can't go. She was livid."

"How could she be when she did the same thing!"

"She said me and your dad were nothing like her and Will. I told her that's right, because your dad would never run out on me like Will did."

"Oh no!" I smack my palm on my forehead. "Don't you know the rule about never bashing someone's ex in case they get back together?"

"I didn't then. I was young and stupid. We never went to teach abroad, I married your father and had you, and yes, my life wasn't filled with adventures like Cassie's, but I've been happy. Will came back and they had the twins, and Cassie continued to have adventures with Will and the kids until he died."

"And you two never made up, even after Will's death?" I attended his funeral two years ago, but at the time I didn't think much about mom and my aunt because Cassie was surrounded by her boys and Will's parents most of the time.

"We had started to—we were making progress, but we ran out of time. Three months ago we met for coffee and I asked how she was doing. She said she had no regrets, that she wouldn't trade her time with Will for anything, even knowing how short it all was. She said without him, she didn't know who she was anymore."

"Because she could no longer see herself reflected in Will's eyes..."

"That's right."

The funeral is a more somber occasion than the wake, with the priest performing his duties with an air of gravity, and the loss of Aunt Cassie finally feels real to all the family assembled here. I see now why all these rituals are important, how they help move us through the stages of grief, finally leading to the soft pillow of acceptance.

I know it will still hurt for a long time to come, and my mom might regret not having fully reconciled with her sister until the day she dies, but she seems a little better than when I first arrived, and I know dad will be there for her.

I promise my mom I will visit again soon, and I mean it. Aunt Cassie gave us a special gift, forcing us to spend this time together and I think our relationship will be different moving forward.

My dad drives me to the airport. He's quiet the whole way, listening to his classic rock station. When he drops me at the gate he simply says, "Thanks for being here for your mother. Have a safe flight home, Katherine."

Staring out the window, the clouds below me as we cruise at thirty-six thousand feet, I feel strange, that I'm leaving what used to be my home, traveling to a place that's becoming my new home. I feel strange about my new relationship with my family, and about mourning an aunt I barely knew, which is a different kind of loss.

I think about what Aunt Cassie said about Will. I think about what my old therapist used to say, that I was the only one who saw me as dark and damaged. Maybe that's true for all three of us, whether I'm Katherine, Kat, or Katie. I'm still not convinced that the darkness doesn't seep through no matter what I'm wearing, but now I'm also not sure that in this new age people assume that a goth person is necessarily gloomy. There will always be some fraction of people who make snap judgements based on appearance, or a first impression, like Gloria did with Paige and Luna, but I'm taking the positive side and saying that might no longer be the norm.

Catching myself looking on the bright side makes me think of Nick. He's a psychologist, and he didn't know I suffer from depression until he accidentally found my meds. Doesn't that mean something? Was it only because of the clothes that professional Katie wears? He saw me in my gym gear, and we spent enough time together that I think he saw the real me, yet he didn't know. Maybe I'm much more than just my darkness.

Damon saw my Kat persona from day one, but I also shielded him from seeing me on my dark days; I showed Damon only the light side of me, even in goth clothing. He didn't even realize I was in a bad place that day he came to ask for the concert ticket, which now annoys me since he broke up with Paige anyway.

I know that I am under no obligation to attempt a relationship with either Damon or Nick, but I can't decide if pushing them both away is to prevent future heartbreak, or the sensible decision of a woman who is trying to establish herself in a new city. The thing is, I want to be someone who can fall in love. Maybe I'm strong enough to handle it now, even if things fall apart. Don't I deserve that chance?

As the plane descends into the Austin airport, I make up my mind. I know what I need to do.

48

⚬≫≪⚬

I drop my suitcase in my living room and look around with satisfaction. I can't believe this is my home, that I really did it, really moved here to Texas. Now that I'm back it feels more like my home, not just because all of my things are here, but because all my favorite people and places are here now.

I give the mint, Heartleaf Skullcap, and periwinkle a drink of water and marvel again at my cute patio space. That's my patio. This is my bathroom. I wash my face, brush my hair in the mirror, change my clothes, and run up the stairs to Damon's apartment.

The second the door swings open I ask, "What do you see when you look at me?"

He squints like he can't see clearly.

"Katie—you're back! Where have you been, I was worried."

"It doesn't matter." I repeat, "What do you see when you look at me?"

"Uh, I'm not sure what you mean."

"If a friend asked you to describe me, what would you say?"

"Oh, uh, you're cool, and edgy, fun, you work a lot, you're easygoing. And hot, but that goes without saying," he says with a wink. "Why are you asking?"

Poor Damon has zero understanding of the implications of this conversation. How could he? But his answer was honest, and congruent with everything I know about him. He's a nice guy, uncomplicated, fun, a good kisser, and we could belong to the same, or at least adjacent, scenes here in Austin. A girl could do much worse. But it's not enough and would never be more than just a short-lived fling, fun in the moment, but not worth losing a friend over.

"I'll tell you later. I'm sorry—I have to go," I say, and I fly down the stairs, leaving him with his mouth hanging open, bewildered.

My car zooms to Nick's house, my heart thumping the entire way. It seems like each traffic light takes an eternity to turn green and each obstacle gives me more time to worry about what I'm about to do. Finally, I arrive at his house, and I bang on his door.

When I see his soft, smooth-shaven face, his kind eyes, his strong arms, I don't know how I stayed away this long.

"Katie! What's wrong?"

"Nothing's wrong, I mean I don't know what is right or wrong, but Nick, just tell me. What do you see when you look at me?"

He reaches out for my hand and gently pulls me into the foyer. He brushes my hair away from my eyes and says, "I see a savvy, independent and ambitious woman, who brings out the best in others. A woman who is kind and introspective, who finds the joy in a packet of astronaut ice cream but has empathy for a community facing gentrification. I see a disciplined woman who knows what she has to do to stay on a forward path in a world full of dark alleys. And who has become an incredible person in the process. I see you."

I want to scream and cry and laugh all at once, my emotions are overwhelming. Nicolas Stone sees me as a whole person, the person I want to be, and it feels incredible. How could I have doubted him?

I push the door shut gently behind me and press myself against him. He wraps his arms around me, then kisses the top of my head. Our bodies fit together like a puzzle, and he tilts my head up to kiss me on the mouth, tenderly. His familiar coconut scent sends me to a tropical paradise, where Nick and I are the only people for miles, and he slowly explores my lips, my neck, my collarbone. I tug his shirt out from his jeans and run my fingers across his toned back, pulling him tighter against me.

Nick pulls my blouse over my head and runs his finger along the edge of my black lace bra. The intensity in his eyes as he admires my body drives me insane and I push him towards the leather couch, loving the impatience building between us, both wanting to prolong this moment when we've waited so long to get here. I straddle him, squeezing him with my thighs, while he runs his hand down my sides then reaches under my skirt and discovers my black satin panties. Now I'm tired of waiting and I unhook my bra. He groans and his mouth finds my breast. I can barely stand it anymore and he knows it.

"Come with me," he whispers, and this time nothings stands in our way as I tighten my legs around him, and he carries me to the bedroom.

Lying naked in Nicolas Stone's bed, I sigh with contentment as my head rests on his chest, watching the rise and fall as he breathes. This must be what heaven feels like, sleepy euphoria, complete relaxation.

I jump when a furious bark erupts from nearby.

"What was that?" I say.

Nick smiles like the Cheshire cat and sits up. "Throw this on and I'll show you," he says, and hands me a t-shirt as he pulls on some boxers.

He leads me through the living room and kitchen to the back sliding glass doors.

"Is that-?"

"It sure is," he says.

"Brownie!" I squeal. Nick opens the door, and my favorite four-legged friend nearly bowls me over. I know he remembers me this time and he's wagging his tail with delight.

"Why didn't you tell me?" I say.

"I never got the chance to. I fell in love with him that night at the book launch and adopted him a few days later. He's a very good boy—aren't you Brownie?" Nick says as he pets the back of Brownie's neck.

"I never thought I'd see him again. This is amazing—I can't believe it."

Nick smiles and my heart fills with joy. If this isn't a sign from the universe that Nick and I are meant to be, I don't know what is.

He cooks me a healthy dinner on the grill while I play fetch with Brownie. It's like a dream, a sunny Texas day, backyard BBQ, a handsome man, and a fine dog. It's a ridiculous dream that I never even considered, especially for a goth from New Jersey, but it's real.

Cuddling on the couch leads to round two, not surprising with all the repressed, unanswered heat between us since that first day on his couch, heck, since that first day at the hotel gym. He asks if I'm staying over, but I decline.

"I want to take this slow."

"It's a little late for that," he says, his hand grazing my thigh, and I give him a lascivious look as his fingertips send a shiver through me.

"I'm serious. Not slow like that, I'm all for blazing ahead in that department. I mean taking it slow about being together as a couple. I still need to become my own person here, keep growing in my professional career, living in my own apartment."

Nick considers all this. "Of course. You take things as slow as you want. I'm not going anywhere; I'm not in any rush."

Oh crap. I forgot about the other reason we can't be together. I suddenly feel woozy and faint. Maybe this was a dream after all.

Nick helps me into a chair and sits next to me, holding my hand. "Are you alright? You look like you just saw a ghost."

"There's something I forgot to tell you…"

His eyes get as big as Brownie's. "You're scaring me."

"The thing is, I don't want kids…I know you want a family someday so maybe this—"

He pulls me in and gives me a hug. "Stop—don't say it. I understand why you would feel like that, I do. But it's not a dealbreaker for me, put your mind at ease."

That's easier said than done, because I know later he could change his mind and it could become a problem. But a million things could happen between now and then. I could get hit by a bus, there could be a zombie invasion, or we could break up for a hundred other reasons. I decide to try and let it drift into the background, just be with Nick and see where it goes.

We share a long kiss goodnight, and I'll admit it is very hard to leave him, and just as hard to leave Brownie. But I need to get settled back in before work tomorrow.

49

"**M**orning darlin', welcome back. I'm sorry about your aunt."

"Thanks, Amber."

It feels good to be back in my normal routine again. I know how many people hate coming to work, but I can't wait to read my e-mails and get started on my day. I'm lucky that way. Today I need to focus on Zulimar and I'm looking forward to getting lost in the search, find my flow.

When Roxy comes in a half an hour later, she stops in my cubicle and does the sympathetic head tilt. "Hey Katie, glad you're back," she says, and I take a moment to bask in the glory that is not just Roxy's acceptance, but that it actually seems that she missed me. Wonders never cease and I will file this situation under lessons learned, category 'Nothing is Impossible.'

"I'm glad to be back! I just know we can find the perfect site for Zulimar now that I can focus on it again."

Roxy puts her bag in the cubicle and comes back and leans against the edge of my desk. "I'm glad that you are doing well, but I have to say, you seem pretty chipper for someone who just came back from a funeral."

My face begins to warm, and I know Roxy will pick up on it since she has a sixth sense when it comes to gossip. I turn my head towards the computer, but it's too late.

"Wait, did something else happen?" she says.

I give a coy shrug,

"No, can't be, not you and Mr. Positive!"

"Keep your voice down," I say, and look around to see if anyone else is within earshot, but it's still early and no one's in our section. "But yes, we got together yesterday."

"Got together, like you're dating, or *got together*," she says, dripping with inuendo.

"Ugh, Roxy, you're too much. That's private."

"That's a yes, then. Well good for you, I don't know why it took this long, I saw it from day one," she says with a smug look of satisfaction.

It annoys me that Roxy was right, from that first day she said he was my type even though she didn't know either of us. I don't believe in type anymore, that's what I've learned since I moved here, it's meaningless. On paper, Damon and I are a great match, but Nicolas Stone, he gets me in a way that Damon never could, no matter how much I might try to explain things to him.

"Fine, I admit it—you were right, happy now?"

"Very," she says. "And I'm happy for you, too. Are you going to tell Gloria?"

Ugh, Gloria. Ever since I knew there was a spark between Nick and I, there has been a horrible dread of it impacting my career at Purple Cactus. What kind of professional falls for her very first client? It's not a good look.

"Do you think I have to? I mean technically the project is over, right?" I say.

"Yes, but Gloria will definitely want to try to keep him on as a client, in case he writes another book, or says something stupid down the line and we need to clean up his mess."

"Shit, you're right. It's just so new, right now, I don't know if it's even necessary."

"I won't say anything," says Roxy, "but I doubt this will stay secret for long and it's better coming from you than if she finds out by accident."

She's probably right. I would never want anything to mess up my job, but Nicolas Stone and I, we were an inevitability; I see that now.

"Did you come up with any leads on a location for Zulimar?" I say.

She graciously accepts my change of subject with just a minute eyebrow raise. "Unfortunately, no, my leads were all dead ends. I think we need to get the word out somehow, have more people in on the search."

"Hmmm. Who knows buildings besides architects?" I say, tapping my pen on the edge of the desk.

"Real estate agents?"

"Yes! Corporate real estate agents."

Now Roxy is getting excited. "That could work. Do you know any?"

"I don't think so," I say and both our faces fall.

"Not like we can ask for their help when we're not looking to buy property," she says.

"True, but let's not give up on this. I'll ask Gloria if she knows any, or if we can send out an e-mail to the staff for leads. Somebody must know somebody who knows one. It's just a numbers game."

Gloria is with clients all morning, so it's not until after lunch that I get a chance to approach her.

"Katie—how are you doing?" she asks when I knock on her door.

"Fine, thanks. Glad to be back. And thank you for sending the flowers, that was very thoughtful."

"Of course, you're part of the Purple Cactus work family now." My previous company used to talk about workplace culture and being like a family, but it seemed artificial. With Gloria, it feels genuine, we really do care about each other here, but without the pressure to socialize outside of work. It's perfect.

"Thanks Gloria, I'm really happy here. That's why I hope what I'm about to tell you doesn't mess anything up."

"Oh dear, you'd better close the door," she says and waits for me to be seated again.

"The thing is... Nicolas Stone and I are seeing each other. Not while we were working on the project, not while we were on the lecture tour, but just since yesterday. Going back home made me think about some things, and I realized Nick and I, there's something special there and I need to explore it."

Gloria doesn't look as surprised as I expected. "I'm not blind, you know. The way Dr. Stone looked at you was not the way a client looks at their project manager. I appreciate that you didn't let it interfere with your work, but the project is over, so you have my blessing."

"You're not worried about potentially losing future work? I mean, don't we usually try to convert single projects into lifetime clients?"

Gloria shrugs. "That's one of the things I like about you, that you see the business side. You've disclosed this to me, and I appreciate that you did that, because we trust each other. We can worry about the rest as it happens."

I feel like I can breathe again. I don't know what I would have done if Gloria had been angry, or if I lost this job. But it's all okay, and I feel like a kid springing on a trampoline, weightless and free.

"On another note," I ask, "do you know any corporate realtors? We are still trying to find the right spot for Zulimar."

"Actually, I do—my brother. He's in Houston. I'll let him know you'll be reaching out to him, and then I'll send you his contact info."

"That's fantastic. Thank you, Gloria, for everything."

She swings her aubergine scarf around her neck, which I know by now means the meeting is adjourned.

I give Roxy the thumbs up on my way back to my cubicle, to let her know I'm not fired. I'll fill her in on Gloria's brother later. Hopefully, he will be the answer to our problems.

Nick texts me a photo of Brownie being a ham, asking for belly rubs, and my heart swells. I'm still in dream mode, that not only are Nick and I together, but that he gave Brownie a forever home. It doesn't feel quite real yet. I'm trying not to jinx it or let my stupid negative brain convince me that it won't last and I'm just kidding myself. Just focus on the present, Kat, that's all you can do.

He asks me if I'm coming over later, but I tell him I have some things to take care of tonight and I will see him tomorrow. I'm not playing games with Nick, not purposely keeping him at a distance, even though I don't know how else to take things slow. No, tonight I feel like the right thing to do is to fill Damon in on the latest developments. I can't leave him hanging, even though I know he is going to be pissed when he finds out I'm with Nick now. Maybe I'll tell him in two stages, let him down easy.

While I'm doing my post-work cardio I have a revelation. I don't know why I've been so resentful about my routine. It's like Nick said, if you knew something would make you feel better and you simply didn't do it, wouldn't that be crazy? I tell myself that now whenever I'm feeling unmotivated or undisciplined. It's not someone else telling you what to do, it's you helping yourself. The subtle shift in thinking is hugely impactful. Now I realize these thirty minutes on the treadmill are a gift, even though I still despise every moment of exercise. I just turn up the music and go.

Shower, chicken and veggies consumed and there's nothing left to aid in my procrastination. I can hear Damon's music bleeding through the ceiling, so I know he's home. I should get 'the talk' over with.

50

"Hey, can I come in?" I say from Damon's doorway. Damon stands back and I walk through. I sit on the couch and realize I'm wringing my hands. "So, about yesterday..."

"Yeah—what was that?" asks Damon and he flops at the other end, resting his arm on the back of the sofa.

"The thing is, you're a great guy—"

Damon holds up his hand. "Let me stop you right there. I don't need another friend zone speech."

"I'm sorry," I say. "I really like hanging out with you, but we're just not in the same place."

"I know. You work too much," he says.

"That's just it, well, part of it. I love my work, and that's something you just can't understand. Nick understands that."

"Nick?!" Damon's face contorts in disbelief.

Oh shit. I didn't mean to mention that yet; I was hoping to break the news slowly. Too late now.

"Yes."

"I can't believe this. That guy judged the way you looked—how could you end up with him?"

Thinking of things from Damon's perspective, what he's seen, what he's heard, his point of view is not unwarranted. I know he is just looking out for me because he is a friend, and he cares about me. "You're going to have to trust me that there is a lot you don't know about Nick. He gets me."

251

"Yeah, okay, I will have to take your word on that one. You didn't have the nicest things to say about him, especially in the beginning."

"I know. But I didn't really know him then. He's a kind and generous guy. He even adopted a dog from the shelter."

Damon frowns. "I just hope you know what you're doing."

"Who ever does? There are no guarantees. I'm sorry you broke up with Paige though, she seemed nice."

"It wasn't really about you—Paige and I just didn't click, that's all. It's no big deal, we only dated for a couple of months."

Now I see lazy river Damon again and I'm less worried. I'm not that conceited that I think he'll pine over me endlessly; I'm sure he'll float around the next bend in a flash.

"Can we still hang out?" I ask.

"Yeah, sure. Someone's got to make sure you don't miss the best food in Austin."

"And one-hundred-degree days are right around the corner."

"Truth."

As I get up to leave, Damon grabs my hand. "Bye, neighbor," he says, and holds it a little too long before he lets it drop.

This feels like an end, but I hope it isn't. Maybe when Damon starts dating someone else, we can go back to the way things were. Only time will tell.

When I'm back in the apartment, I text Nick.

Katie: Changed my mind, can I come over?

Nick: Always (smiley face)

Screw taking it slow. I wasted all that time protecting myself and worrying about the future, when I should have been enjoying the things I have right here, right now. Cassie's death taught me that life is too short to be cautious and we have to make the most of the time we have.

Nick and Brownie greet me at the door. Nick wraps me in a hug and then gives me a kiss, and for a second I think we're never going to be able to keep our hands off each other. But then he says, "I was going to take Brownie for a walk before the sun sets, want to join me?"

"I'd like nothing more," I say, leaning down to give Brownie some pats. As I stand in the foyer, something new catches my eye, a framed photograph that must be a teenaged Nick, his sister, and his parents.

Nick follows my eyes and then rests his gaze on the photo. "I realized it wasn't healthy, hiding the memories away. There were some happy ones too. And I need to reconnect with my parents. Especially now that I will want them to meet the girl of my dreams."

I blush, thinking about meeting his parents, and realize my mom is going to be ecstatic when she hears about Nick. I was going to wait until I felt like we were solid before sharing the news with her, but maybe that's silly because I feel it in my heart that this is so right. "That sounds like a good shift. I'd love to hear stories about your family someday if or when you feel like sharing."

"I'd like that."

We walk through Nick's neighborhood, and I think of the landscaping in New Jersey, and how I never appreciated it. Now I do, I appreciate every Texas Persimmon and Mexican plum tree, every bright red Flame Acanthus, purple Texas sage, every rock rose. I never knew Texas could be so lush and colorful, with such a variety of plants and flowers.

Nick holds Brownie's leash in one hand, and my hand in the other.

"I told Roxy and Gloria about us today," I tell him.

"That was fast. Must mean you believe in us as much as I do."

I squeeze his hand. "I do, I really do."

"What did Gloria say, is it going to affect your job?"

"No, Gloria appreciated that I waited until the project was over, and that I was open with her."

"That night on the couch we weren't going to wait," he points out.

I snort. "She doesn't need to know that. I'm not that honest," I say.

"Fair enough. I'm relieved she wasn't upset. You know I'd never do anything to hurt your career. Especially when you've done so much to help mine."

"I do know. How's the book selling?"

"Pretty well, for non-fiction. We knew self-help is a competitive market, but they are pleased with the numbers so far."

"And think of all those people you've helped," I say.

"I hope so."

"I know so. You've changed my life."

Nick stops walking and kisses me. I return the gesture, his mouth soft against mine, until Brownie gets impatient and pulls us forward. We both laugh.

"Brownie was used to being my number one for a while," says Nick. "He might not want to share the attention."

"That's okay, Brownie is *my* number one," I say. "Aren't you, boy?" I give him a few pats on the back, but he's more interested in sniffing some bushes.

"He's going to be one spoiled dog," says Nick.

"As it should be," I say.

Back at the house, Brownie curls up in his favorite plaid pillow bed, lined with fluffy cotton, like a little prince keeping court.

Nick and I snuggle on the couch with me resting back against him, and he tells me all about the book tour and the people he talked to along the way. I doubt I'll ever get tired of the enthusiasm he has for his work, his passion for helping people be just a tiny bit more satisfied with their lives. I love that Nick used his inquisitiveness to ask and answer such important questions, ones so central to our existence.

When I hear some of the positive outcomes people have shared with Nick in e-mails and letters, I have to admit a bit of envy. Nothing I do at Purple Cactus is meaningful at that level, more than just me finding meaning in being good at something. I'm glad we helped the young Mina Marin get a second chance, but who knows what she'll do with it. Maybe that's why Zulimar's project is so important to me. Because we are trying to help someone who in turn is trying to save the world, instead of just sell more perfume, or make up for bad behavior.

Nick traces circles on the side of my ribs as he talks, perhaps absentmindedly, perhaps not. I listen to his soothing voice but also enjoy this closeness, his warmth beneath my body, the touch of his fingertips making the hairs stand up on my arms.

I'm enjoying the tease, encouraging him to keep talking, but soon he pushes my hair aside, and kisses the side of my neck from behind. I sigh, and he slowly brings his hands to my chest and caresses my breast, making me moan. His warm breath on my neck is driving me wild, but I love that Nick takes his time. With Nick I believe that we have all the time in the world, a whole lifetime to be together, in more ways than one.

Soon I can't stand it, and I flip over so I'm lying on top of him, needing to feel his lips against mine, his tongue in my mouth, longing for more, much more. He grips my hips and pulls me even closer, and I feel him against me, and our flame is burning brighter and brighter until I tell him I can't wait any longer, and we stumble, kissing along the way, to the bedroom, until we're both satisfied.

51

⚭

Three months later

"This is incredible," I whisper to Nick as we walk hand in hand. Before us is a re-creation of the lost city of Atlantis, made entirely out of garbage collected from the ocean. The pavement is marked in chalk with a curving trail, guiding visitors through the exhibit of fluted columns made from crushed plastic bottles and seaweed crafted from decaying fishing nets. The concrete beyond the walkway is a wash of blues and greens, expertly chalked like swirls and eddies, even a whirlpool that looks so three dimensional I don't walk too close, for fear of falling in and drowning.

The seafloor is dotted with aquatic life, shells made of melted bottle caps, molded and formed into scallops and conches, starfish made out of oyster spacers, an octopus made from a deflated beach ball with arms of rope.

Further on stands a six-foot statue of Poseidon, draped in a toga of worn sailcloth, grasping a trident topped with eel trap cones. He sports a beard of tangled fishing wire and a crown of wooden coffee stirrers.

The installation culminates in an arch that leads to an altar, with a mermaid draped across the tabletop, a sacrifice to the sea. Each scale on her tail is the top half of a plastic spoon, painstakingly layered, and finely shredded grocery bags form her luxurious long hair, swooping in a wave down over her hips.

That Zulimar was able to bring so much humanity to a plastic garbage mermaid is a testament to his skill as an artist. Each component was a labor of love, his gift to the world, and his plea for change.

"This is something special," says Nick.

"It really is," I say.

Past the exit, Roxy and Gloria are standing with Zulimar. He looks good, relatively speaking, thin and weathered, but energized by the day, finally seeing his vision come into fruition. We walk over.

"Katie," Zulimar says, "I was just telling these ladies that I'm forever in your debt. This location exceeded my wildest dreams. Thousands of people will see it. I can't thank you enough."

"It was our pleasure. This is fantastic—I'm not an artist like Roxy, so I didn't know what it would look like, but it's truly magical. And thought provoking," I say.

"Thank you, thank you," he says, bowing his head.

This will surely stand out as one of the greatest moments in my life, helping another person try to make the world a better place and achieve his dreams, his destiny. The wheels start turning in my head and I wonder if eventually we could market Purple Cactus as a firm for positive change. Or who knows, maybe someday Roxy and I will start our own business. As Gloria said, the sky's the limit.

Roxy pulls me to the side. "We did it!" she says.

"Did you have any doubt?" I say.

"Honestly, a little. But that doesn't matter now because we fulfilled our promise. I wish we had more projects like this."

"It's like you're reading my mind," I say.

Gloria joins us as Nick chats with Zulimar.

"My dream team did it again. I'm so proud of both of you. Such talented young women, the future leaders of Purple Cactus," says Gloria.

"You must be very good at hiring," says Roxy and winks at me and the three of us grin, Gloria shaking her head.

Nick and I drive back to Austin. Gloria offered to pay for us to stay overnight at a hotel, but we didn't want to leave Brownie with a sitter because we love him so much.

On the way back, I think about everything that's happened since I moved to Austin, since I decided to become a closet goth. I'm glad that Gloria is finally seeing Roxy's true potential and looking past her outward appearance. That's the way it should be. But at the same time, I like Katie's professional look, and I don't plan to dress goth at work anytime soon. That should be okay too; it's my choice.

But there's still something that bothers me. Now that Nick is comfortable with my full range of outward expression, professional office attire, evening casual goth clothes, and my full on goth club outfits, there's still one thing I haven't been able to reconcile.

My name.

The Katie from work, a successful career woman, the Kat from high school, who suffered with the onset of depression and learned to manage it with something akin to finesse, and the Katherine my parents see me as, their only daughter.

Maybe it doesn't matter too much if my parents call me Katherine and Gloria calls me Katie. But it matters what Nick calls me. I want him to know and love Kat as much as Katie, so I can be sure he accepts all of me.

I bring it up when we get home, after we dote on Brownie, playing tug of war and giving him belly rubs.

"Hmm," he says. "That's a tough one. I first knew you as Katie, so that's certainly in my mind, but I will call you whatever you want. It's only a name, not what's inside. People change names all the time."

"You were pissed when you found out I called you Mr. Positive at first," I point out.

"Yes, but that's different. That was something you said out of spite, out of lack of understanding about who I was and what I was trying to accomplish."

"You're right, I'm sorry about that."

"No worries, it's long forgotten. We had a few missteps, but we got there in the end," he says and strokes my hair.

"We sure did." It's been quite a rollercoaster, but one I'd ride a thousand times to end up here with this amazing man.

I lean against him on the couch, enjoying the moment, but still continuing to ponder my predicament. "I'm just not sure. Kat is a big part of me, of who I am. But Katie is a good match to Dr. Nicolas Stone because of the way we both value our careers."

"Every part of you is a perfect match for every part of me," he says, and then kisses me to prove it.

"Mmm, that's true," I say, enjoying his lips on mine.

Nick pulls back and says, "You let me know when you decide, okay? Until then, I'll just call you the love of my life, how's that?"

"Perfect," I say and my eyes well up with happy tears. Nick holds me in his arms until Brownie breaks in, wanting to be part of the hug, and the three of us snuggle up on the couch.

Note from the Author

First, I'd like to thank you, dear reader. I am honored to share this story with you. If you enjoyed this book, please consider leaving a review or rating to help others decide if this is the right next read for them.

This book is near and dear to my heart. I moved to sunny Austin, Texas many years ago and fell in love with this energetic city. I also have a keen interest in positive psychology. If you would like to learn more about this fascinating topic, I recommend:

- *Flourish: A Visionary New Understanding of Happiness and Well-being* by Martin E. P. Seligman.
- The *Positive Psychology Center*, University of Pennsylvania (https://ppc.sas.upenn.edu/).
- *The Greater Good Science Center*, University of California, Berkeley (https://ggsc.berkeley.edu/).

If you or someone you know is struggling with depression, please seek help from a mental health professional or find support at the National Alliance on Mental Illness (www.nami.org).

ABOUT THE AUTHOR

Rain Nox is a multi-genre author. She currently resides in Texas, where she enjoys gardening, nature, and cats. For more information, visit www.rainnox.com and sign up for her mailing list to receive updates and exclusive content.

Other books by Rain Nox:

<u>Midlife Magic Fantasy</u>
Animal Charmer
Magic & Melody

<u>Women's Fiction</u>
Nothing Blooms in the Shade

<u>Kids Horror</u>
Haunting at the 18th Hole